All The Truths Between Us

LIZ AMOS

First published in 2023 in Great Britain by
Liz Amos, in partnership with whitefox publishing

www.wearewhitefox.com

ISBN 978-1-915635-34-1
Also available as an eBook
ISBN 978-1-915635-35-8

Designed and typeset by seagulls.net
Cover design by Emma Pidsley
Project management by whitefox

To Rebecca, who was there from the beginning.

And Anne, because I promised when I was seventeen.

Content Guidance

This story contains instances of strong language,
online bullying and violence, and references
to drug misuse, racism and sex.

one

BEN

I'm practically running out of the building.

I sweep the freebies into the old leather satchel I've been dragging into the office every day – loot from my act as a grown-up. I doubt I'll look at any of it again.

Summer's been rammed with work placements at prestigious law firms in London. I'm supposed to be grateful. I've tried – I'm not a complete arse. Obviously, I'm privileged – studying law at Oxford. I get that not everyone's wined and dined by City solicitors, quick to claim you belong with them.

Most people are passed over.

I've done four of these placements in the last ten weeks. The black and mixed ethnicity lawyers I've seen wouldn't fill a conference room. The women who look like my mum are mainly secretaries. It's not for me to hate on powerful middle-aged white men; my dad was one. But I feel caught out by the contradictions.

So, basically, I know I'm lucky. Being here is a dream come true.

Someone else's dream.

I check the time on my phone. I consider trying to track down the associate I've been sitting with to say goodbye. I think the better of it. He's probably getting dinner in the canteen before he settles in for the night. I can picture him now: surrounded by colleagues, all eating alone.

I leave a note on his desk instead, and leg it.

The glass lift whisks me from the sixteenth floor to the lobby. I step out into the atrium and there she is. 'Butterflies' doesn't begin to describe the churning that starts in the pit of my stomach. All the assessment centres, the panel and partner interviews, the presentations, the written exercises – everything from the last few weeks pales in comparison to the conversation I know we need to have.

I could be about to alienate my best friend.

I hear Harriet a beat before I see her. She's laughing, chatting with the Jamaican security guard. Everything about her is incongruous with these surroundings. It's not just the slogan T-shirt dress or her undercut afro – often in braids, but today styled in a carefree fauxhawk. Or the mismatched earrings. Or the well-worn ballet pumps.

It's the fact that she's not trying to impress anyone.

Harriet is mostly happy in her skin; she always has been. Not invincibly confident, but quietly OK with herself. I've always loved that. Seeing her is an instant boost – a stupidly big grin spreads across my face as I approach them.

'Here he is!' She reaches out and kisses me on the cheek. 'Ready?'

'Yeah, let's get out of here.'

'Aright, yuh two luk afta unuself now.' Her new friend nods at me too.

We're walking through London – it's surprisingly easy to do.

Even back when we lived here as a family, before Mum and I moved out to Harriet's hometown, walking was my first choice. I liked being rooted. I liked knowing how the streets fit together, which alleys to duck into and where I would emerge. I guess it helped that we lived in a posh postcode. Now, it's the best of limited options. I can't take the Tube.

'Are you OK?' Harriet has an incredible radar.

'Long week.' It's true, but not the whole truth.

She doesn't push me. She just links her arm through mine and we walk in the assured silence of people who don't keep secrets from each other. She knows I'll tell her, eventually. Sometimes the level of trust she has in me makes my chest physically ache.

Like heartburn.

Liverpool Street becomes Moorgate. Moorgate turns into St Paul's. The suits give way to a more eclectic crowd. We duck out of other people's photos, crossing the Millennium Bridge. Harriet snaps a couple of her own with the old-school film camera she takes nearly everywhere. I'm watching her too closely. I'm being weird.

'So . . .' I fake confidence as the Tate Modern looms ahead of us. 'What's first? Art or food?'

She laughs. 'Talk about tough choices! Maybe art? Unless you're starving?'

'No, that's fine – whatever you want.'

'Whatever I want?!' She puts her hand against my forehead in mock concern, pretending to take my temperature. 'Who are you? And what have you done with the Ben I know and love?'

'Harsh! I let you have your own way. Sometimes.'

'Ben, you're a dictator. A benign one, but still. This is highly suspicious.'

I would laugh, but the comment cuts a little too close to the bone. The best I can manage is a smile and eye-roll. 'See if I ever treat you to anything again.'

She's suddenly serious. I'm thrown by the way she stops – right in the middle of the bridge, in everyone's way – and takes both my hands in hers. 'I've been so excited about this. Thank you.'

I don't know what to say. I refuse to believe this is my opening. For starters, it's too early in the evening. We're also surrounded by a surging mass of strangers. And the fact is, I'm not nervous – I'm scared shitless.

'You're welcome.'

Such a cop-out.

two

HARRIET

Being in London with Ben is The Plan.

I'm not a die-hard planner, but there are things I'm convinced about – things I weave into the fabric of who I am. People I can count on.

Waiting for Ben in the law firm's lavish reception, I find myself telling Dennis far more than he needs to know about our history. He reminds me of my uncles and I can tell he is amused to see me here, looking so underdressed for my visit to the beating heart of capitalism. When he asks if I'm meeting someone – because I'm clearly not a client or employee – I tell him about Ben.

I'm early – I have plenty of time.

I tell him I've known Ben my entire life. He was three when I was born – my surrogate sibling, my boy-next-door best friend, despite the fact that we've only shared a hometown in recent years.

I tell him about summers spent with Ben's family in their Bloomsbury flat when my parents couldn't get enough time off work to cover the long break. Uncle David's academic timetable meant a little more flexibility for him. And Clara (never 'auntie' after the age of ten, when she told me double figures were a milestone and made me her equal) worked intermittently: a writer/activist/curator before portfolio careers were a thing.

'An yuh parents dem? How dey know each odda?'

Dennis seems to be enjoying my rambling – I get the impression not many guests of the firm stop to make small talk. I'm not surprised. Ben told me these places charge their clients hundreds of pounds an hour. He said the lawyers record their time in six-minute increments and have daily billing targets, so they're probably not hanging around in the lobby having long conversations with the security staff either.

'Oh, our mums go way back. Through church – a Pentecostal one in West London.'

He nods knowingly. 'Mi nuh hav time fi it. Buh mi wife hav ah lickkle group ah fren deh. Dem a tight-tight.'

'Sisters in the Lord.'

'Um-hmm, is ah community ting.'

That's the short answer, but Ben still hasn't arrived so I give Dennis the longer version too. I tell him, in outline, about the fateful Saturday night when the hall that the church used was booked by a couple of very amateur musicians. Mum and Clara caught the last few songs when they came to set up for the next day's meeting, and the rest – as they tell it – is a history of double-dates and speedy weddings.

By day, these alluring men were students. My dad would go on to take his IT degree in-house, working in a suburban business park and moving out of London with my mum at the earliest opportunity. Uncle David eventually became a professor of anthropology, one of the youngest to be offered a permanent position, a rising star in his field.

And then I'm back to Ben – I can't help myself. 'We're moving here together next year, hopefully, if Ben gets one of these jobs.'

Dennis shrugs, non-committal. 'London can bi aright. Whereabouts?'

'So, we haven't decided yet, but I'll be applying to do art foundation and fine art at Central Saint Martins.'

'Art? Fi real? Yuh gwine bi poor?'

I laugh. 'We'll see! Not intentionally. But there are student loans; Ben's offered to top up the rent as well. We might still need a few other flatmates to chip in, but it should work out.'

'Yuh parents nuh mind? Dem nuh waan yuh tuh bi ah docta ar ah lawyer?'

It's a classic question – I know where it comes from and I get that a lot. I try not to feel too stereotyped. 'Well, I don't think my dad is ever going to be bragging about his daughter the painter. But they're OK. They're not pushy.'

I know I've said a lot – far more than anyone needs to in these sorts of situations, but I like the connection. I never know what I'm going to unearth in a conversation with a stranger.

I hear colours in people's voices; I see shapes in their sentences. I visualise myself differently, reflected back from someone else's perspective. People are my eighth wonder of the world – especially from the safe distance of a one-off interaction. I take all that idiosyncrasy and make art out of it, in whatever way I can. So, it's fair to say I talk to random strangers quite often.

But I didn't tell Dennis everything.

I didn't tell him the thing I barely admit to myself, even though it's been so breathtakingly clear for months now. I didn't tell him the thing I'm not sure Ben knows, despite how blindingly obvious it really should be.

I'm in love with him.

I am in love with Ben.

Just thinking about The Plan makes me feel like I'm free-wheeling with pure joy. Everyone around me is freaking out a bit with university applications and exams. It's all coming at us

– our inevitable collision with questions that are too big to look in the eye: *Who are you? What are you going to do with your life?* It feels like we're all on the edge of ourselves, frantically tracing the face of the unknown for clues, trying to read the Braille of the great beyond.

But for me it's pretty simple. Art and Ben. That's a life that makes sense to me. And surely, at some point, everything else – all the unacknowledged things between us – will click into place.

A lift descends and I see Ben spring out of the glass box, his face breaking into a luminous smile as soon as his eyes meet mine.

I know we'll find our way.

three

BEN

I cheated. I see that now.

Standing in line to scan our tickets, Harriet's radiating hope. She fidgets with excitement. She's talking a mile a minute about the artist whose work we're going to see. When I came across the promotions for the exhibition months ago, I knew straightaway that she'd love it. Abstract art, sculpture, jewellery and more – all by the same woman? Tick. A non-Western artist getting the recognition she deserves? Big tick.

I knew it would make her happy. Somehow that feels manipulative now. I've shamelessly used the things she loves to set the scene. That feels underhand. A cynic could say I'm trying to buy her approval. I'm just putting myself at an advantage ahead of the gamble of a lifetime. Well, to be honest, I am. But also, I do really want Harriet to be happy. Whatever happens.

This is an ambush. Waiting isn't going to make it any easier.

'Harri, I need to talk to you.' I touch her arm. I need to anchor myself. I've practised this so many times in my mind. I need to feel her next to me to make it real.

We've moved through into the exhibition space. We're in front of a medium-sized canvas: blue, black, light yellow – zig zags and triangles. It doesn't mean that much to me, really, but part of me knows I'll remember it for the rest of my life. I've interrupted – she was telling me something about it. I was trying to listen.

She's looking at me now. The heartburn starts up. I force myself to keep speaking. 'You know you're really important to me, right?' This normally goes without saying. Today I need to check.

'You're scaring me – spit it out.' She's only half-joking.

'OK. OK, it's a big deal but at this point I just really need you to know . . .' I wait for a second or two, because the words feel heavy. Then I say it: 'I want to become a monk.'

Her laughter is a punch in the gut.

'Please don't.' My voice catches. I realise I may actually cry.

'You're serious?'

'Really.'

'Oh, wow.' Her hands play with the camera still slung around her neck, eyes glued to the ground. 'Oh wow.'

'I know.' We're blocking the canvas. I steer her to one side.

'Is that even a thing? That people do?'

'Yeah. Clearly, not that many people. But yes.'

'But you mean like way, way down the line?'

I exhale. She seems to be shivering. It's as if the air conditioning has been turned up too high. I automatically rub her arms. There's no easy way to say this. I know I'm derailing The Plan. 'No, I mean right now. It's a process, but I've been thinking about it. A lot. And I start next month.'

It's like I've slapped her across the face. She flips from catatonic to manic, shrugging my hands off her shoulders, finally looking at me properly. Her eyes are wide with fury.

'You can't be serious!' She's louder than I'd like, but asking her to keep it down is absolutely not an option. I try to ignore the spectators. 'Ben, you *cannot* be serious. Next *month*? What about Oxford? Finals? Your mum must be –'

'I haven't told her yet. Please, you can't say anything to anyone. Not yet.'

It's a lot to ask. But Harriet is the one who's always looked out for me. So, I trust her. I've put my heart in her hands. From the look on her face, she wants to tear it to shreds.

'Please, Harri. You're the first person I've told.'

'Why?'

The question is so quiet, I think I imagined it until she repeats it again, to herself. Why do I want to do this? Or why is she the first to find out? Either way, I don't get a chance to answer. She's in my arms before I can respond and I can feel how fast her heart's beating, her camera lodged awkwardly in my ribs.

I hold her.

I'm about to speak, but she pulls away. She thumps my chest with a tight, closed fist. And turns. And leaves, moving much faster than seems possible for someone who claims she's not athletic.

I know if I don't catch her immediately, I'll lose her in this crowd. She'll be swallowed up by the city, refusing to answer my phone calls.

That can't happen.

This can't be it. There are still a million and one things to say.

I run.

four

HARRIET

Of course I laughed when he told me – it was the only sane response because it had to be a joke. But, apparently, it's not. It's a nightmare that I can't shake myself awake from, no matter how fast I sprint through this labyrinth. I need to get out – the walls are closing in on me; there's no way I can stay here.

I push past a family dithering in front of the lift, debating which floor they need for the gift shops and restaurants. I'm pounding the down button, willing the doors to close before Ben has a chance to throw himself through them. If he's even coming after me – who knows anything anymore?

I don't understand a thing that he's telling me.

A *monk?*

I thought the only people still signed up to that were Buddhist. Or Hare Krishna devotees. Or really old white men. Life in a religious order is supposed to be for people who are really, exceptionally wise and noble, or else can't cut it in the real world. Ben is neither of those things. What is he playing at?! He would literally be throwing his entire life away.

He'd be throwing *my* life away.

I escape the gallery, falling out of the doors, embarrassed to be stumbling around like someone concussed – like this revelation has knocked me off-kilter. But it has. There's no denying it has. I'm barrelling nowhere fast, barely managing to sidestep two lovers engrossed in an intimate clinch. Irritation rises in my throat like bile. I fight the urge to walk right through them, breaking up their smug embrace. Tears are threatening to overpower me, and that's so not OK – I don't cry in public.

Where am I even going?

Now I'm out here, I don't know what's next. This whole evening is completely unmoored. I head off along the South Bank and the worst thing is I start to drag my heels. I shouldn't. After a stunt like that, Ben really doesn't deserve it. But, despite the fact that I did *not* see this coming, I do know him. Ben will be looking for me.

And I do want him to find me.

I gravitate towards the river, leaning against the railings. The water swirls below me. A tour boat drifts past. The daylight is shifting. Electric lanterns stutter into life along the riverbanks – they twinkle, standing to attention in the parallel avenue of trees. Across from me, the building lights blink out against the darkening sky, their blurry glow reflected in the water. A slow summer sunset paints the glass and brick soft gold.

The whole view is magical, but I put my camera back into the cloth bag on my shoulder – this is not a night to remember. It will already be impossible to forget.

The air is buzzing with collective conversation – people passing by, relaxing on benches, dining on the pavement, laughing in clusters outside bars. It's an audio-stream of perfect togetherness – the universal sounds of belonging.

Everyone else has their tribe.

I've never felt more alone.

'Don't jump.'

I look towards him, then back out over the water, trying to decide where to pitch my response.

'You're not worth it.' It seems I'm only capable of banter laced with bitterness. He doesn't mind. Even without looking, I can feel his quiet smile as he comes to a halt right next to me – our shoulders almost touching.

When I glance his way to double check, he's looking towards the river too. But relief is hiding in the edges of that smile, in the corners of his eyes. He's being kinder to me than I would be if the roles were reversed – if I'd told him something massive and personal, and he'd lashed out and run off.

'Ben, I'm sorry I hit you. That's not OK.'

'I probably deserved it.'

'Don't be a sexist idiot. Can you imagine what would happen if you hit me? That's never allowed.'

He nudges me with his shoulder – apology accepted. I don't want him to move away, but he does, turning his back to the river to look at me. I can't take the scrutiny. I look over my shoulder, following the progress of a cyclist as she weaves between pedestrians and out of sight.

'I know this is a bit shit for you.'

'What kind of monk swears the way you do?'

'I don't know – a shitty one?'

'It's not funny!' He's taking his cue from me, keeping things light because I keep deflecting. But I need answers. 'This makes no sense to me, Ben! You're twenty – if you need to find yourself, go backpacking!'

'It's more than that. It's more complicated than that.'

'OK, well, explain it! Because all I'm hearing is that you're running away.'

'I'm not. I just – I need a different life. I know this leaves you in the lurch with moving to London next year; I feel awful about that.'

'London?! Ben! How can you not –' I stop, slamming on the brakes before I make a hideous evening worse. It's enough to discover Ben is living in an alternate reality. I don't want to humiliate myself with confessions I won't be able to take back.

The silence that fills the gap is tense. Awkward – like a heavy breather with no respect for personal space.

'What?' Ben seems genuinely perplexed. I will have to help him out, at least a little.

'It's more than that! We've always been together. We've been through *everything* together! Practically. And now you bring me to London on some pseudo-date, ruin the Choucair exhibition and kill one of my favourite galleries – all so you can feel slightly better about telling me you basically don't care about me at all!'

He fidgets with his satchel strap, and for a minute I think I see a blush rise in his cheeks – barely detectable under the light brown of his skin. 'I do care! Of course I do.'

'You're leaving me! And for what? To pray by the sea for the rest of your life?!'

'Not everything's about you, Harriet.' I've flipped a switch. His eyes are narrowed, his voice caustic.

I shouldn't have belittled him. He shouldn't have ambushed me. We shouldn't be having this mad fight about an impossible future. Somewhere in a parallel universe we're still inside the Tate Modern and I'm linking my arm through his as we walk from room to room, laughing about nothing and everything because we so enjoy each other's company. Instead, we're here.

I can't do this.

'Whatever. You don't want me around? I don't want to be with you either. I'm going home!'

He softens. 'I'll come with you. Waterloo's that way.'

'I know! I'm not totally lost without you.' I'm being a bitch
– petulant and cruel, and I'd stop if I could but the words keep
coming. 'I'm going to Paddington.'

Even as I say it, I can't believe how low I've sunk.

For Ben, the whole of London is a minefield of unexploded
grief, but I've just thrown a hand grenade. His whole face drops.
There's no way he will follow me there. Paddington station is our
most direct train line, but instead – by silent agreement – we've
been taking the local stopping service in and out of London for
the last three years.

'All right.' He nods slowly. 'Your call.'

I want to undo it. He looks utterly crushed, and I'm sorry.

But my mind is swimming, my body aches and if I look at
him for a minute longer I'll dissolve into tears – right here, right
now. I clutch my bag to myself, shrugging a little as I back away.
I leave him there, without a proper goodbye, retreating into the
pulsing throng of people criss-crossing the city, their dreams and
disappointments hidden in plain view.

Maybe I'm the one who's running away.

five

HARRIET

Three Years Ago

Something was very wrong.

As I entered the kitchen, Mum looked in my direction with bloodshot eyes, but her focus was elsewhere – her phone held limply in the palm of her hand.

'Sit down, Harriet.' Her voice was clipped.

I obeyed. School always left me ravenous and today was no different. Raiding the fridge had been my only thought. But in her shaking inhalation, I heard a vulnerability that hit me somewhere between the ribs. I held my breath.

'It's Uncle David. There's been an accident.'

The relief was instant. Dad was OK. My parents were still together. No one was making me move to the other side of the world. I crossed possible catastrophes off my mental list, thanking God that the universe was still in order. Accidents happened – how bad could it be?

'But he's all right?'

'No. No, he's not. He fell. We think he fell. From the Underground platform at Paddington station.' A sob almost eclipsed her next words, but part of me already knew them. 'He's gone, Harriet. There was a train. He died immediately.'

Reality fractured.

It was impossible to compute.

Mum moved towards me, arms outstretched. The hug that

enveloped me was fierce and unrelenting. I mechanically returned the pressure while my mind scrambled around in shock.

This couldn't be right, because I'd just spoken to him last week. It had to be a mistake, because we'd talked about the summer. He'd told me about an exhibition some of his anthropology students were curating with the art faculty – he was going to send me the details so I could see if I wanted to check it out with Ben next month.

Ben.

My tears were quiet but they wouldn't stop.

A moment ago, I was celebrating my family being intact. What kind of hell must he be going through? The thought of him cut through the confusion – lucid awareness that anything I was feeling would only be a fraction of his pain.

Mum cleared her throat. 'It's impossible to . . . but if you . . . Together, we're just going to have to . . .' She gave up trying to articulate anything comforting, cradling me for the longest time instead.

When she finally released me, I wiped my eyes in a useless attempt at composure. Ben's family was a second home, all the more loved for being totally different to mine: full of fire and feeling. There was an energy to their dynamic that was a little stunning, like front-row tickets to a spectacular show. But imagining the Wilkins family without Uncle David? It was impossible – like a solar system without a sun.

'How are they? Ben and Clara?'

'They're completely devastated. Uh, it's completely unimaginable!' She shook her head, looking past me. 'This is the kind of thing that changes you forever.'

I sent Ben a message – later that night after far too long spent online, scrolling through speculative coverage of the 'incident'.

It was short and unimaginative:
Ben, I'm so sorry Xx
By the morning, it had been read. There was no reply.

The day of the funeral was hot, even for the end of June.

The Underground was a sauna; the air above was just as stifling. We arrived to more people than I had imagined. Students were lining the covered walkway that led to the university's chapel, congregating in quiet clusters.

Despite the crowd, it was eerily still. I could hear the echo of my heels clopping as I hobbled along behind Mum and Dad, struggling in a skinny pencil skirt and shoes that I regretted. I'd dug out a former work experience outfit, trying for a sophisticated look to show respect. Now, I realised just how uncharacteristic the whole ensemble was. I imagined Uncle David raising an eyebrow sceptically. The image made me smile and well up, conflicting emotions fighting for an outlet.

'She's over here.'

Dad spotted Clara as we retreated into the chapel's cool gloom. It took a moment for my eyes to adjust, but I would've struggled to recognise her anyway. Her whole posture was completely transformed. She seemed both smaller and straighter – like a lone soldier determined to face down the enemy of life-altering loss.

Dad directed us up the centre aisle, into the pew behind her.

Clara had insisted we meet her there, insisted we didn't need to come early, didn't need to escort her from the flat. Even so, as they reached over to her, she collapsed into my parents' arms – clutching them like a human lifebuoy, adrift in a sea of sympathetic onlookers.

'Where's Ben?'

Clara pulled back from their embrace, turning to me. She stroked my cheek. 'He's bringing David in.'

The lump that had formed in my throat began to expand. Ben was carrying his dad's coffin? It was too much for him. It was an impossible weight to bear. Clara seemed to read my mind.

'I know.' She sighed. 'I know, but he insisted. And you know Ben.'

I couldn't watch.

I studied the floor as Uncle David came in. I kept my eyes averted as the coffin was lowered onto its stand. I didn't want to see all of his brilliance and warmth snuffed out and boxed up in that too-small world of gleaming wood.

Ben sat directly in front of me, the tight curls of his hair glistening a little at the nape of his neck. He was so still, so insular. There had to be a way to help – to transmit even a little of his pain over to me. The urge to touch him was overwhelming. I sat on my hands, forcing myself to respect his privacy.

Time took on an odd dimension – in what felt like a heartbeat, it was all over. The chaplain began the closing prayers, his voice hushed and reverent.

'The Lord gives and the Lord takes away.'

I knew how I was supposed to respond – the correct thing to say. It was written right there in the order of service, the lines in bold for the congregation. I just couldn't.

'Blessed be the name of the Lord.'

Ben's voice was audible in the collective murmur, low like a man's – not the boy from my childhood. His head fell forwards, his shoulders slumped. And my belief in the unshakeable goodness of God began to disintegrate.

six

BEN

My key is barely in the lock. The front door to the flat flies open.

'What's going on, Ben? Maggie's been on the phone to me! Harriet's a mess but no one's getting anything out of her. Why was your phone off? What happened?'

Mum has a gift for asking ten questions when one would do. She stands in front of me. She fills the hallway, despite being so petite. People who admire her say she has 'presence'. Her detractors have called her a bully. It's a thin line.

'I'm doing fine, thanks.' I'm tempted to lift her out the way.

'Don't give me that! Of course I'm worried about you too! But you're not the one who came home early in tears.'

'Maybe I'm crying on the inside.'

She stops. I can see her mentally consulting her parenting books. I take advantage of her indecision, sidestepping past her. She follows me into the kitchen.

'Sorry. I'm worried. Sit.'

It's only nine in the evening. Today feels like the longest day. I can't believe I was at a desk this morning, pretending to want to be a lawyer. Honesty is brutal. It's taken a knife to my life and carved it up: before truth, and after. I have nothing in the tank for another round. But I sit anyway, taking my seat across from her at the small table pushed up against the wall.

It's just easier.

The clock ticks between us, time marching over our heads.

A calendar hangs below the clock. It's August now, but it won't be long until we're into September, then October, with the start of term marked in block capitals. I know I need to tell her.

'Where were you?'

'Walking.'

'Did you . . .' Because she hesitates, I know exactly what she wants to ask.

'No, Mum. I didn't drink anything, smoke anything, inject or ingest anything.'

Her hunched shoulders relax a little. 'So, you were just walking? To clear your head?'

I nod. I think of Harriet – her face as she left me. I'd anticipated this would be a big one for our friendship. I'd expected she might feel betrayed on some level, because of the secrecy. And we've been talking about living in London together for a while. But the way she left! For the second time this evening, tears are a possibility.

'Oh, Ben!' Mum clutches at my forearm, resting on the table. 'What happened?'

It's easier to look at her hand than her face. 'We just had a conversation that didn't go so well.'

She shifts in her chair, but manages to resist interjecting. That in itself is a small miracle. I'll take it. I'll confess.

'We were talking about next year. I've been rethinking my plans. The whole lawyer thing isn't for me. I made another application, a while back. I found out I've been invited to take it further. So, I'm going to.'

'Uh huh.' There's nothing explicitly discouraging in her response, but I know she's waiting for the rest. For the details.

'I'm going back to Scotland, to the monastery I was at before. Until Christmas, initially. And if I pass that stage, it's roughly a year for the next bit. Then another three or four. And after that it's permanent.'

Her hand on my arm is stiff, too still.

The ticking clock shouts into the silence. The ceiling creaks under the footsteps of the neighbours above. The fridge-freezer hums tunelessly.

Eventually, she recaps what I've said, the way the therapist told her to. So that I know I've been heard. 'You're saying your new plan is . . . what? To be a monk in the Hebrides?'

I nod. She's almost robotic with the effort of trying to keep her tone neutral. It still sounds more ludicrous coming from her. 'Yes. That's the new plan.'

'And what's this about being there until Christmas? Which Christmas?'

'This Christmas. From September until Christmas.'

She pulls her hand back, stung. 'Not possible.'

This is exactly why I don't tell her things. It's never a conversation. Just a string of assertions: me against her. Dad was our mediator. Three years on, we're still hopeless without him.

'It's done, Mum. It's happening.'

'Absolutely not! You're in the middle of your education. In a year, maybe. We'll see. But you don't drop out of university on a whim just as you're about to finish!'

'It's not a whim!'

'Then why is this the first I'm hearing about it?'

'What would you have said if I'd told you sooner? "That's great, Ben – you go for it!"'

We both know I have a point. She takes a moment to regroup. The onslaught isn't over. I feel a hundred years old. I'm weary with the weight of trying to justify this all over again. There's something else too. Something old and familiar. It comes at me like a cloud descending.

Anger. Real, genuine fury.

This is dangerous territory.

'I'm going to bed – we can do this another day.'

'No, Ben, we can't. You need to listen to me. Your degree isn't something you just throw away. It's a privilege.'

'Mum –'

'An expensive opportunity to set yourself up for life.'

'Not now! I can't –' I get up from the table, leaving the room. My vision's tunnelling as I concentrate on breathing. Does no one care enough to just hear me out? My heart rate is climbing. I need to focus on solid things. Anything. Whatever I can find to help me stay together.

My fingers trail the wall.

The edges of my self-control are fraying. It always feels like I'm drowning, being hammered by waves of adrenaline and the roar of my pulse in my ears. I fall into my room and collapse onto the bed.

'You have to graduate!' Mum's followed me into the bedroom.

She's unbelievable. I pull the pillow over my head. Breathing.

'Afterwards, that's your problem.'

My arteries are on fire with mounting aggression. Every nerve is on high alert.

'But while you're under my roof –'

Suddenly, I'm on my feet. She's startled, finally quiet. There's a moment when anything is possible and I'm terrified by what I could do.

I yank a few clothes out of various drawers, throwing it all into a sports bag I haul from the bottom of my wardrobe.

'What are you doing?'

'Packing.' I head for the bathroom. She follows me again. A tenacious shadow. Monitoring my every move.

'Why? Where are you going?'

'I don't know yet. I'll figure it out.' I return to the bedroom with my toiletries. I'm jamming a book into the bag, looking for my phone charger.

'Are you punishing me? Because I told you what I think, that's it – you're out of here? End of discussion?'

The bag is done. I finally turn around and look at her. Mum is wringing her hands. She looks totally bewildered. It's as if someone is pranking her and it's gone too far.

'Look – I need you, Mum.' She seems taken aback. She opens her mouth to speak. I plough on – there's more. 'I need you to come with me to Oxford. I gave notice to withdraw from my degree, and I have to meet the dean and the proctors with my tutor next week.'

Now she's truly speechless. She's a cartoon character, her mouth hanging open in a perfect 'O'.

'You don't have to agree. You don't have to support me. But will you at least be there? They're probably all on your side anyway.'

Mum is a lot of things – dynamic, principled, affectionate when it suits her. She's annoying and stubborn. I'm apparently just like her. But that doesn't help me guess what's coming. This one could go either way.

She nods. 'Yes. Yes, I'll come.'

For a second, I almost forget I'm holding back a rage-spiral. We've found the calm in the eye of the storm. I smile at her. She manages a slight twitch at the corners of her mouth, shaking her head simultaneously.

'You'll be the death of me, Ben!' The hiatus is only temporary. 'This is absurd.'

I can't stay here dodging bullets all week. I pick up the bag, kissing her cheek briefly as I move past her out the room. *Don't let the sun go down on your anger.* 'I'll call you with the details. Thanks for agreeing to come.'

'You're going to Maggie and George, aren't you?'

I stamp on my shoes in the hallway, heading out the front door. 'Yeah. If Harriet will have me.'

She might not.

She could slam the door in my face.

It's a possibility I'm not ready to consider, so I don't wait for Mum to point it out. 'I'll be in touch.' I head down the communal stairwell and out into the night.

seven

HARRIET

Three Years Ago

The pub was packed for the funeral wake.

We had all migrated to the first-floor function room, spilling down the stairs and mingling in the street. When Ben finally saw me, he raised his eyebrow quizzically, just like Uncle David – an unmistakable likeness.

He nudged his way over to where I was standing alone by the buffet. 'Hi. I kind of didn't see you there. You look –'

'Ridiculous?'

'No, not especially.' He smiled and it felt like an achievement. 'Professional.'

'A professional mourner?'

He smiled again but this time it didn't quite reach his eyes. 'Corporate – like a fancy receptionist.'

'Oh good, that's exactly what I was going for.'

The pause that followed felt eternal. I badly wanted to say something helpful but the scenario was worlds away from anything that hanging out in the holidays had prepared me for. Stupidity seemed inevitable; I was already cringing on the inside.

'I'm so glad you're here, Harri.' He looked me in the eye for a moment – long enough for it to feel like a spotlight had been turned on us, everyone else dissolving.

I smothered my surprise and kept quiet. It seemed the best way to avoid putting my foot in it.

His voice dropped to a desperate whisper. 'I can't deal with these people! Half this lot never bothered with us before.' He gestured to a nearby group of his relatives, a blend of both sides exchanging small talk. We watched as they piled their plates high with rice and peas, ackee and saltfish, jerk chicken, yams – their laughter loud and jarring.

'Plus, the students and all the faculty lot –' Ben broke off. A figure queuing for food caught his attention. 'Oh, shit!' He grabbed my arm, pulling me away with him as a voice called out.

'Ben? Ben!' The man approaching us was determined to be heard.

Ben stopped and turned, his fingers digging deeper into my wrist. 'Professor Lewis. Harriet, this is my dad's colleague.'

'Ian, please.' He extended a hand in my direction but Ben continued to clutch me. I gave a small wave with my free hand instead.

'I wanted to . . .' Ian stalled, his eyes flitting between us briefly. 'I'm so very sorry for your loss. I wanted you to know that I understand these are difficult circumstances.'

I could feel Ben stiffen next to me, his face shutting down. He dropped his grip on my arm, stepping towards Ian almost imperceptibly. He'd grown taller and broader since I'd last seen him; I noted the change as he eyeballed the startled professor.

'Which loss?'

'Well, I –' It was hard to know if Ian was confused or playing dumb.

'Which loss? What exactly makes you feel bad, Ian? The fact that my dad is *dead*? Or the fact that you *stole* our *home* before his body was even in the *fucking* ground?'

The steel in Ben's voice shocked me. It cut through the small talk. People glanced in our direction. I saw Clara in my peripheral vision, a hand flying to her face as she darted across the room.

'Now, son, let's watch the language.' Ian straightened. 'You know it's more complicated than that.'

The air thickened, toxic with testosterone. Ben seemed suspended on the edge of himself, seconds from explosion.

He caught himself.

He deflated just as Clara appeared at his side.

'I –' He punched his own chest, turning his force inward. 'I am *not* your son.'

Ben stalked off, propelled by rage. I heard Clara apologising for him as I fought my way through the whispering bystanders, chasing after him.

She didn't sound sincere.

The ridiculous shoes and restrictive skirt slowed my pursuit. I eventually located Ben in a corner of the beer garden, his jacket and tie discarded, a pint glowing amber in the afternoon light.

'You got served?'

'It's the suit. And if you're here to lecture me –'

'I'm not. Scoot over.'

He made space on the bench and we sat in silence, watching the people around us live out their everyday dramas, oblivious to the wake unfolding just a stone's throw away.

'What was all that about?'

He put his head in both hands, studying the wooden table and the bubbles rising in his ale. He exhaled. 'We're being evicted. We're homeless.'

Homeless people were bearded men on street corners with questionable body odour and dodgy histories. Homeless people were bedraggled women with yellow teeth, their entire wardrobe tucked in a couple of plastic bags. Not Clara. Not Ben.

'I don't understand.' I knew my questions could make him

angry again but I simply couldn't grasp what he was saying. 'You live . . .' It clicked.

'Exactly. It's the university's flat. An employee benefit. Dad's gone; that tosser finally has his job – he's always been after it. He gets the flat. We're out at the end of the month.'

'Can't you buy something else?'

The look he gave me was incredulous. 'This is Central London.'

'Or rent?'

'In theory. It's crazy expensive, though. And Mum's free-lance. You should see some of the places we've looked at! When they even let us in the door. I don't know. I guess we'll find some-thing somewhere, but . . .' He picked imaginary fluff from the sleeve of his shirt. 'Honestly, Harri –' His voice faltered. 'I know you're trying to help but I can't talk about it right now.'

'Sorry.' My gut flipped. It was more awful than I could've anticipated. 'Sorry, I didn't mean to pry. You were just so mad! I was worried.'

'No, I get that, thank you.' He grimaced. 'His face really got to me!' He thumped the table, making his drink quiver. 'Can't believe he had the nerve to show up!'

I took his hand; it felt like the right thing to do.

I uncurled his fist, interlocking our fingers. I lifted our hands off the table, wedging them into the space between our legs. He flinched. The warmth of his palm felt foreign next to mine, the back of his hand grazing my thigh.

I didn't let go.

He settled. He leant back against the wall behind us, gradu-ally downing the ale as it warmed, droplets sweating on the side of the glass. The blue sky above us was inappropriately beautiful and I turned my face to the sun, letting my mind drift for a while. I caught him looking at me.

'What?'

'You do seem a bit different. It's not just the office wear.' He smiled again. 'Or maybe it's everything else that's different, and you're the same? I don't know. But I'm so glad you're here.'

'Said like someone who's drunk.'

'On one pint? It's true, I'm serious. I think maybe you're good for me? Because you actually know me. Means a lot.'

He was right.

There were no fireworks and it wasn't exactly an epiphany, but I noticed it – maybe for the first time: he was completely familiar to me. This person I'd memorised without meaning to. This person who was now looking at me with curiosity and a little bit of awe, like newfound treasure.

His appreciation sank deep into my bones – a feeling of being extraordinary, special in a way I'd never considered myself to be.

The glow was euphoric.

'Thanks. You're good for me too.'

He snorted. 'Am I? Look – haven't even offered to get you a drink. Do you want something? Non-alcoholic, obviously. Not going to get you into trouble.' He sat up and let go of my hand, rooting in his jacket for his wallet.

Before I could answer, my phone began to vibrate. 'It's my mum – we should probably go back upstairs.'

'I guess.' He visibly wilted at the thought. 'United front?'

Something expanded in me as I met his gaze. These were unfixable things, disaster on top of disaster.

What could I possibly do?

'Of course!' I forced myself to sound positive. 'I promise, I won't leave your side.'

eight

BEN

Getting to Harriet's house is a mission.

Her hometown has always felt misshapen – ever since we moved here. It's not that London makes sense, either. Central London's a mismatched jigsaw puzzle of old and new. It's connected, though. Here, you're easily stranded. So much of this place is a network of residential streets, ending in cul-de-sacs miles from the nearest bus stop. It's assumed you'll drive.

I don't have a car. I can't be bothered to wait half an hour for a bus that will only take me part of the way. By the time I trek for an hour, it's late and I'm exhausted. I ring the bell and hold my breath, stepping back from a front door that's more familiar than my own. Maybe I should've messaged Harriet first. Too late now – the door is opening.

'Ben! Your mum just called.'

Of course she did.

'So, you know I want to be a monk and everyone thinks I'm crazy?'

Maggie beckons me in and closes the door behind me. She smiles in sympathy as George appears from the living room. 'Not crazy. Unconventional.'

It's so much easier to appreciate other people's parents.

'Evening, Ben.' George points to my bag. 'Did Clara kick you out or are you running away?'

Maggie swats him. They exchange the type of look that

people who've been married an age use to communicate. 'We'd love to have you. We're always happy to.' The living room door clicks shut from the inside and Maggie lowers her voice a little. 'If it's all right with Harriet, it's fine by us. I think she's just . . . Well, you can talk to her.'

'Mags, he can't exactly go anywhere else tonight. Look at the time! Let the boy stay and be done with it. Yes?' He turns to me. 'I'm off to bed. See you in the morning. Keep out of trouble.'

I smile. 'I'll try.'

Maggie points at the closed door. She mouths at me, exaggerating her words and gesturing theatrically. 'Talk to her.' She pats my arm, then heads upstairs too. I'm left alone with Harriet, a wall between us. I knock on the closed door. I choose to interpret the silence as permission to enter.

The room is in semi-darkness. There's just a floor lamp shedding light on the couch in the bay window. It's a sofa bed. They bought it for me. Harriet's sitting on it, staring into space. Seeing it brings back memories. That, and the jumper she's wearing – an old one of mine. I must've left it here at some point.

She's got her satin bonnet on, hair ready for bed. Small shorts. Thick socks, despite the summer heat. Classic heartbreak uniform. She's hugging her knees. The jumper sleeves are pulled right down, clutched in her palms. I flop onto the sofa next to her, sighing more dramatically than I mean to. She uncurls and looks at me. It almost feels like nothing's changed.

'You told your mum?'

'I told her.'

She nods. 'You can stay.'

The gratitude I feel is immense. I'm weightless again, reenergised. 'I promise I won't be here too long – we have a meeting in Oxford next week, but until then . . .'

'You'd kill each other.' She smiles slightly.

'Thank you so much, Harri. I know you hate me a bit right now.'

'I don't hate you.' She moves closer, raising my arm and dropping it over her shoulders. She fidgets herself into a comfortable position, leaning back against me. She's warm in a way that's calming.

'Nice jumper.'

'Do you want it back?'

'Nah, it's OK. If things go to plan, I'll be giving up most of my stuff anyway.'

We sit together in silence. I'm drifting off, ready to be through with this day that's been so draining. Then I hear her sniffling.

'Hey? Do you want to talk about it?'

She shakes her head vigorously, head-butting my collarbone.

'All right. When you do, though . . .' I kiss the side of her forehead. I may as well have turned on a tap. She can only be described as weeping.

People are easily hurt, I'm realising.

I feel horribly powerful. And, also, completely at a loss to know how to fix this. A wet patch spreads across my shirt where her cheek is pressed. I hug her. I stroke her shaking shoulders. After a while, she shifts away and dabs at the fabric she's drenched.

'Harri, we're going to be OK. Me and you. We always are.'

A lightning flash of irritation rearranges her features. Clearly, I'm not saying the right things today.

'OK,' she exhales, 'I have to go to sleep. You remember how to put the bed out and where to find everything?'

'I remember.'

'Good. I guess I'll see you in the morning.'

'I guess so.'

She tiptoes out of the room without a backwards glance. The house is quiet in a way that middle-floor flats never are. I'm left alone, sitting on the sofa bed. I'd hoped I would never have to sleep on it again. But here I am. It's proof: life is bigger than all of us.

We never really know what's coming.

nine

HARRIET

We are four days into our little sleepover, and Ben is in the bathroom.

There are things you shouldn't know about a person outside of your family – bathroom habits are on that list – but when Ben and Clara moved in with us after Uncle David died, I got a crash course in intimacy. The 'morning dump', the 'late-night leak' – his words, not mine.

I guess the exchange was mutual: he's still the only person to join my ritualistic plaiting sessions, watching endless films with me while I braid extensions into my hair ahead of the start of term. It's a rhythm I've fallen into – changing my hair with the seasons: freeing my afro for longer periods over the summer, protecting it with braids in the busyness of term-time.

At the end of that horrendous summer holiday, our first hair/film fest was comfortable – a little bit of light relief. He filled the hours complaining that the plots were predictable, mocking anything with a love triangle and teenagers played by impossibly good-looking adults. He passed me the braid strands when I asked for them, and even plaited a couple in for me: 'Just in case I have a daughter one day.' It was fun.

This is not.

I thought I could handle him being here – we spent well over a year in that strange extended family set-up, before Clara managed to complete on the flat they have now. So, I thought this would be bearable, maybe even nice: seeing him at the dinner table, lazy brunches at the breakfast bar, being together for the last days of the summer holidays just like old times.

But he's everywhere.

And having him everywhere just emphasises the craziness he's dropped in my lap. How can he go from being so completely entrenched in my life, to willingly vanishing into thin air?

Plus, the bathroom-hogging is unforgivable.

I hammer on the door. He emerges, half-naked in pyjama shorts and looking vaguely sheepish. I avert my eyes from his bare chest. It's been a while since I've seen him topless and the sight makes my insides somersault.

He grins at me. 'You might want to give it a minute before you go in there.'

'Eew!' I duck in and grab my deodorant and a towel, holding my breath.

'Body's got to do what it's gotta do.'

'Where are your clothes?'

'Huh?'

I gesture, wishing I hadn't brought up the subject – it just slipped out.

'Oh, sorry.' He smiles. 'I thought we were past dressing up for each other. Anyway, what have you come as?' He nods at my approximation of an exercise outfit.

'I'm going to the gym with Annie.'

On cue, the doorbell rings. He follows me down the stairs, wrestling on a T-shirt he'd previously flung over the banister. Ben is not tidy; I'd forgotten that about him. I fish out a bag from under the stairs, and open the door to the first friend I made at secondary school.

'Great! You're ready! Let's go!' She's talking before the door is fully open, flying high on a whirlwind of energy that always inspires and exhausts me in equal measure. It takes her a minute to register the sight of Ben behind me. 'Ooh, Ben – hope I'm not interrupting.' She squints slyly between us, ignoring the daggers and *shut up* signals I'm firing in her direction.

'Hi, Annie.' He smiles at her tentatively. He's never quite known where he stands with her – the other best friend. 'Wait, hold on.' He turns to me. 'You're going to the *gym?* Since when do you go to the gym?'

'Since Justin got a job as trainee fitness instructor.' Annie dives in before I can open my mouth. 'I've been a member for ages but this newbie was lured along by the thought of watching Justin on an exercise bike.'

It's a complete misrepresentation of the whole situation. My face is on fire; I can feel Ben's eyes on me, asking questions I don't want to answer. 'I wouldn't put it like that.'

'Who's Justin? Do I know him?'

Annie leaps in again. 'No, he's after your time – joined our year group at the start of sixth form last year. I'm surprised Harriet hasn't mentioned him! He's the new person everyone wants to get to know – kinda like you were, but less moody-broody.'

Ben's laugh has a defensive edge. 'That was grief, not brooding. There's a big difference.'

This conversation is getting out of hand – one uncomfortable subject after another. When Ben and Clara moved in with us, Ben transferred to my school for the last year of his A levels. The way he was with everyone that winter is a version of himself he hates being reminded of. Annie's not always the most tactful person but this is insensitive, even for her.

'All right, reunion over. Let's get going, Annie.' I bundle her out of the door before she can bring up the monastery.

Something about the way this turned into a bit of an assault makes me want to reassure Ben. I hug him goodbye without thinking – despite trying to cut down on our rampant physical contact, now that he's living under my roof and also on the verge of abandoning me.

It could be my imagination, but I swear he holds on to me for a fraction longer than normal.

ten

BEN

Three Years Ago

I took a deep breath. I pushed through the doors.

The common room was the worst. Basic. A few tables and chairs. A vending machine that rarely worked. In my old school, I could've lived with it. Here it was an ordeal – every time.

The blank space left me vulnerable. People watching me. Whispers about my history. Girls trying to coax sad stories out of me ... OK, that part wasn't always awful. But I never knew where to sit. I didn't belong anywhere. Today was no different: a whole free period avoiding eye contact, head down, ear buds in.

I spied an empty corner and made for it.

Mum thought switching schools for the last year of A levels would be unideal but manageable. And it's not like we'd had much choice. The offer to crash with Maggie and George was salvation we couldn't pass up. She seemed to think having Harri here would help. Not sure she'd factored in the chasm between sixth form and the rest of the school.

I sat down. A good spot. On the far side with a clear view. No one could sneak up on me. Anyone who approached would also attract the attention of the whole room. So, I would be safe. No one was that desperate to talk to me.

The window looked out over a handful of other blocks – perfect for spying on everyone. I didn't want to talk to anyone, but there was still something hypnotic about seeing people doing ordinary stuff. In their ordinary friendship groups. With ordinary problems.

Except it was a sick joke, really – the way things carried on. Just kept going. It was insulting that everything was still so normal.

The world didn't end.

It basically didn't care.

For a little while things had been a whirlwind. Dad's status at the university initially got him some attention: *Notable Professor Dies in Tube-line Tragedy.* Then there was the investigation into how the 'incident' had happened. Did someone deliberately push him? Was it suicide? Was it the ridiculous overcrowding? The manic shoving? All those commuters trying to shave a few seconds off their travel time?

But once people got their answers – once they figured out it was the shitty outcome of a poorly timed fainting spell – they decided no one was directly to blame. Except perhaps Dad, for inconveniencing everyone's journeys.

People got back to their lives.

No one was to blame. Not the people who failed to install air conditioning. Not the people who didn't put up barriers. Not the people who wouldn't move back when he tried to leave the platform for air. It was just an old network, strained by a bloated city. Just one of those things. They had said that. In official language, but basically that. Just one of those things.

What the fuck does that mean?

Not. Good.

I put my head in my hands. I squeezed my temples as if that could possibly make it all stop. This was exactly why sitting alone in the common room pretending to listen to music was a bad idea. I wasn't listening to music. I was listening to my mind trying to make sense of something senseless. Again. And again. And again. And again.

I picked up my phone. Scrolling. Endless photos of happy people doing happy things with all the other happy people. Interspersed with rants I couldn't care less about.

And that's another thing: I'd thought I had friends. People who knew and liked me. And then I left. Turns out all I'd been carrying around was a pocket full of indifference. Hundreds of people with enough time to update their status, but who couldn't pull their finger out to drop a line saying, *We miss you. Are you OK?*

Six words. Six!

No, I'm not. Thanks for asking.

Time was crawling. Only ten minutes killed by my toxic thought-vortex. I stood up, not knowing where I was going. In theory, free periods were for studying so the library would make sense. But what was the point when I was already ahead? I owed it to Dad to stay on track – predicted high grades, preparing to interview for law at Oxford. He had been so excited when I brought up the idea.

He'd said he could see me there.

He'd assumed he would see me there.

So, I had good reason to keep on top of things – for him. It just didn't take a whole lot of effort.

I jogged down the stairs and out of the sixth-form block, drifting. I picked up my pace as I went past the art block. I didn't know Harriet's timetable – maybe she was in there making something magical. I wouldn't want her to even glimpse me like this: dark and distracted. Again. She'd worry and ask questions. I'd end up dragging her down and feel bad for doing it. Lying to her was something I could never do. But hiding was different – that, I was starting to get good at.

I found myself at one of the school gates. It was the least public of all the exits. It led to a footpath that meandered for a while until it hit a main road and some housing. The path was overgrown but overlooked: CCTV cameras spied on a spot that would otherwise be infamous. I kept walking until I was out of range.

'Ben, wait up!'

I spun round. It was a voice I didn't recognise.

'You looked like you could use a friend.' She smiled, slipping her bag off her shoulder and holding it out to me, half-open.

I peered in. I looked at her. I didn't even know her name.

'I know somewhere we can go. Follow me, new boy.' She took my hand, pulling me along with her.

And it was clichéd on every level – ending up high and horny in the woods.

But I wasn't thinking.

Finally, I wasn't thinking.

eleven

HARRIET

'Annie, what was that?' I still can't believe the way she painted everything so inaccurately back at the house. 'All I'm trying to do is get over my gym phobia! We both know you're the one who's into Justin.'

She hushes me as the gym doors buzz open. Her eyes scan the weight room and she lowers her voice, as if the whole place might be bugged. 'Everyone's into Justin. I'm just a bit more determined.' She flashes me a bright smile followed by a mock pout, trying out her flirting, and I can't help but laugh. We head upstairs to the studios, finding adjacent bikes to warm up on before the spin class starts.

'But seriously' – we adjust the machines and settle ourselves – 'Ben is going to stew over that all morning.'

'You're welcome.'

'What's that supposed to mean?'

'Would it be the worst thing in the world if he gets a little jealous? Feels a little threatened? You and Ben, you're like yin and yang – you balance. You belong together. But someone has to break your ridiculous deadlock.'

She ups her resistance, standing to cycle, while I go for a more leisurely rhythm. We don't talk for a while and her words echo in the gap, filling my mind with possibilities I grasp like a lifeline.

Maybe there's still time.

Maybe I can change Ben's mind.

It's not like this whole becoming a monk thing is even really happening yet. Apparently, it's on the horizon – OK, fine. But everyone knows the horizon is mythical – a receding line you never really reach.

Maybe losing him isn't inevitable.

For the first time in days, optimism breaks on me like the dawn, the colour seeping back into my world. This is fixable.

'Annie! Have I told you lately you're my hero?'

'Meh.' She shrugs, grinning, 'I just call it like I see it.'

I'm about to say more, but the studio has filled up and a hush falls automatically as Justin steps up to the platform and mounts his bike. His smile is gregarious – like he's the perfect host of the perfect party, instead of someone unlucky enough to be tasked with whipping us into shape.

'Morning, everyone. Let's start slow, see how we're doing. Any injuries? Anyone need help getting set up?'

An older woman near the front raises a hand. He hops back down to the floor and chats with her privately, his voice too quiet for most of us to hear. She laughs, relaxing, and just watching the exchange makes me feel less tense too. If she can do this, so can I.

'I see some new faces.' His eyes find mine. 'Thanks for making it out today. This class is forty-five minutes. You'll feel it, but in a good way. I'll give you options to take it up or down a level as you need. Have fun! We'll start with a quick warm-up.'

His enthusiasm is contagious. I sit up a little straighter as he cues up the music, getting ready to give it my best shot. Glancing around at the mix of people in the room, it's obvious I'm not the only one. From the fitness faithful to the uninitiated, almost everyone is smiling, eyes fixed on the front. I look across to Annie, beaming and more buoyant than ever.

She's right. Everyone is into Justin.

The music does most of the work for me. It's not the over-rated hits I was expecting: crap lyrics pumped out over a relentless beat that almost disguises how misogynistic the words really are. These tunes are anthems that I want to ride my heart out to – melodies that make my breath soar, basslines that my legs immediately fall into sync with.

I forget I'm uncoordinated. I forget my cardio is rubbish and I haven't participated in any sport or exercised in months. I forget I'm in a baggy T-shirt and cotton leggings instead of the expensive, figure-enhancing outfit any real gym-goer would have.

It's fun.

Justin is part-coach, part-cheerleader – alternating between stern and encouraging, making it all look easy while assuring us our pain is legitimate. It's the fastest forty-five minutes I've experienced in a long time. The class is ending before I'm ready to stop. I know Annie wants to try and catch Justin afterwards so I hang back, lingering over extra cool-down stretches, until she waves me over.

I'm nervous – I don't know why.

Maybe because Annie's such a fan, I feel like I'm meeting a minor celebrity.

'Hi, Harriet, isn't it?' Up close, Justin is every bit as charismatic as he seems on stage. He's smiling like I'm a long-lost cousin. 'I've seen you around but never had a chance to say hi. Was the class OK?'

'It was great! I'm not really a gym person but I loved it!'

His self-depreciation is kind of sweet. It seems he really isn't aware we've all been hooked. A couple of other people are loitering to talk to him and he acknowledges them before turning his full-wattage smile back to us.

'Thank you both for the support. Great to meet you, Harriet
– hopefully see you soon.'

Sitting in Annie's car, my thighs are burning and sweat is pool-
ing in places I didn't expect to get sticky. The ache tomorrow
will be an invasion, infiltrating everywhere, but for now it's
worth it to be so alive.

'Not bad, huh?' Annie backs out of the gym car park, nudging into the usual A-road congestion. 'You look happier, anyway.'

'It's like I've conquered Everest or something. I can definitely
see the appeal.'

'Justin's pretty amazing, isn't he?'

I laugh; she's so eager, so earnest. 'The appeal of exercising,
not Justin! But, yes, he's very motivational.'

'Fine, mock my devotion – I don't care. Not all of us were
lucky enough to meet our soulmate straight out of the mater-
nity ward.' The lights turn red ahead of us, and she takes the
opportunity to examine me, tough love all over her face. 'Really,
though, what are you going to do about Ben?'

It's like I'm teetering on the edge of two versions of myself.

There's the me I've been for months now, the one who has
kept quiet and hoped for the best – hoped he'd see, realise, figure
things out for himself. And then there's the me I think I need
to become. Someone more assertive. Someone prepared to risk
calling the shots.

'I think I need to just tell him the truth. Tell him how I
really feel.'

'Eee!' She drums on the steering wheel with excitement,
twisting awkwardly against her seatbelt to throw her arms
around me. 'About time!' The lights change and the car behind

us honks. She glares into the rear-view mirror and we move off again. 'I'm so excited for you! When?'

My phone pings. It pings again and again, a stream of notifications interrupting us. I check the screen – a reflex reaction. And then I check again, because surely this can't be right. Justin?

Found you through Annie.

Hope that's ok.

Glad you enjoyed the class.

You did really well.

I can see he's still typing, so I wait a second.

Don't mean to be patronising, sorry!

'Wow, you're popular today.' Annie's eyes are on the road but her voice is loaded with curiosity.

'Sorry, what were you saying?' I sidestep the question in her comment, but I'm not quite paying attention. Justin is still online; I should answer. I don't want to come across as touchy – I appreciate the compliment. It's nice to be told I've done well at something so far outside my comfort zone. I send a quick reply.

Thanks! Not patronising.

You're really good at making exercise fun.

The moment the message is sent, I find myself analysing it. Does that sound too eager?

'I asked when you're thinking you'll talk to Ben?'

I turn my phone face-down in my lap, focusing on Annie again.

It's one thing to hypothetically confess to your lifelong best friend that you really want more. It's another thing to actually do it – say those words out loud, never to be erased. And it's a whole other thing to do it when you're agnostic at most, and they've just told you they want to make a religious commitment that involves a lifetime of celibacy. No romantic relationships, no sex, nothing.

'Don't chicken out, Harriet – I know you!' She's virtually inside my mind.

'I won't – I know I need to! But I think maybe I'll wait until he's been to Oxford – who knows if he can even just drop out of uni like that?'

Annie draws up to the kerb outside my house and turns the engine off. She sighs, like a worn-out parent about to reason with a child who is being slow. 'Just promise me when you do it, you'll do it properly. Everything out in the open. None of that avoiding verbal confrontation thing that you do. Tell him straight, OK?'

My phone pings repeatedly again. I can't resist; I flip it over.

Have you ever done parkrun?

It's good if you're not a gym fan.

Maybe we could do one together some time?

If you're interested . . .

'Who *is* that?!' Annie peers over, and I shove the phone in my bag.

'No one. And I hear you about Ben. You're right, as always.' Flattery is bound to distract her. 'I promise, I'll tell him everything.'

She looks at me for a moment and I wonder if she saw Justin's photo before I could get the phone out of sight. I don't know why my first instinct was to hide this from her – he hasn't said anything earth-shattering. But now I've gone down that route it would be a bigger deal to tell her about the messages. Anyway, maybe he got in touch with her too. I concentrate on the real dilemma.

'I mean it, Annie. I know you're right about talking to Ben. It's just hard. There's a lot of history and the timing is beyond rubbish.'

She nods. 'I'm with you all the way.'

I blow her a kiss, jumping out of the car. I head towards the house, towards Ben and back to pretending as best I can that everything is normal and we'll be all right. I hear my phone ping again and dig it out from the bottom of my bag.

No pressure btw

It makes me smile – Justin's funny mix of magnetism and deferential awkwardness. He probably won't follow through anyway, but it's nice to be invited.

Parkrun sounds good. Just let me know.

twelve

BEN

'You're quiet.'

Mum and I are walking up from the Oxford train station. She's right. For once, I don't mind the observation. It doesn't feel like she's trying to prove a point. It just feels like concern.

'Are you worried about the meeting? Have you thought about what you're going to say?'

'Well, I think they just want to get to the bottom of why I'm leaving before they sign off on it. But actually' – I push my hands into my pockets, sighing – 'I'm kind of worried about Harriet.'

The pause that follows is longer than I expect. 'This must be very difficult for her. She cares about you a lot, Ben.'

'Yeah, that too. I actually meant this Justin person. According to Annie, he's a new potential boyfriend or something.' Even to my own ears I sound possessive. 'Which is fine. Obviously. I mean, it's none of my business. But.'

'She's a big girl. She can take care of herself now.'

'I know. I do know that.'

'Well, then. Good. So, focus! You're about to throw away fifteen years of education and several thousand pounds of debt.' She squeezes my arm, taking some of the sting out of her words.

'You really are unbelievable.' Mum's so predictably blunt, I have to smile. 'That was me baring my soul.'

She laughs, but it ends abruptly as we reach college. The sight makes something in me go quiet too. It's a wonderland.

Ethereal. Formidable. I can't count the number of times I've walked under the huge bell tower. Or ducked through the small, inconspicuous door instead – swiping myself in after-hours when the giant gates are closed. Approaching from the other entrances is just as momentous. Being waved in past the tourists by Vinnie or one of the other custodians – that never gets old.

This is a home from home.

It's hard to compute the reality of leaving it behind. The idea of suddenly being an outsider again, after belonging somewhere so breathtaking. It's difficult to swallow. I'm not going to lie. But should everything be easy?

There was some debate about where to hold the meeting. They wanted it to feel neutral, despite the panel of five officials in attendance. Apparently, that ruled out the deanery – I'm fairly sure that would've been the most comfortable option. Some deep armchairs. Coffee. Maybe cake. Instead, we're meeting in a small seminar room, up a staircase hidden behind one of the many arched doorways dotted around the quad.

We take the stairs and pause outside a closed door. Voices are audible inside the room. In normal terms, I'm overdressed: black shoes, black suit, white shirt, white bow tie. But I'm supposed to be in subfusc – full academic dress.

'Can I?' I motion to Mum's oversized shoulder bag. She pulls out my gown and mortar board. I shrug on the gown. Its large sleeves hang down over my suit like batwings. I don't wear the mortar board. Until graduation, this cap is just for carrying: a symbol of the end goal.

Only, now, the goal has shifted.

I can feel the rightness of that choice in my gut. But putting words around it has proved elusive – with Harri, with Mum. Today, that has to change. Today, I need to nail this. I need a coherent argument. Because if I can't convince every single person on the other side of this door that I know what I'm doing, it all ends here.

And I'm not ready for that.

I knock on the door. The voices go quiet. I hear someone get up; a chair scrapes the floor. In the seconds before the door opens, I turn to Mum – doing everything I can to make her my ally.

'Ready?' I smile at her. 'Game face, OK?'

She suppresses a small smile as the door opens. She's worried. No amount of banter is going to calm her nerves. She's here, and that's something. But, really, I'm on my own.

'Ben, come in!' My law tutor holds the door for us as we enter. 'Mrs Wilkins, pleasure. Please, take a seat.'

Small windows face into the quad, letting in a haze of natural light. Reading lamps struggle to project into the gloom. There are no portraits on the walls – an anomaly in a college steeped in history. For all the talk of neutrality, the room is set up like a job interview.

The panel are sitting in a row behind a table. Chairs for me and Mum are set facing them, with another table for our use. Notepads and pens are laid out for us. There's still and sparkling water, self-service tea and coffee, various biscuits individually wrapped. And a box of tissues – a compassionate afterthought.

'I'll do introductions.' My tutor takes her seat. 'I'm Dr Kiran Varma, one of the undergraduate law tutors here and Ben's pastoral tutor as well. This is the Very Reverend Dr Amy Stuart, dean of the college – so, in charge of both the college and the cathedral. To my left is Professor Richard Coombes, junior censor, with responsibility for non-academic undergraduate matters.'

Everyone apart from Mum is wearing a gown of some kind. They nod and smile politely as Dr Varma rattles through the list.

'And finally, from the wider university proctors' office, we have Professor Timothy Yates and Professor Gerhard Mueller – senior proctor and assessor, respectively. And I'm sure I lost you a long time ago!' She laughs, rolling her eyes at the absurdity of the gathering. 'The long and short of it is, we're all here because we care about you, Ben.'

I've sat across from her on a weekly basis, defending my essays, talking through the reading list. It's nice that she's taking the lead here.

'We see it as our collective responsibility to understand and guide your choices to the extent that we can. So, talk to us. We have your statement. You want to withdraw from your degree?'

'Yes.' I centre my breathing. I stick to the facts. 'I have an offer to explore entry into monastic life. It's a pretty long process, but there's an opportunity to start really soon and I want to go ahead with that.'

The panel exchange sideways glances. It's the junior censor who speaks first. 'Ben, leaving your degree after two out of three years is an enormous step to take. And as a college, we would be very sad to lose your contribution. You've been a wonderful ambassador for all our BAME students and prospective students –'

I barely contain my inner groan. I sat in on one access talk, answering questions on underrepresentation and feeling like a fraud for all my privilege. I doubt he even knows about that. By my 'contribution', he basically means that I'm not white and I'm here. I'm still figuring out how to respond, when I see Mum straighten.

'Uh-uh.' She's seething.

I try not to smile.

'Don't you put that on him. If we're seriously talking about equality, he should be equally free to do whatever is right for him. As an *individual*. Just like anyone else.'

They probably think she's finished. She's not.

'And please! Don't you be talking about his "contribution" when we all know losing him will cause a drop in your diversity statistics, and *that's* what you're really worried about. Come on now. Be real.'

Now she's done. Keeping a straight face is a struggle. The junior censor coughs. I almost feel sorry for him. Dr Varma glares at him. The others stare at the table.

'Ben, as your tutor, I can unequivocally state that I value you. Your mind, your prospects. This is about you, not the college or anyone else.'

The assessor speaks up. 'The proctors' office – we're concerned with enforcing the rules and policies that govern academic life across the university. Since medieval times.' He laughs lightly. I've never laid eyes on him before. When he looks at me, his gaze is steady, calm. 'But, as assessor, my particular area of responsibility is how the university handles welfare issues. So' – he leans back – 'I don't know if this is relevant, but it would be remiss of me not to ask. Are there any underlying difficulties we should be aware of? Financial problems? Worries about the pressures of finals? Physical- or mental-health concerns?'

Mum and I lock eyes, briefly.

'Nothing relevant.'

He nods.

I know I'm being evasive. It's time to speak up. I just don't know where to start. 'Look, I know this is unusual.' Understatement. 'But this isn't out of the blue for me. I did a guided retreat at the monastery when I was eighteen. I've done my research. I know what it's about. And, honestly, monastic life is not a million miles away from what you're all doing here.'

I'm suddenly struck by the hypocrisy of this particular group of people trying to talk me out of my decision.

'I mean, look around! You work in this beautiful, historic environment. We live communally. We eat together every day. We study. We have these term rhythms and traditions that dictate the timetable of our lives: Michaelmas, Hilary, Trinity. And, let's face it – it's a bubble here, too.'

'But we expect you to leave – we're preparing you to join the real world.' The junior censor has recovered enough to speak again.

'Well, you didn't, did you?' With every word, I have less and less time for him.

There's stifled laughter from the other panel members. I relax into my argument.

'And what is the real world? What's so great about it? I tried the stuff you push us towards – I went to the City, I did the work experience. And as far as I can see, the status quo is . . . broken.' I stop myself from swearing in the nick of time. 'If I want to live an alternative lifestyle – a more humanitarian, holistic life that's less materialistic and kinder to the planet – now seems like a pretty good time to do it. Because if we don't all drastically change the way we live, we're . . . screwed.'

Dr Varma is smiling, shaking her head. 'I listen to you arguing with us, and it just reminds me of our tutorials. You are one of my most passionate, truculent students – and I mean that in the best sense. You know your own mind, that's for sure. And your academic work is so promising. So, I guess, my real question is: why now?'

I can see Mum nodding in my peripheral vision.

Dr Varma pushes the point. 'Why not wait a year? Do it after graduation. If it's right now, won't it be right then?'

I'm thrown, and she knows it.

I can't deny the logic in what she's saying. Dropping out is drastic. It's a leap of faith. I don't know how to explain that.

I don't know if it's the right thing to do – it's definitely not sensible. But I still think it's valid, even if I can't pin down exactly why.

'It just . . . it feels urgent.'

There's a pause. It's like I can hear their thoughts. They think I'm immature. They think I'm reckless and spoilt – someone who doesn't know how good they have it.

I don't know what to say to that.

'You might not think so, Ben, but I do understand.' The dean is smiling at me, empathy etched on her face. I immediately feel less alone in the room. She knows me from chapel. If rational intellect and religious belief are two different languages, then we're both bilingual. 'Look at me: I'm female and I'm clergy. I'm head of a college critics still try to write off as an Etonian stronghold. I understand desperately wanting to change the narrative. I know that . . .' She waves her hands in the air, trying to pull down the exact sentiment. '. . . driving impulse towards revolution.'

I'm nodding. That's it. That's exactly it. I want change, and I want it now. Yesterday, actually. I don't want to go on being part of something that doesn't feel relevant anymore.

She leans forwards. Her voice is gentle. 'I understand why you want to throw everything you have into a new path, now that you've identified where you want to go. But –'

My heart sinks.

'Ben, in my experience, if you want to walk through certain doors, certain keys are useful. Finish your degree. It doesn't have to close anything off. It just gives you even more options.'

I slump in my chair.

It's a poor negotiating tactic – pretty much a white flag. But I can't help it. This is a rollercoaster. I wasn't ready for it. I didn't seriously consider the possibility of being forced to stay. It's not like a degree is mandatory. If I stop showing up, they can't drag me back here. But the offer from the monastery is conditional:

they won't accept me if my time there would cause 'irreconcilable conflict with prior commitments'.

So, I need this.

I need them to let me go.

Mum puts her hand on my shoulder. I'm suddenly so glad she's here. I feel ground down. Smaller than small. Powerless, where before I was so confident.

'We can see this is very important to you. And we respect that.' The assessor's voice is soothing. He reminds me a little of Dad. I take a deep breath. Now is not the time. 'We would like to invite you to at least consider an alternative proposal. Instead of withdrawing altogether.'

My head snaps up, alert again. He nods at the senior proctor. So far, he's been quiet, taking notes in the corner.

The senior proctor moves his pen and paper to one side. He pushes his glasses up the bridge of his nose. He rests his hands on the table.

'You do have the option, within the rules of the university, to rusticate. To suspend your studies for one academic year. In doing so, you would remain eligible to sit your finals the following year. Whether that means coming back into college or potentially relaxing the residency rules to enable you to somehow finish your studies remotely at the monastery, well – we just don't know. This is truly unprecedented. All parties would need to co-operate very closely.'

There's light. There's hope.

'It is a compromise. But one we hope you can live with. Because we would be very sorry to see you walk away entirely at this stage, after all your investment. So, we ask you to please think about it and let us know. Ideally within twenty-four hours, given the timescales of your proposed plans. I understand you'd like to be in Scotland by the end of next week?'

I look across to Mum. She has tears in her eyes – maybe relief, maybe shock. My hands are shaking, adrenaline going crazy in my veins. I want to fist-pump the air and give them all high-fives. I want to laugh at the improbable becoming real, right in front of my eyes. I'm doing this! I'm actually doing this. By next week, I'll be at the monastery, on the edge of a new life. The first step.

'Yes.' I nod. Repeatedly. Emphatically. 'We'll talk about it.' I smile at Mum. She tries to smile back. 'We'll talk and I'll get back to you.'

We don't talk.

We leave college and walk the meadow's tree-lined avenue in silence until the path meets the river. I think of Summer Eights – the intercollege boat races in Trinity term. It will stay with me. People rammed along the riverside. Boathouse balconies bursting with spectators. The cheering. The chants. It will all stay with me. But knowing I can leave is like winning the lottery. A long shot. A game-changer.

'Thanks for having my back with the censor on the whole diversity thing.' It's easier to start the conversation with something we both agree on.

'Ridiculous man.' Mum kisses her teeth. 'But you're playing into a dangerous stereotype. The black male drop-out.'

'And you played the angry black woman.'

She snorts. 'I guess we can't win.'

I feel her waver next to me. The shift is subtle enough. A slight change of pace. But her posture is her tell. She's readying herself. No messing about. This is it. This is where we get into it. I swallow, hard.

'Just. OK, just help me, Ben.' It's a statement, not a question. An instruction. 'I heard you in there. But . . . help me understand. You don't have to keep it secular for me. I'm a Christian; you're a Christian. But a *monk?* I just don't get it.'

I feel the way I always feel. I can argue about almost anything, indefinitely. But faith? Belief? It runs too deep. It's too personal. Words can't carry the full weight of what it feels like – in my cells, in my synapses. And I'm trapped. I feel trapped. Because who plans their life by something they can't even articulate?

She stoops, fingering the mud-orange gravel at our feet. She finds a loose stone. Two, three – a little collection. She hands them to me. 'Watch out for the ducks.'

I smile at the stones in my palm. 'But ten points for the rowers?'

I lob the stones across the river. Forcefully. One at a time. It's been an age since we've done this. There was a time when it was a ritual. Her way to help me get it all out. When I was small. And the feelings were so big. Fears. Frustrations. Sometimes bullies. Sometimes boredom. Sometimes this gnawing ache that didn't have a name but looked like monsters under the bed or 'natural' disasters on the TV news.

We'd take a bus. We'd find a large pond, or a lake, or a river. She'd give me stones. I'd throw them away. The water would ripple. The stones would sink. And the weight was gone. Temporarily. It was my idea – I started it. And she noticed it made me feel better. So, then she encouraged me to keep doing it. To cope. And I was, like, seven. So, I never asked.

I didn't ask what I'm wondering now.

All those stones disappearing into the dark, never to resurface again. Was it release?

Or repression?

'Ben.' Mum moves to stand next to me, quietly – she's almost cautious. 'Is this about what you did? Is it guilt? Are you still trying to make amends?'

'No!' My volume startles me. I try again, with more self-control. 'No, it's not about . . . It's not that.'

She turns away from me. She continues our walk, moving on from the water and re-joining the path. I'm left to catch up in my own time. I can tell from the hunch of her shoulders: she's not convinced.

'I mean, when I went there, after . . . everything that happened . . .' I try to think it through, without reliving the specifics. I have to give her something; Mum won't let me off the hook. 'They were so good to me. Even though I was in such a bad place. So, maybe it is about that. A bit. Maybe I want to be like them. To have that level of goodness. Or at least be around it.'

'But how well do you know them? You only really spent time with a couple of them. I'm not saying they're not good people. Possibly great people. It's just such an extreme choice. And, remember, they're still just people.'

'Yeah, but it's like they've really thought about it.' I'm staring ahead. Beginning to rant. 'They've figured out how they want to be. Their lives aren't superficial. They're brave enough to say "fuck the system" –'

I see her smile in my peripheral vision. 'Probably not those exact words.'

'You know what I mean. They've chosen these really, extremely altruistic values. And people write them off, but the monks aren't actually bothered. They just get on with living these quiet lives. And you know what? Everyone is so caught up in the fact that this is unusual. But really! I feel like that kind of misses the point. Fine. Dismiss them. They're "abnormal". But what about the rest of us?! Look at the state we're in!'

She shifts again.

Her chicks are coming home to roost. Or whatever that saying is. This is her. Almost word for word. Her influence on me. It's the books she raised me on. The documentaries she sat me in front of. This is just a different version of a choice she would make.

Trying to be part of a sea-change.

I can feel myself reaching boiling point. Somewhere between irritated and emotional. Probably too defensive, but incapable of calming down. Yes, I'm changing The Plan. I'm dropping out. I'm quitting, failing, escaping: whatever. But maybe it's actually just sanity. To want to escape *this* version of reality – where it's all a competition. And everyone and everything is a resource. Or a rival. And the only way to win is to be the last one to die trying.

Maybe I'm weird.

Or maybe the real question is – why would *anyone* want to live like that?

'But you're doing so well, Ben. At everything!'

I've argued with Mum enough times to hear it. She's caving. Right now, she's not even buying into her own rhetoric.

'Maybe. But, Mum, it's the whole game. I hate these rules. I don't want to play anymore.'

She nods. And sighs. 'But why?'

Unlike with Harriet, I know what Mum means. She wants me to get to the point. My true motives. At the heart of it all. And I flinch. She's reaching into rawness. She's hitting a spot that endlessly reverberates.

It's love.

And shame. And gratitude. It's history. And awe. And anticipation. And things I don't say out loud to other people because it's easier to be silent than to be misunderstood.

Mum prods again, more insistent this time. 'Is this just about what you want?' She shakes her head. 'No, it's not. Is it?' She's putting the pieces together. Deciphering the puzzle. Seeing the whole picture for what it is. 'You think this is something God is asking you to do, don't you? That's what you believe?'

'Yes.'

'And, actually, you don't know *exactly* why.'

I don't answer.

'I'm right, aren't I?'

'Yeah.'

'But being asked is enough for you? You're willing to go along with it, and hope you find out?'

I nod. 'Yes.' It's as simple, and complicated, as that.

Mum exhales, rubbing her hands over her face. Processing.

I shouldn't rush her. But it feels like no amount of time would really be enough. 'It made you feel better, though? That I can do this, and still graduate?' We've followed the path as it loops round from the river, back into the woodland along the edge of the meadow. She doesn't answer straightaway.

'Do you know the worst thing about losing your dad?'

'Just one?'

'So often when it comes to you – parenting you – I don't know what he'd say. That blank! That silence! It's like losing him all over again, each time. And then I think I should know, and maybe I didn't really know him. Maybe I didn't pay enough attention.'

I'm so used to her bravado. I'm used to her defiance. The strength she shows to, and demands from, others. Hearing her insecurities makes me feel like Dorothy in Oz. I'm not sure I can cope with the wizard being all smoke and mirrors.

'Of course you did, Mum! Don't do that to yourself.'

'Well.' It's like she can sense my fear. With just one word, she's composed again. 'About this, I'm pretty sure. I had a lot of thinking time when you were at Maggie's. And – now, this is not meant as a guilt-trip, but – I think he'd want you to graduate. That's definitely what I want. And I think we'd agree. So, if you can do both, that's good. That's better.'

My pulse quickens. Hearing something close to acceptance

from her means even more than I anticipated. As usual, she speaks again before I've found the words to respond.

'Also, think about it from their perspective. The monastery. You're talking about potentially making a lifetime commitment? In the long run? All the vows: poverty, celibacy, obedience. For the rest of your life?'

'Yes.'

'Well, how can they believe that – if you can't even commit to finishing a three-year degree?'

I have to admit, it's a good point. As much as I believe in going down this route right now, withdrawing to do it could come off as flaky. Trying to hold it all together will stretch me in ways I can't even imagine. But I can at least try. Especially if that means some kind of truce with Mum.

Honour your father and mother.

'OK. So, I won't quit. I'll take the year off like they're offering, and we'll all go from there. That can work. And then everyone's happy.'

'Slightly happier.' She chuckles quietly. 'Let's not get carried away.'

This is impossible.

Mum's hard enough to please at the best of times. But this? After all the shit I've pulled in the past? I must be crushing her. I can't ask. I don't want to hear it. How much I'm disappointing her. Again.

It's actually incredible that she's still here. Talking to me like this is normal. Trying to take my wild dreams in her stride. Yes, we fight. All. The. Time. But she's a warrior.

'You're not too bad, Mum. You know that? You're all right.' I put my arm round her shoulders, and she laughs.

'High praise, thank you.' She hugs me back. Squeezing me with the full force of mixed emotions. 'I'm quite fond of you too.'

We've walked the full loop round to the college again. Tomorrow I'll get back to my tutor. I'll update the monastery too. For now, there's nothing left to do except head home.

'Right.' I'm suddenly decisive. 'I'm ready for ice cream. Let's do it.'

Her laugh is a cackle. 'You're always ready for ice cream. I remember when you and Harriet used to make ice-cream soup for breakfast.'

'Ice-cream soup!' It's a blast from the past. I'm transported back to London and summer holidays in early secondary school. 'Yeah! We'd warm it up in the microwave. Until Harri burnt her tongue one time, and we were like – "Hot ice cream?! What are we even doing?!" So, we stopped.'

'Probably for the best.'

The floodgates are open. My mind is full of summers and Harriet, and how much she's shared with me. I have to tell her about the meeting. I can't wait to tell her.

'Actually, do you mind if I call her real quick? To let her know how it went. What? What's the face for?'

'Nothing.' Mum raises her hands – the universal posture of surrender. Of neutrality.

I raise my eyebrow at her. It's not like her to hold back.

'No, nothing. Go on.'

She walks a few paces behind me. I call on our way to the ice-cream café. Harriet picks up within the first couple of rings.

'Hello?'

'It's me.'

'Obviously.' She sounds breathless. 'So, don't leave me hanging . . . ?'

'Really good news!'

thirteen

HARRIET

It's Saturday and Ben and I are going out for dinner.

Tonight.

Ben and I are going out for dinner tonight – to 'celebrate' the fact that he's leaving. And that's the only explanation I have for hauling myself out to try parkrun with Justin this morning: I need the distraction. There are too many hours to fill, too many emotions to keep a lid on.

So, here I am.

It feels like a festival – people milling around, congregating on the field and in the car park. Volunteers in hi-vis jackets are stewarding participants into some semblance of order, but I'm still not quite sure what this involves or where I'm supposed to be. I should've read the link Justin sent. I regret my spontaneous, late-night 'yes' to a message that took me completely by surprise.

My phone vibrates and I scan the horizon, scouting for the landmarks he's described. I see the tree, the woman in the fluorescent pink tracksuit. I see Justin, beaming his trademark smile. Even jogging over to him, I'm self-conscious.

'Hi! What did I sign up for?'

He laughs, reattaching his phone to some kind of bicep gadget-holder. '5k?'

'Are you serious?' My jaw swings open.

'You'll be fine, it's completely relaxed. We can walk and you don't even have to finish. But that would be a real shame.'

We make our way through all the starting procedures. It feels so bizarre to just begin running for no apparent reason, but we plunge in and the stream of people carries us. After a while my mind wanders away from the mechanics of pumping my arms and legs. I sneak a peek at him out the corner of my eye. I'm obviously holding him back – he is totally at ease. Annie's told me so much about him, it's easy to forget he's a total stranger.

'So' – I try to talk and breathe – 'this is your idea of Saturday morning fun?'

He smiles. 'It helps. I have ADHD.'

'Oh, sorry.' I feel like such an idiot – insulting him right from the start.

'Nah, don't be. It's kind of helped me figure stuff out. Like, I know I wouldn't want a desk job – school's bad enough, and that's with doing PE.'

'What about next year – will you go full-time at the gym? Your class really was great.'

'Ah, thanks.' His unbelievably stretchy smile expands. 'Actually, I want to become a physio as well as doing the personal training thing. So, hopefully university. I can keep on top of my ADHD symptoms pretty well these days – I was diagnosed really young, so. It's my life, you know? Just gotta get on with things.'

'It's so good that you have a plan.' I can't keep the wistfulness out of my voice.

'How about you – what's next?' He slows down a little, letting me catch my breath.

'Art, I think.'

'Wow, that's really brave.'

'Brave?' I get a lot of adjectives thrown at me in response to my degree choice, but that's not normally one of them.

'Yeah, I mean – it's great. I guess it's just not straightforward, is it? You sort of have to be prepared to hustle and really be the one to keep yourself going. Believe in yourself when no one else does.'

I don't know what my face is saying, but it can't be good because he immediately starts to apologise – backtracking, digging.

'I really do think it's great! Sorry, sometimes I don't stop talking when maybe I should. I'm just thinking out loud. You'll do great. I'm sure.'

'It's fine . . .' I'm not convinced it is. 'You make a good point.'

I slow down to a walk. It's as if my mind can't keep my body running and wade through the rising tide of insecurity at the same time.

How have I never considered the possibility of failing as an artist before?

When it's not about grades, when no one is being paid to take an interest in what I'm making – it's true, it's a lightning bolt to my psyche: there's a high probability that no one will care.

Justin is walking now, too – long strides, I almost have to jog again to keep up. The runners have thinned out; the path curves across a meadow and the sky is huge ahead of us. It should feel spacious, but a kind of claustrophobia is closing in.

'Why a physio?' I need to change the subject.

'I like the idea of helping people get their movement back.'

I'm nodding, but I'm struggling to listen – still at a crossroads in my thoughts. 'Maths is the other option, for me.'

'Art or maths! Aren't they quite diffcrent?'

'People say that.'

'I'm unoriginal, OK, I can take that.'

I smile. 'I just love any kind of pattern. It's like they help things make more sense. And I love that we have these other, more universal ways to communicate, not just words.'

'You could do loads with maths. You could be the next big thing in STEM.'

'Because I'm black and female?'

He doesn't miss a beat. 'Because you can do maths! And you actually seem to like it! I couldn't wait to drop it. Didn't work for me – I always lost the thread halfway through. So, thank God for apps.' He laughs and I appreciate it – his lightness, his total lack of defensiveness.

'Anyway, shouldn't we be running?' I feel like I'm cheating, strolling along.

'You tell me – you're the one who doesn't like exercise. Why is that, by the way?'

'It's not really exercise – I'm just out of the habit with exercising. I don't like gyms. It feels like they're just for one type of person.'

'Ah, I hate that! I try with my classes – with the music I choose and things like that. Everyone needs somewhere to be active. It's a lifesaver! And I hate that some people are put off even stepping through the door.'

His sunniness is clouded over for the first time – his eyebrows drawn down into a deep frown.

There's more to it than I've said.

We're circling a topic that I don't like to touch on, especially with people who don't know what happened. But I feel like I can't leave it here – with him thinking it's all about the gym.

'Your class was fun. It helped. It's not just . . . I had a horrible, horrible thing happen to me. In May, last year – right at the end of year eleven. Before you joined.'

Justin stops in his tracks.

I stand still too, but that's as much detail as I want to go into right now. I don't re-live it. Not if I can help it. Especially not with boys I've only just started talking to.

'So, it's been, what? Fifteen months. Unbelievable, nearly a year and a half. But I'm still building back. My confidence.' This is me ending the conversation.

He looks excessively uncomfortable – I'm worried his smile is gone for good. I should have kept my secrets to myself. He scuffs the ground with his trainers, kicking at a tuft of grass. Eventually he starts off again, setting a pace I can manage and I fall into step alongside him.

'Harriet, I hope you're OK.'

'I am.'

'For what it's worth, you have a good gait.'

'A good what now?'

He chuckles and it's good to see the brightness resurface. 'The way you run. Lots of people tilt or hunch, but you've got naturally good technique.'

'Thanks!' I feel like I've been given a gold star in primary school – it's ridiculously gratifying.

'Rubbish shoes, though – they'll do your knees and ankles in. And shins. And back. I can help you choose some better ones, more supportive.'

I'm laughing – laughing harder than the comment deserves, but it just sets me off for some reason. 'Am I your new fitness project?'

He grins too. 'Depends. Are you coming back next week?'

Next Saturday is a date I can't wrap my head around. Next Saturday Ben will have left for the Hebrides. I'll need an incentive to get out of bed.

Annie enters my mind for a split second – I didn't tell her about this. I will tell her about this. Probably. Not that this is something that needs reporting: two people running in a field at silly o'clock on a Saturday morning, surrounded by families and fanatics.

Justin's smile is shrinking with the lengthening pause.

'OK, all right – you win.'

'Yesss!' He suddenly takes off, sprinting ahead then circling back – arms aeroplane-wide. He beats his chest and crows like he's Tarzan, like he's king of the world. 'Too much?'

My bemusement is obvious. 'Maybe a little?'

He shrugs, laughing. 'I just love a parkrun convert.'

fourteen

_____

HARRIET

Fifteen Months Ago – May, Last Year

It went through to voicemail again.

'This is Ben Wilkins. Leave a message. I'll call you back.'

I hung up and redialled, my hands fumbling over the sturdy buttons of the landline phone. It was late morning on a Friday; he could be anywhere – in a lecture, the library, a tutorial. He might still be in bed, or doing laundry, or out with friends. I had no idea about the precise rhythm of his life in Oxford, just a crushing need to get hold of him immediately. I coiled the cord around my fingers, my breath suspended in the pause between each ring.

'Hello? Harri, is that you?'

Now that he was there, I couldn't speak. His voice always seemed lower on the phone but there was more to the resonance this time – a combination of warmth and worry that left me choked up. I nodded, pointlessly.

'Can you hear me? Hello?'

'Yeah, I can.' My voice was barely a whisper.

'Shit. What's wrong?'

'Everyone's OK. It's just . . . I'm sorry. I just . . .' The sentence wouldn't complete itself. My chest constricted, a strangled, wheezing sound escaping in place of intelligible words.

'OK. So, OK . . .' He tried to organise his thoughts out loud. 'You're safe right now?'

'Yes.'

'Is anyone with you?'

'No.'

'All right, listen, I'm going to come and see you.'

I sank to the carpet, floored by a cocktail of remorse and relief. It was too much to ask but exactly what I wanted. I put my head between my knees, letting the air slowly refill my lungs. 'You don't have to do that.'

'I want to. I'm on the next train. You'll be OK until then?'

'Yes. Thank you.'

'Of course. Sit tight.'

'Ben?'

'Yep?'

'If you need to get hold of me, use this number. Please don't use my phone.' It was the most I'd managed to say. I shuddered – a sick, sinking feeling coursing through my whole body. I hung up before he could ask me anything else.

Ben hugged me as soon as I opened the door, wrapping his arms around me like a comfort blanket. It felt like he'd arrived in no time, but my stomach started to rumble and I realised I had been sitting in the same spot, comatose, for almost the whole day. My parents would be back from work before long. There was no way I could even imagine facing them – their questions and things I would have to admit.

'Something awful happened at school today and I . . . Everyone is . . . I can't stay here.'

He let go of me, stepping back to assess the damage. 'Come back to Oxford with me. Stay the weekend.' He shook his head, pre-empting my protests. 'You need to. Message your parents, or leave a note or whatever. Or I'll call them. It will be fine. Let's just go, all right?'

Now that he'd suggested it – insisted on it – I could see it was absolutely what I needed. It wasn't until we were on the train, sitting opposite each other, racing away from the carnage, that I was ready to tell him why.

'You can't get worked up over this, Ben. Don't get angry and do something stupid.'

He raised both eyebrows. He exhaled, crossing his arms over his chest. 'I mean, it depends. But I'll try not to.'

'I started seeing someone. I did really like him. Things went quite far. And I sent him some photos, just in a private message' – my voice began to shake – 'but then he did this . . .' I unlocked my screen, opening up the app and passing Ben the phone as quickly as possible.

I didn't want to see it.

My body.

All the reactions and comments. The ways this beast had taken on a life of its own – people like Annie going into battle for me, so many others happy to rip me apart. It had been morphing and mutating for hours, refusing to die down and disappear.

I examined the view from the window – the sun-scorched fields, the deep green oaks stretching their heavy branches skyward, all of it whipping past as the train sped on.

'Fuck.' Ben's voice was hoarse.

I snuck a glance in his direction.

He pushed the phone away, screen down on the table between us. He rubbed a hand across his face, his jaw clenched, his eyes screwed shut.

Why had I shown him?

He'd given up social media not long after Uncle David died – I could easily have hidden this from him. My heart started to hammer uncontrollably, a wild thing caught in my ribcage.

Would he blame me? Think less of me?

The totally manipulated GIFs, the unimaginably cruel captions – those were edits that made me nauseous, but the original pictures? No one forced me to take those. A trembling sensation overwhelmed me, like someone was shaking me from the inside, from my very core.

'Harri.' His voice was quiet but firm. 'Harriet, look at me.'

I raised my eyes to his.

He held my gaze, unflinching, unsmiling. 'I love you, Harriet. You're the best person I know.' His eyes were iron. 'You do *not* deserve this.'

I nodded, numb.

'Do you hear me, Harri? Say it. Say, "I don't deserve this."'

'I don't –' A lone sob surfaced. The anger and fear and horrifying humiliation of it all had chased away my ability to really weep.

Ben got up, moving to sit next to me. He cleared his throat and flexed his fingers, restless with rage. He reached out. He held my hand, leaning back in his seat, closing his eyes. It was like he was closing the subject for the time being, giving me space to hurt in private. Maybe he was, but there was something else too – I noticed as I watched him for a minute longer, feeling grateful for him in every fibre of my being.

I stared in utter disbelief.

He was crying.

Slow tears were descending down his cheeks. There was no disguising it; he didn't bother to wipe them away.

He was openly crying. For me.

fifteen

BEN

It's so good to be back with Harriet in our favourite Chinese restaurant.

Things have hardly changed. The décor is still unpretentious. Red lanterns. Colourful dragons. Fairy lights. Photos of the specials are still blue-tacked to the windows. The neon welcome sign still blinks.

'You two! Long time! I worried you split up!'

I let it go – people have been making assumptions about us for years. Harri doesn't correct her either.

'Usual table? Nice to see you! Very nice. Talk later, OK?'

I'd thought about suggesting somewhere new for our send-off dinner, but as Harriet sits in her chair I'm glad we went with this. She's starting to relax – smiling. The first proper one in a while.

I've missed it.

And I have a feeling it won't last.

We get drinks and order. We talk about everything and nothing. I refuse to be the one to bring up the elephant in the room. After the food arrives, she finally acknowledges why we're here.

'So, they're letting you take a year out to go to the monastery? That's good.'

I love her for trying, but she's massively unconvincing. I play along, aiming for casual. 'Which reminds me – do you think you could write me a reference?'

'You need references?'

'I need everything! References, personality profiling, psychometric evaluations, health check, personal statement. And I'm basically going on a twelve-week interview.'

She pulls a face. 'That's intense.'

'Yeah. But it makes sense.'

I can't let it go. There are so many misconceptions. I have to chip away at the ignorance, even when it's coming from someone I can't bear to fight with right now.

'It's a huge risk for them. This is their family; it's not just a job. They can't just fling the door open to every person who shows up claiming God told them to move to the Hebrides.'

She smiles, but it fades just as quickly. 'I think I'd find that really difficult. What would I say? I don't know what makes a good monk.'

'Well, they're not really asking that. It's just a character reference. Like, four, five questions about me as a person. And then it all goes into the mix and they'll decide.'

I don't know why I'm pushing this, but I really want her to say yes. Maybe because it would be evidence that she doesn't think I'm totally crazy. A tiny shred of support.

'Please? I'd be massively, eternally grateful.'

'Can I think about it?'

'Sure. I can put you down as a maybe?'

She nods, but she's shrinking into herself. It's like I've juiced all the joy out of her. She stops eating. She's ripping up her paper napkin, collecting the fragments into a pile, crumpling them together, then pulling them apart again. I've probably had every dish on this menu – the flavours are insane, but it's turning to ash in my mouth.

'Harri, please, please talk to me!'

I cover her hands with mine; I can't take any more of the paper napkin routine.

'It feels like every time I bring up the monastery, you cry or you're about to. It's killing me! I had no idea it would be this tough for you. I mean, I knew you wouldn't be thrilled but . . . ?'

She flips my hand over, stroking my palm. Her fingers travel to my wrist. Toying with the friendship bracelet she knotted there after Dad died. The only jewellery I wear. It's fraying; I never take it off.

'It's a shock. It's hard to imagine.'

There's more.

There must be more. She's clearly editing. Her sentences are so short, so tight. But I wait, and that's it. She doesn't elaborate. And I don't know what to do. If she doesn't want to tell me, she doesn't want to tell me.

'OK, so, about that' – I'll have to work with what I've got – 'there's this little handbook they've written for applicants, to help you get ready. And one of the things they say can be helpful is if the most significant people in your life come and visit the monastery. Just to see it and hopefully understand it all a bit more. Mum's already been, when she came to get me the last time I was there. But I wondered whether maybe you'd want to come up? Maybe in the October half-term? I know it's a long way to go for a few days. But what do you think? Would that help?'

Her poker face has reached new levels. She pulls away and sips her drink. I have no idea how she's going to respond.

'Yeah, I think I'd like that. I am really curious about it all; I can't help it.'

'Great!' I'm grinning from ear to ear. I feel like I've finally nudged a boulder. I'm dying to keep up the momentum. I hate feeling like we're misaligned. 'Should I have told you sooner? When I started thinking about it?'

'When was that?'

'Hard to say. It just sort of surfaced. Six, maybe nine months ago.'

'Honestly, I don't think it would've made much difference.'

'But it was dickish to do it at the Tate?'

'Dickish?' She smiles and it sticks.

'As in, I was a complete dick.'

She laughs. She picks up her chopsticks again, taking a huge mouthful of noodles, and I know we're past the worst. 'I get what you were going for. Hiding the pill in the jam.'

'I'm so sorry you missed the Choucair exhibition. Wasn't expecting you to do a runner, to be fair. But anyway' – I reach underneath the table for the grand reveal – 'I got you this.'

I pass the present across to her – the curator's book about the exhibition and pretty much every limited-edition postcard I could find in the gift shop. I came by the restaurant earlier – asked if I could hide it here. It was so worth it.

'Ah, Ben!' She wipes her hands on her lap. She touches the book like it's treasure. She flicks through the postcards, examining the details on the back of each one. Her whole face is alight, like sunrise. 'You went back to the Tate after I left?'

'I did. You were talking about the canvas. The geometric abstracts.' She's about to start explaining again. 'Don't tell me – she used ratios to section them off, right?'

'You were listening?'

'They're mathematically balanced and that's why they feel so satisfying to look at. And something about contrasts and colour theory – not sure I totally understood that bit. So, I didn't know which postcards to get, but mainly I just went with those.'

She's looking at me like I've grown two heads. 'You were really listening.'

I feel like I'm being appraised.

'Of course!' I start to blush; I can't put my finger on why. 'Obviously, I was a bit distracted by the bomb I knew I had to drop. But I always try to listen to you, Harri.'

I don't know why this is news.

She hugs the book. She's beaming – but not quite at me, kind of through me. Past me. When her eyes do meet mine, she almost jumps – like she wasn't expecting me to be looking at her. But how could I not be looking at her?

She's being completely strange.

'I, um . . .' She puts the book and postcards into the bag hanging off the back of her chair. She knocks back her entire drink in about three gulps. 'Thank you so much, Ben. I, um . . .' She leaps to her feet. 'I'll be back in a minute.'

She heads for the toilets.

I'm so confused, I have to laugh. I mean, she's not crying – so that's a relief. But, honestly, for someone I've known since forever, she can be totally mysterious.

Sometimes I really, really wish she had subtitles.

sixteen

HARRIET

I can see Ben – I'm like some kind of second-rate spy, studying him from behind a stack of boxes in the little corridor that leads from the toilets to the main part of the restaurant.

He's talking to the owner; she's stopped by our table – clearing away our empty glasses, pausing to catch up.

He's so completely happy. It's obvious. Everything about him makes that abundantly clear. He's tranquil – one knee raised, his foot resting on the bar across the bottom of my chair. He's leaning backwards, leisurely – hands hooked behind his head, biceps curled and elbows in the air. A picture of ease.

Even his clothes are calm: there's something soothing in the casual grey and caramel brown of his low-key T-shirt choice against his skin tone, like a visual manifestation of being comfortable, stable, down-to-earth.

And, significantly, he hasn't sworn all evening – a pretty reliable barometer for the overall health of his soul. He's in a very, very good place.

I'm about to detonate on the inside.

I so desperately want to tell him.

He's being so attentive. I think he knows I'm holding out on him, and he's in such a positive frame of mind – I think he'd listen, even if it's hard to hear.

I order another drink on my way back to the table. Technically, I'm underage, but I'm basically almost eighteen and no one ever asks me for ID – especially when I'm out with Ben. I need a little artificial courage, some extra help to shake off my inhibitions.

When I sit down, he smiles. 'Thought you'd run off on me.'

'I was just . . .' What? Hiding and examining him like a creepy stalker? I sip my drink, buying time to collect myself. Before I know it, I'm draining the whole thing all over again. 'There was actually something else I wanted to talk to you about. Sort of about Justin and what Annie said the other day.'

He sits bolt upright. 'I absolutely wasn't going to ask you about that, but it did freak me out.'

'There's really nothing happening.'

'But if that changed, he's – you know – a civilised human being? Annie likes him?'

'Annie likes him a lot.'

'Great. Good.' He looks so relieved, relaxing again in his seat. 'Not that I don't trust your judgement. I just worry. After last year.'

And I realise we're having two different conversations. And Annie was wrong – he doesn't feel jealous or threatened. He's protective of me – deeply, completely protective.

'You don't need to worry.'

He smiles a wry smile, like that's ludicrous, like I've told him he doesn't need to breathe to stay alive. 'Anyway, is that what you wanted to say? I interrupted.'

This is my moment. This is where I steer things back on track. I feel a little dizzy, pleasantly unhinged, like the alcohol is my puppet-master and I'm free and loose under its influence. Only, I don't feel eloquent. Words are even harder to hold on to somehow, slippery sentences sliding away from me – none of them quite right.

And then a song comes on over the restaurant radio – I haven't been listening to the music; it's background music, it stays in the background. But this song – we love this song. And I say it to Ben.

I say, 'This song! This song!'

He smiles, a slow smile.

'We should go to The Living Room!'

And because we've said it in unison, it's a done deal – everyone knows if you say something in unison, it's like a decree of the gods. It's meant to be.

So, we pay and gather up our things and head out.

The evening is balmy; it feels like summer holidays on the continent used to – our two families squished together in a small self-catered villa, sometimes Portugal, sometimes Spain, the air holding us closely as the skies transition to night.

Those memories are favourites: being poolside at dusk in shorts and T-shirts, playing cards and drinking fizz while our parents overdid it and found themselves hysterical.

We've already lived a lifetime together – I never want that to end.

And I find I'm thanking him again for the book and postcards.

'It's just so kind of you, Ben! You're really very kind.' I link my arm through his.

And he laughs at the repetition – apparently, I've said thanks enough now. But it's a kind laugh because he really is a very kind person, almost all of the time.

The Living Room is dark – it's always dark in there. Tea lights on tables, fairy lights. We seem to like fairy lights; I say this to Ben because I think it's true – there were fairy lights at the restaurant too. We check my bag into the cloakroom and head upstairs. It's so small, so cosy and rustic and intimate with its wooden beams sloping over the attic dance floor – maybe the world's smallest dance floor. And I say this to Ben too: 'Do you think it's the world's smallest dance floor?'

But I don't know what he says in response, because it's also noisy – small but loud, maybe because the space is so small, and the speakers are right there. They're right there! In your face! In my face! A speaker, right in my face! The bass goes right through me, so I dance because I can feel the music. I can *feel it!*

A cocktail is a very good idea because the colours are so vibrant, it would be a crime to say no. It's blue, but it can't be from blueberries because they're more of an indigo really and this – this is cerulean. There are so many different shades of blue. And I say this to Ben, because he listens to me when I talk about colours. He does!

'You do!'

'I do what?' He leans in.

But I'm dancing, and he's dancing – fluid, brazen, ridiculous moves – and why repeat myself when words are inadequate, and there's magic between us anyway. We're dancing together in the heart of the magic, and music surrounds us, people surround us, and we're so connected – by the music. And atoms! We're all just atoms, so alive! We're outside of time – eternal atoms, mingling with the soundwaves and I like it. I will live here forever and always, yes! I don't need anything else. Maybe another cocktail?

'You haven't finished that one.'

And I look, and he's right – it's true! So, I drink and drink and it's going, going, gone. I dance my way over to the bar, but it's moving and that's awkward – inconvenient, inconsiderate. Why is the bar moving? Wouldn't it make more sense if it stayed still, so people can reach it? Because otherwise, people might fall, reaching out for it.

But I don't fall because Ben catches my wrist, and he pulls me closer and I look at him – I look up at his face, and I just have to put my hand on his cheek, just for a minute. I tap it – is it real? It's so lovely. And I say this to Ben, too: 'You have a lovely face, Ben.'

And his eyes are wide, and getting wider. And they really are the nicest colour, even though it's dark in here – too dark to really tell. But I know what colour they are, sort of – they're difficult to place, somewhere close to hazel. I want to talk about his eyes, but he seems to want me to drink this, drink this, drink this. What is this?

'Water.'

'Oh, OK – thank you, Ben.'

'No, don't thank me! You're totally wasted. I can't believe I got you drunk!'

'I'm fine, I'm fine, I feel fine.' But maybe I said it too many times, because that's a classic give-away and he's smiling and groaning at the same time. And he really is beautiful. That jaw! Those cheekbones! So, I tell him again. 'The thing is, you're too beautiful to be a monk.'

We seem to be leaving The Living Room.

Bye, bye, Living Room!

He has my bag from the cloakroom and his arm is round my waist and I like it – I like it a lot, a lot, a lot. He feels and smells sooooo good . . . ! But I don't say that, no! I don't. Because I'm making a good point and I have to concentrate.

'You're too beautiful to be a monk. You shouldn't be a monk; you should be a model!' I'm pleased – it sounds poetic, the alliteration. Is that the word? Assonance? Too many words.

We're in a shop, very bright lights – too bright. Why so bright? More water. OK, OK, I'm drinking it. We're walking, slowly. He's shielding me, holding me up, stone-cold sober – he hasn't had a drink in years. I think he forgets; I think he forgets that alcohol can make you see. Well, it makes me see. It makes him violent. But me, I can see – everything. I'm so insightful, as I explain:

'But really, Ben, it's not right. It's not fair – for society, you know? To deprive society. Ooh! Don't hide . . .' There's a saying in the Bible somewhere that backs me up, I know it, and I'm excited because he can't argue with that.

What is it? What is it?

'Don't hide your . . . candle in a cupboard!'

He bursts out laughing, and it's such a wonderful sound. 'Don't hide your light under a bushel?'

'Right. *Jesus* said that! So, you're basically arguing with Jesus here. And you . . .' I pat his chest for emphasis. 'You don't argue with Jesus.'

Triumphant, I'm triumphant because: mic drop! Case closed!

He's still laughing to himself but then he's talking to me and I have to watch his mouth closely to catch the words, but also it really makes me want to kiss him, but he says, 'Drunk theology. The best kind. Anyway, I do argue with Jesus. All the time.'

And I'm a bit confused, because how does anyone argue with Jesus? And why are we talking about Jesus? Why are we always talking about Jesus?! Also, I'm still touching Ben's chest and it's hard to stop touching him, but I do – because I might be a teeny bit tipsy, but I still know groping is not OK.

Oh, I'm getting tired! Why are we walking?

'Why are we walking?'

'Because you need to sober up, or your dad will slaughter me.'

But I'm not drunk, or maybe only a little drunk. But the thing is, I'm too drunk – even though I'm hardly drunk. I'm too drunk because he isn't taking me seriously, even though I'm really very serious. I tell him, 'I'm really very serious.'

But he laughs and I shake his arm because I *am! I'm serious.* I also have so much insight, too much – it's overwhelming. I keep losing my way; my thoughts are an intricate maze of amazing insights, and I'm a bit confused about what I'm trying to say. But anyway: 'Do you understand?' Imploring. Pleading. 'Do you understand what I'm telling you?'

'I'm beautiful. Too beautiful to be a monk.'

'Yes. Correct!' I'm so relieved; he's such a good listener. 'You're *so* very beautiful.'

'Thanks, I guess?'

'You're welcome. Any time.'

He laughs quietly. 'Good chat, Harri. Good chat.'

I feel like I'm leaving a dream behind. It's hard being so insightful.

'I'm very sleepy now, Ben. Ever so tired. Maybe I could just sit here.' The kerb looks clean enough.

'No, don't sit there. It's OK, you're nearly home. Please try and be quiet – seriously, your dad will actually skin me alive.'

'Don't worry! He loves you. Like a son. He says so.'

'Yeah, well. You're still his only daughter.'

'Also, I love you! Yes! Did I say that?!' I really am tired – but this is *important.* 'I meant to say that. Did I already say that?'

'OK, shh, we're here.'

It's my house. How did it get here – it's right here! Look at that. 'I'm home!'

He's shaking his head, wrestling my bag from my shoulder, digging around for my key. He opens the door and sighs: no parents.

'They don't wait up when I'm with you.' I'm clearer; my head is clearer.

'They should.'

'Ben, I love you.'

He stops. And he beams. 'I love you too.' He gives me a hug, and I hold him and hold him. Maybe if I hold him long enough, he won't go. He doesn't have to go.

He's going.

'I'll message you in the morning. See you in a few weeks. Please, please be quiet, all right?'

He can't love me. He doesn't mean it. He doesn't mean it because he's leaving.

He's still leaving.

seventeen

BEN

The journey is like unpacking one of those Russian dolls.

Taxi. Train. Coach. Each stage helps me shed more of my everyday life. Leaving the South East. Leaving England. Leaving family and friends and expectations. I reach Oban and the landscape enlarges. I get smaller. Another stranger passing through.

It's comforting.

It's like being put in my place. My plans are reduced to small talk. Chatting to people in the B&B, I don't mind admitting I'm on a spiritual quest. Waiting for the ferry, it's an admission that doesn't raise an eyebrow. No one asks why – they ask where. Iona? Holy Isle? I'm not the only seeker.

Everyone has their own reasons to be heading west. An escape. A routine homecoming. There's a sort of tension, boarding the boat. Weighty anticipation. We've had some false starts. The weather wasn't co-operating. But now we're within reach of far-flung places.

I study the people I'm travelling with. A handful of us have ventured out into the elements for a better view of our surroundings. I try to guess their stories, listening for Gaelic or English. I imagine silent worries hovering over their heads: fears of people who've been fixated with a dot on the map.

Will romanticism buckle under the strain of reality?

Have the outsiders altered things beyond recognition?

And, for me: can I seriously hope to find a community at the end of all this? A home with thirty men on an island with only a couple hundred inhabitants?

What on earth am I doing?

We slip through the early morning mist – Peter Pan sailing on air. Land masses materialise, then disappear just as quickly. A lighthouse. A castle. Houses are dropped across the terrain like sprinkles on a cake. The clouds hang low enough to touch. Light breaks through in shafts so straight it's as if someone took a ruler and drew them.

I watch the water churn and foam as the ferry slices an endless sea. It's fascinating. Humbling. The boundlessness. The unending continuum of waves and currents circulating the globe.

There's a commotion further along the deck – it brings me back round. A shriek of laughter, squeals of delight. I look, too. Casually at first, but I'm soon just as caught up in the wildlife-spotting as everyone else. A woman swears she saw four or five dolphins. Her friend puts money on six.

It's been almost three hours. And then – there it is.

The island's contours aren't the most dramatic on offer. It lies squat, close to the water. Gentle. Self-assured. Like it doesn't need sheer cliffs or rugged mountains to be special. Like it doesn't have anything to prove. The white-washed cottages of the island's only village are visible flecks, further along the coast.

I don't want to get ahead of myself.

I don't want to prejudge anything.

But as the ferry manoeuvres, sidling up to the pier that juts out into the sea, I can't help wondering if this docking ritual will become my new normal.

I take the steep gangway to disembark. I make my way onto land and head off through the car park and along the single-track road shared by everyone: people on foot, cars willing to pick up any potential passengers in sight.

Today, I walk alone.

The view is the best company I could hope for – looking out across the sea loch on one side, grazing sheep on the other. It's calming: being welcomed by the vast indifference of nature doing its own thing. We didn't agree a specific meeting place, but the options are limited. In less than ten minutes, the road has taken me to the edge of the village.

I'm about to pull out my phone, when Father Graeme rounds a corner. He's wearing his habit – the long monastic robe common to all the monks in the community. And a bulky waterproof, zipped up to the chin. He greets me, grinning, arms outstretched.

'Ben! Welcome!' He folds me into a vice-like embrace. 'Welcome back. You made it!'

He's the same.

Visibly older – the grey hairs have taken over. But still instantly recognisable. Joy and grief erupt in me, unexpectedly. I'm eighteen again, full of gratitude for his generosity.

'Thank you so, so much for having me.'

His laugh is a chortle, a real throat chuckle. 'Don't thank me yet. Give it a few weeks – you're not on a summer retreat this time. But it's good to see you. You look well.'

'Yeah, I'm doing a lot better.'

'Good. Excellent. This way.'

He directs me to a car, throwing the small rucksack I'm travelling with onto the back seat. In no time, we've left the village behind. The scattered buildings recede as we take the only road to the monastery.

I remember it confused me the last time. I'd imagined something imposing. In reality, it's fairly new and low-key. Mostly single storey. Understated, sympathetic to the landscape. Spaces with different functions are clustered around a courtyard – the chapel, the small guesthouse and community rooms. An internal corridor links the open areas to the monks' private quarters. I'm surprised to be ushered through.

'You'll get the full tour in your orientation, but let's drop your things off before we meet Brother Richard.'

'I'm not staying in the guesthouse?'

He smiles over his shoulder. 'You're not a guest.'

I've imagined this moment for months. It still feels like a dream.

'This is you.' He hands me a key and points straight ahead. 'I'll wait here.'

My heart is pounding. I don't know what I expect to find on the other side of the door – it's just a room.

In fact, it's more like a suite.

Modest, sparse – but in a relaxing way; it's not soulless. Bed, small chest of drawers, table, two armchairs. A basic bathroom. The windows overlook part of the monastery grounds. A low stone wall marks the outer boundary. Beyond it: the rock-strewn fields that make this land so impossible to navigate in neat lines. I want to take it all in, but I'm conscious I've left Father Graeme standing in the corridor.

I hesitate, back on the other side of the door – do I need to lock it?

'Up to you.' He reads my mind. 'It's not about trust. We have to work quite hard for a sense of privacy here, as you'll come to appreciate. The silences, having a key – it's to give each other space. Your cell is your home. No one will ever come in uninvited.'

'Cell?'

He chuckles. 'This way – Brother Richard is waiting for us. This won't take long.'

We find him in an austere office.

Even though Father Graeme is the community leader, I can't help feeling like I'm meeting the headmaster. Knowing this person is the novice guardian is paralysing. His opinion of me matters. If they're going to invite me back, it will only be with his say-so. And if they do, he'll oversee the next stage – deciding whether I'm ready to make initial vows.

'Father Graeme.' Brother Richard nods to him. They shake hands. 'Welcome, Ben. How was the journey?'

'Long. Fine. No complaints.'

'Well, I won't keep you – you'll do a full induction later in the week. I just wanted to give you some context for your first few days.'

'Thank you.' A nearby chair is calling to me – I can still feel the motion from the ferry. I want to sit, but no one else is.

'We're a relatively recent presence on the island, as you know. Other communities in the Hebrides have centuries of legacy, whereas our particular religious order only settled here in the 1980s.' He's a short man. Wiry and a little grim. I'd feel like I was being lectured if I wasn't already so interested in the things he's telling me. 'We don't take our warm welcome for granted. If you progress with us as a novice, you'd be expected to learn the language and histories of these islands, alongside deepening your understanding of our monastic rule of life.'

I'm nodding. Nervous. Super keen. He seems to be in full flow, leaning on the desk.

'But for now, you'll have two weeks of retreat to help you to connect to our spiritual rhythms. And then we'll get you contributing to the work we do here and we'll concentrate your study on our core texts.' He rifles through a pile of papers, plucking out a sheet and handing it to me.

I glance it over. I feel my enthusiasm drain away, like someone pulled a plug. The reading list assembles all the usual suspects: straight, white, Western thinkers. Dead men other men have been talking about for centuries.

'Is there a problem?'

I look at Brother Richard. His arms are folded across his chest. Nothing about his posture encourages me to be honest. I look at Father Graeme and his eyes dance – a dare. I don't know how to begin.

'I'm just wondering . . . It just seems to me that if these are your "core" texts, and they're all from . . . a particular perspective – isn't that sort of writing everyone else off?'

'We do have an extensive syllabus.' Brother Richard is immediately defensive. 'As you advance, we have several specialisms you can explore – environmentalism, liberation and decolonial theology, feminist theology, queer theology . . .'

'But isn't it all just theology? The way you're structuring the reading list – I mean, there's no neutral theology, is there? So why split it out like that? Why are these texts "core" and everything else is niche?'

He straightens, standing back from the desk abruptly. 'We have our traditions, Ben. I thought you'd be prepared to respect that.'

'Come on, that's unfair!' It's my turn to be pissed off. 'I don't have a problem with traditions. My dad was an anthropologist. And I've spent the last two years at Oxford.'

Father Graeme intervenes. 'I think Ben is identifying and questioning an implicit hierarchy of ideas. It could seem like we're saying some viewpoints are more valid than others.'

'Yes, exactly. I'm just asking about the labels. And the thought process behind them. Couldn't some of your core texts be written by, I don't know, Global Majority authors? Women? People who are still alive?'

'Five minutes off the boat and you expect me to rewrite the entire course to suit you?!'

'Richard!'

They look at each other.

I'm speechless. I know I raised the question, but I had no idea I'd be poking a sleeping bear. The pause is deafening. It doesn't take a detective to pick up on an undercurrent. Something is being said. Something in the silence that I can't decipher. They lock eyes. There's kindness in Father Graeme's face. Or pity. Either way, I'm out of my depth.

Brother Richard looks away. Father Graeme turns back to me. 'I, for one, think it's a valid challenge. Put it in writing would you, Ben? We'll look into it.'

I nod. The sheet of paper is shaking in my hands.

'Well, I think we have everything we need, thank you, Richard. Let's head back together, shall we, Ben? Walk and talk.'

I barely make it out the door before the words start falling from me.

'He hates me. He's the novice guardian and he already hates me.'

'He doesn't hate you. Community life – let's just say: it has its complications. Rest assured, that wasn't about you.' He pauses, smiling. 'As such.'

'I know I'm argumentative. Believe it or not, I try to rein it in.'

He laughs. 'Well, working out whether to adjust yourself for the sake of others is the job of a lifetime.'

We reach my cell and he turns to me, putting both hands on my shoulders. 'Shake it off and get yourself settled. Brother Martin will come by in an hour to give you the grand tour. You *are* welcome here, Ben.'

I let myself in.

The glow has gone. The room feels empty. The view is bleak and desolate. I fall onto the bed, kicking off my shoes and cursing my stupidity.

Who does this?

How could I drop out of university to study monoculture theology on an island with old men? How could I leave everyone who actually cares about me to be with people who don't think I'm worth the effort?

The doubt is crippling. Worse than the fatigue of the goodbyes. Worse than the exhaustion of the journey.

I don't know what I'm doing.

But.

I do know how I got here.

eighteen

BEN

Three Years Ago

'Do you want to come to church with me on Sunday?'

I was sitting next to Jonathan during afternoon registration. Half the tutor group had already signed out: the ones with frees last thing, the ones who just couldn't be bothered.

I knew next to nothing about him. People mainly called him Jono. He was gay. He seemed nice. That was it. Apparently, he was also religious – and not shy about it either. I had no clue how to respond. *Fuck no* seemed a bit harsh.

'Don't worry.' He bulldozed through my awkward silence. 'I'm not hitting on you. Even if that was your thing, I'm not into the whole bad boy routine you've got going on.'

'I didn't – that wasn't why I . . .'

I had kind of assumed my sneaking around with various girls and getting shit-faced had gone unnoticed. Officially, there'd been no comment. The quality of my work was still where it needed to be. My university applications were in. The law tests and Oxford interviews had gone well enough, although outcomes were a few weeks off. I'd thought I was pretty discreet. It was unnerving to be called out. Embarrassing. I could feel myself blushing.

'Relax. Deep breath.'

'I just wasn't expecting that. And, honestly, church is the last place I'd want to spend my Sunday morning. God and I are on a break right now.'

He smiled. 'Fair enough. Have a good one.' The room was emptying. He got up to leave.

That threw me too. I thought he'd push it. I was sort of disappointed he didn't.

'The thing is . . .' I caught up with him in the corridor, surprising myself – why was I telling him this? 'It's just . . .'

He waited.

I sifted through my internal baggage. I tried for a succinct explanation. 'I did the church thing for years with my family. I thought I believed in God. But now, it's like that certainty feels . . . kind of offensive?' I shook my head. This wasn't coming out clearly. 'There's too much I don't understand. I can't be around it. I can't be around people who are so sure they have all the answers.'

He was quiet for a minute. I liked that. He seemed to be thinking. Maybe what came out next would be worth hearing – unlike all the platitudes I'd been treated to after Dad died.

'I would be there. I definitely have more questions than answers. Which way are you going?'

I pointed towards the art block and we started to walk there together.

'Look, you probably don't want to hear this but I guess I just feel sorry for you. Your dad . . . that's awful. And having to move on top of that.'

Funnily enough, his pity didn't grate on me. I had enough self-pity of my own. It felt good to hear someone acknowledge it was legitimate.

'You seem lonely. And I've been lonely.' He smiled but it was thin. It barely covered over the kind of pain I glimpsed in my own face these days. 'I don't think church is necessarily the solution. Actually, for me it was a huge part of the problem. But I trust this group – it's a fairly safe space. No guarantees, though!'

'You go every week?'

'Every week. But if it's not for you, that's fine. I figure, Jesus was so inclusive the establishment killed him for it. So, I'm just trying to be more like that. Open invitation.'

'Right. Well, I'm not going to kill you for the invite. But if someone tells me that "all things work together for good", there's a real chance I'll knock them out.'

He laughed. I wasn't sure I was joking.

Lately, it was as if my body was host to parasitic fury. My emotions were short-circuited; they defaulted to numb or enraged. The anger felt like an external force on a mission to conquer every inch of me. I watched it happening with eerie detachment. It was like living someone else's nightmare.

'So, is that a yes?'

We had arrived at the art block. Harriet often put in extra time there at the end of the day. If I wasn't 'otherwise occupied', I'd go and sit in. Seeing her paint or play around with her ideas was mesmerising. After a while, she'd forget she had an audience. I'd blend in and she'd be soaring somewhere untouchable. Somewhere she belonged.

I didn't have that – somewhere to go and find myself.

Losing myself was easy. A joint and a hand job was pretty much all it took. But finding myself – remembering who I'd been, the person my dad was proud of . . . it was getting harder every day. Harriet was the link. She was quickly becoming the only safe place I had left. That was too much to ask of her. I had to try something else.

If not for me, then at least for Harri. 'Yeah, I guess so.' I nodded, feeling more decisive once the words were out of my mouth. 'Yes. Give me the details and I'll be there.'

'Great!'

I smiled. 'We'll see.'

nineteen

HARRIET

The first art class after the summer is usually a highlight.

Especially when the course leapfrogs the holidays and September is a continuation of the same, ramping up towards a final project – an end expression. I normally have momentum. I normally have a whole six weeks' worth of independent exploration: a stack of postcards from exhibitions, a sketchbook exploding with initial ideas. Spreading it all out on the table to be critiqued by everyone else is when it all comes together – I see what's working, what people connect to, what I want to take forwards.

This time it's different.

The A level class is small – only six of us taking fine art. The group is too small to hide in. It will be my turn to share soon and I'm nowhere near ready.

I'm usually so at home here.

The atmosphere in the art block is unlike anywhere else in school. It feels more informal. The minute we slip on our paint-splattered overalls, covering up a uniform of charcoal grey and canary yellow, we're signalling the switch. Conversations get personal and political – everyone speaking their mind. Music is encouraged. We take it in turns to dictate the playlist from our phones, remotely connecting to speakers subtly hidden in the corner of the classroom.

It's the one department that feels light and spacious. The rooms flow into each other, separated by partition walls covered with work in progress and shelves overflowing with reference books. Everyone works differently but it's all here: a printing press, easels, a kiln, the digital suite – equipment strewn around the block like an obstacle course.

And for us, the sixth formers, there are individual work bays. From the early days of year seven, I envied those little cubby-holes – a three-walled mini-studio, all to myself? It was the dream. Somewhere to pin up my ideas and leave my work to come back to. A creative space of my own.

Now I have one – my bay is next to Annie's.

It's bare.

We took down last year's work in July, anticipating the next phase. It should be thrilling – standing on the verge of a brand new deep-dive. It's an exciting moment – beginning to whittle down a host of influences to find a starting point, maybe discovering a different type of media to use.

I should be jubilant. Especially this year. For those of us who want to do art after A levels, it's also the time to pull together our portfolios.

The task is monumentally important.

A portfolio is the vital first step in art school applications – the opening ticket. Make or break. A chance to state who we are, artistically speaking. A chance to show our potential and prove what we're capable of.

The January deadline will come around in no time.

If there was ever a time to be buzzing with creative energy and inspiration, this is it.

Only, I'm drawing a solid blank.

A brick-wall blank – impenetrable, thicker than a fortress. And, for once, that blank space is intimidating.

'All right, thank you, Annie.' Ms Harrington's voice snaps

me out of my trance. 'Some promising first thoughts. Harriet, shall we look at your work next?'

The question is rhetorical – she's already moving around the table towards my firmly closed sketchbook.

I feel the weight of six pairs of eyes shifting in my direction. The expectation is tangible – like a noose around my neck. I set the bar high last year. My paintings focused on the intersection of identity and physicality, and the things I explored landed so well with everyone. I won a national prize – the Examiner's Choice award in the 'One to Watch' category. It was unexpectedly topical: there was even interest in the local news – celebrity for a day.

Finding the next project was never going to be easy. It was always going to be hard to follow up on something that flowed so organically from such a personal place. Even in ordinary circumstances. But these aren't 'ordinary circumstances'. Nothing feels normal. Not since the Choucair exhibition. Not since my drunken attempts to be honest with Ben backfired in my face.

I'm losing my grip.

When I sit down to draw, it's just scribbles. When I mix paints, it comes out like mud. All the things that felt stable – the things I took for granted – they're deserting me. I haven't made a single thing I'm satisfied with, let alone anything I want to show a class full of people who are expecting a masterpiece.

But I don't have a choice.

I open the book.

Ms Harrington flicks through the pages.

'Hmm, OK.' She goes back to the beginning and flicks through again. 'So we're a little thin on the ground here, aren't we? Did you do any larger works, or is this it?'

'That's all.'

'It's early days.' Her smile is encouraging. She doesn't seem concerned, but the questions aren't over yet. 'This page here – talk me through this one.' She spins the book so it's side-on for both of us, leaning across the table. People crane their necks, trying to get a better look.

The painting is basic – reds: magenta, crimson. Abstract shapes are accented in greys and whites. Simplistic. In this context, it's the kind of painting that can only really be justified by way of a little spark of genius. A visual twist or a decent narrative – some kind of social or historical significance to elevate what is basically something a seven-year-old could make. It's the kind of 'art' that sceptics put in quotation marks.

And I haven't done it justice.

'Well, um' – I suppress a sigh, dragging words out from somewhere deep beneath my embarrassment – 'it's referencing Saloua Raouda Choucair. Her Composition works, like *Composition with Arcs*. I think I was trying for a sense of balance?'

It's ridiculous that I'm even asking. I already know there's no balance. Ms Harrington nods, but she answers with a question of her own.

'And this is acrylic?

I nod. Misery is seeping through me – it's just not good. I know it.

'OK. All right. Well, it's a little underdeveloped, I think. I know these are just preliminary explorations, but it feels a little rushed. Like here – this section, that feels a bit like filler to me. A bit like you were running out of steam and just dumped the colour on.'

Nothing in her tone is particularly harsh, but the critique still stings. It's just so ruthlessly astute.

'And I'm not sure acrylic is working for you. I think it's drying out before you have a chance to really layer the colour.

Here – see, this corner. The tones, the brushwork – it's very, very stiff. It jars a bit. Can you sense that? Which, again, is fine if it's intentional but I'm not getting that feeling – more of an unhappy accident, yes?'

I have to nod again.

'So, gouache might work better for building that density and depth in a more blended way. What do you think?'

I think I never want to pick up a paintbrush again. But I nod in agreement to that too.

'Did you go to the Choucair exhibition?'

'Briefly.'

'And what did you think?'

'I had mixed feelings.'

'All right, well, it's the start of the year. There's still time – I thought you'd get a lot from it, actually. But if the resonance isn't there, Lee Krasner is on at the Barbican, which is a brilliant one. So, don't worry – OK? You can always find someone else.'

I nod. I don't trust my voice to speak without breaking.

'I mean it.' She closes the sketchbook and taps the cover. I can't meet her gaze – not with so much sympathy in her voice. I look at her painted nails and chunky jewellery. I find myself wondering how old she is – maybe forty? What a niche and arguably pointless thing to spend decades doing: teaching art to teenagers.

'Harriet, I know you're disappointed, but I promise I'll tell you when it's time to panic.' She looks around the semi-circle. 'Right, Dylan, what do you have for us?'

I finally allow myself to look up. Annie catches my eye, mouthing to me across the room: 'Are you OK?'

And I nod, even though she knows I'm not.

How can I be?

It shouldn't matter. It shouldn't even be relevant right now. But all this talk of exhibitions, and art, and the search for inspiration – everything is circling the void, the great big chasm in the centre of my chest.

It all makes me think of Ben.

twenty

HARRIET

May, Last Year

I woke with a start, disoriented in a hard bed on the wrong side of the room. I reached an arm out from under the covers, groping the floor for my phone on autopilot. Then it hit me – where I was, and why.

I covered my eyes – as if that could possibly erase the memory of finding photos of my body online. The panic, the trolling, the slut-shaming. This couldn't be me – those words couldn't be describing my situation. Even the label seemed to point the finger: accusing me, focusing on my behaviour instead of his.

I swallowed the sick feeling, pushing it all to the back of my mind. I allowed my eyes to open again, slowly examining my surroundings.

Ben's Oxford bedroom was not much bigger than a box room, with plain cream walls and a sash window that opened over a cobbled alley below. The real view was in the other direction, from the adjoining living room of the 'set' he shared with another student.

I'd been automatically drawn to those tall, grand windows on arrival yesterday.

Natural light flooded the room, offsetting the dark wood-panelled walls. The view overlooked manicured lawns and a library that seemed more like a stunning Greek temple. Its columns and symmetry made my heart sing – the balance and

sheer immovability of it. I had stared at it most of the evening –
watching the skies change and people scurry around – while Ben
sorted out my life.

He called my parents, pacifying them with the vaguest
details and assurances that I'd be back on Sunday morning in
one piece. He messaged Annie, asking her to report the worst of
the abuse and take screenshots for evidence. He confiscated my
phone, turning it off and tossing it into a drawer, slamming it
shut with satisfying force.

I had skipped dinner in the stately communal hall – my stomach growled in protest, but I couldn't face meeting his friends or
making small talk. I overheard him, tactfully downplaying the
situation to his roommate in hushed tones: 'bad break-up' and
'can we get some space?' Later, he'd done a dash out of college
to the nightly kebab van, bringing me back a mound of cheesy
chips and beans that I inhaled in no time. He had taken care of
everything – all the practicalities.

But, more than that, he sat with me.

We sat, and I didn't have to say anything or think anything
or explain. He read a little, listened to music. He was just there,
next to me – with me. The way he occupied himself quietly
without intruding – it was like he created a little cocoon of stillness around me: a place of rest where the noise and aggression
couldn't reach me.

When I eventually collapsed into the bed he gave up for me,
it was almost as if the nightmare that drove me into hiding had
happened to someone else.

Waking up again, having it all resurface the second I opened
my eyes – it was heartbreaking. Would it always feel like this?
Would I really have to start from scratch every single day?

I peeled myself off the bed, directing my eyes to the carpet
and angling my body away from the full-length mirror on the

wardrobe door. I wasn't ready to see myself again – not yet, not with those captions running through my mind. I gave myself a shake and stumbled out of the room.

'Hi, how are you?' Ben was sitting at his desk on the messy side of the living room. He looked up from a textbook, smiling as I emerged. 'You were knocked out.'

'What time is it?'

'Nearly lunch. I got us a picnic. Sort of.' He pointed to a baguette and an assortment of snacks on one of the sofas. 'Thought we could go punting.'

'Ah, thanks' – I tried to muster up at least a little enthusiasm – 'but do you think we could just stay here?'

He rocked back in his chair, tipping onto the back legs. 'I don't think so. It's a beautiful day – look!' There was no denying it. The weather begged to be enjoyed: cloudless skies, heat on the right side of bearable. 'I don't want you to hide here. I want you to enjoy it.'

I sighed, perching on the arm of the sofa, thinking. I'd never really been to Oxford before – not properly, not with someone who could steer me away from the tourist trail and give me an inside experience. Ben was finishing his first year already – the time had vanished; each term was only eight weeks long. He'd already done his exams for the year. He was free and I was here.

It wasn't that I didn't *want* to enjoy this chance. I didn't feel capable.

He twisted towards me, tapping my knee to recapture my attention.

'Trust me. I'm not going to make you do anything you're really uncomfortable with. Of course I won't. But you're here! That's a really good thing. I think we could have a great day.'

Punting was harder than it looks.

The whole charade of effortlessly gliding along a gently winding river, Pimm's in hand – not real, at least not for us.

We took it in turns to bump our boat from bank to bank, narrowly avoiding being decapitated by low-hanging branches, apologising to other punters for holding everyone up. It took all my concentration to figure out the rhythm: standing to push off against the riverbed with a pole that extended way above my head, shifting my hands along until the pole was at my waist and we had drifted forwards by the tiniest distance.

And repeat.

By the time we arrived at our picnic spot, we were sweaty with dead arms and my sides ached from laughing at Ben's technique and his relentless teasing of mine.

'So, clearly we're both naturals.' He moored us at a jetty by the edge of a meadow and offered me a hand up out of the boat, grinning.

'Olympic gold medallists for sure.'

'Because punting is an Olympic sport now.'

'It should be! You need serious upper body strength for that.'

We wandered up from the river, finding a shady spot under a sprawling sycamore tree. The long grass and wildflowers thinned out beneath it, leaving a kind of natural picnic blanket at the base of the thick trunk. Munching through our food supplies, catching up on everything apart from the reason I was there, I knew that Ben had been right to push me.

This was more than a distraction.

It was one of the nicest things I'd done in a while.

Even before everything blew up, I'd been so preoccupied with coursework and revision. Study leave was about to start – the looming pressure of GCSEs just two weeks away, the first exams to really count. When was the last time I'd switched off like this? Even the bread had more taste, more crunch.

Ben had wolfed down his food and was lying on his back, sunglasses obscuring his eyes. His breathing was so even I wondered if he had drifted off, until he turned his face towards me and held out his hand, motioning for me to join him. 'You'll appreciate this.'

'What?'

'This pattern.' He pointed to the leaves and branches criss-crossing overhead.

I slid down next to him, smiling.

'Harri, I don't want to ruin the moment but I have to ask you.' He took off his sunglasses and rubbed his eyes. 'Why didn't you ever talk to me? About him? You know all about me and Charlotte.'

It wasn't an accusation. If anything, he sounded confused – like he'd unexpectedly failed a test and was asking for extra feedback. It was a fair point – Ben's girlfriend had been a topic of constant conversation between us ever since they'd met at a pub in freshers' week.

'I don't know. Obviously, I had no clue he'd turn around and do something so vile.'

'Did he put pressure on you?'

'No.' I thought about it for a moment – it wasn't that clear-cut. 'Not exactly. I think maybe it all felt kind of inevitable. But until the photos showed up, there wasn't a point when it felt scary or out of control.'

'So, if you thought he was a decent person and you were basically happy with how things were going, how come you never even mentioned him?' He sighed, shifting away from me slightly. 'I'm sorry this is an interrogation. It just seems so odd.'

It was odd. Especially as we were in touch all the time – exchanging family gossip; dissecting everyday events; filling each other in on what we were watching, reading, listening to. But the truth was I hadn't known how to talk to him about this.

'I guess I thought maybe you'd judge me. For not slowing things down.'

'Why?! I'm the last person who should be judging anyone.'

'But you said you and Charlotte aren't sleeping together.'

'Yeah. That's new for me, though – it's not exactly the approach I've taken in the past!' He laughed a little. 'I'm trying to figure some things out. But it's not like I would expect you to automatically think the same way.'

It seemed to really bother him; he wasn't ready to let it go.

'Honestly, I'm gutted you thought I wouldn't respect your choices.'

His dejection was obvious. I turned my head towards him, finding his shoulder, resting on him. He had been nothing but good to me since he picked up my desperate phone call – I should have known all along that I could trust him.

'No, you're right. I shouldn't have assumed. Anyway' – I groaned, covering my face with both hands as the visual of the posts resurfaced yet again – 'we're on the same page now. I'm totally swearing off anything to do with sex too.'

He laughed. 'Really not what I'm doing, just FYI. Still a big fan. And you just need a much, much better vetting system.'

I felt the heaviness come back with a blow, like someone had dropped a small car on my chest. The thought of ever allowing myself to be that vulnerable again was utterly overwhelming. A wave of fear engulfed me – a riptide dragging me away from all sense of security. Without warning, tears started leaking from the corners of my eyes.

'Harri?' I didn't know if it was intuition or obvious but he sat up, leaning against the tree trunk, gently pulling me up next to him and putting his arms round me. 'You're going to get past this. I know it. You are.'

'How?'

He thought for a while, brushing a bug off my leg, picking grass out of my hair. 'I have an idea.'

Ben was cryptic – he said he would explain once we got there.

We left our secluded picnic spot, returning the punt and making our way on foot through the crowded shopping streets of central Oxford. The heart of the city was a meeting of past and present – college walls and dreaming spires mixed in with high-street brands. As Ben made a beeline for our destination, I struggled to keep up – dodging street performers and preachers, homeless people and tourists, students and locals: everyone jostling to occupy their own slice of a surreal world.

'You need to talk to your parents.' He spoke over his shoulder, striding ahead.

'I can't.'

'You have to! Harriet . . . ' He slowed down as we turned into a quieter side street. 'What he did – it's a total violation! Of your body and your trust. He can't get away with it! And since you've expressly told me I can't hunt him down and kick his head in –'

'Ben, please don't even joke like that.'

'You need to talk to them. And to someone at your school. For you, but also – what if he does it again? What if he goes even further next time? Or it's someone younger?'

'But just think about how they'll react.'

There were advantages to having lived in each other's pockets. I didn't need to describe the disappointed silence I would be confronted with. I didn't have to tell him how my throat would

constrict and my skin would crawl with so much embarrassment, I wouldn't be capable of stringing together a sentence –
never mind properly explaining myself.

'Point taken.' He stopped at a corner, turning to me with a
half-smile. 'OK, you'll think I've lost it, but hear me out. I think
you should tell my mum.'

'Your mum? Seriously?'

'All right, we don't always see eye to eye. But the woman is a
rock, and she's feminist to the bone. I promise, she'll be on your
side. She'll tell you to "Still I Rise" the shit out of this.'

I had to laugh at his reference to Clara's favourite Maya Angelou
poem – required reading throughout our childhood, the themes of
resistance and empowerment internalised at a young age.

Would Clara really help me?

Ben's support had already made me feel lighter than I
would've thought possible only yesterday. Maybe he was onto
something here as well.

'I'm right.' He smiled at me. 'You know I'm right. She'll deal
with your mum. And your mum will deal with your dad. And
they can all handle the official stuff. Think about it?'

It felt good to have options – a chink of light filtering
through. 'I'll think about it.'

'Good. Anyway, we're here.'

I glanced around me, noticing for the first time that we had
stopped in front of a gallery. Posters advertising the solo exhibition stood out against the slate-grey brickwork. 'Jenny Saville?'

'You've heard of her?'

'Of course! Young British Artists. But she's like the old soul
of the group – she's this completely phenomenal painter.'

'OK, well, I know nothing about her. But I've walked past a
few times and I've seen her stuff has lots of naked bodies –'

'Nudes. When it's art, they're nudes. Often it's her.'

'Right, so that's my point. You shared those photos. And, OK, there's an argument to say it wasn't the wisest or safest thing you could've done. But on the other hand –'

'Ah, you're such a lawyer! On one hand . . . but on the other hand . . .' It was easier to tease him than face what he was saying.

'No, listen, I mean this – on the other hand, it was also so incredibly brave and sort of . . .' He searched the air for the right words. '. . . a really generous, truthful thing to do. He's just a shithead. He didn't deserve it.'

I exhaled, tears stinging in my eyes.

Ben understood.

He really understood where this had come from – how this had all come about.

It wasn't thoughtless. It wasn't peer pressure.

Not for me.

It had been about hope and the excitement of believing someone valued my body like I did. I had trusted someone who turned out to be a total arse; my intuition had let me down completely. But part of me – the part Ben somehow seemed to get – part of me didn't want to accept that I had been entirely wrong.

Ben took my hand, bringing me in close for yet another hug. 'Harri, he's the one who flipped it into this madness. He took it way out of context. And, I don't know, I guess I hoped this could inspire you. To take it back, somehow. Be the one in control again.'

He held me.

It was unbelievably comforting.

The steadiness of his heartbeat; the warmth of his arms; all his belief and support being poured into me, filling me up – recharging my soul; just a simple hug stretching on. And on.

I felt his phone vibrate against my leg.

Ben leapt backwards like he'd been stung.

He put a hand on his pocket, but he didn't take the phone out. His expression shifted through gears I couldn't gauge. For the first time since I'd arrived, he seemed distracted.

'I can't look round with you. I was supposed to . . .' He didn't finish. 'I really need to catch up with Charlotte.'

'That's fine! I've completely monopolised you.'

He smiled. 'It's been nice.' He paused, wavering on the verge of saying something else, lost in thought.

I waited.

Eventually, he cleared his throat. 'All right, you don't have your phone. So, I'll come and meet you back here in a couple of hours?'

'Sounds like a plan.'

I watched him jog away.

twenty-one

BEN

I feel like I've run away.

Harriet did say that. It hurt that it was basically the first thing out of her mouth when I told her about my plans. It made it all seem so escapist. But I've been at the monastery for two weeks now and I do see her point.

Retreat is a luxury.

It's sort of like a spiritual honeymoon, I guess. Normally, I'd never have this much time to just be with God. I'm never entirely surrounded by people who feel the same pull. It's special. We're navigating by the same compass. I don't have to struggle to fit God into a secular timetable. God is the timetable.

From the moment the bells ring for morning prayer, the day is punctuated by an awareness of Someone beyond us. The magnetism pulls us together. We gather three times a day to refocus. In between, so far, my time has been my own.

I've walked.

I've walked and walked. I don't even really know why. It felt like the right impulse to follow in such a beautiful location. I've scrambled down the dunes and discovered abandoned beaches – wide arcs of rock forming sandy bays: distinct alcoves all along the coast. All the different bays have names. Characteristics. People have their preferences – the one that feels like home. Like visiting a local bar, only the entertainment is spotting seals clinging to rocks offshore. Or seeing otters take crabs from the water back up the dunes to eat in the rock pools formed by the rain.

It's quiet. It's addictive.

My favourite bay is walking distance from the monastery. I've stood there, captivated. For endless hours. Staring out at the sea, watching clouds collect and disperse. They shape-shift here in ways I haven't seen anywhere else. Sometimes it's as if the island has its own force-field – storms flicker in the distance, hovering over the neighbouring shorelines but never quite striking here. But the wind – the wind is unrelenting. It goes right through me. It's buffeting my face raw. I like it.

Powerful.

Invisible.

It's like a metaphor.

Some people think it's easier to connect with God in certain geographies. People talk about 'thin places' – locations full of sacred heritage. Places where wider dimensions of reality are more tangible. The spiritual equivalent of infrared light or ultrasonic sound waves. I guess that's the whole point of pilgrimage.

I don't know.

If God is speaking to me, I'm not sure I'm hearing it.

I wouldn't say I've had a single profound experience since arriving. I like the quiet. I like experiencing a kind of minimalism. But I can't help feeling I should be doing something – contributing somehow. And if I'm not having any life-changing insights from all this time spent contemplating, it feels like I should at least get on with some of the work the other monks spend the majority of their time doing.

So, I'm excited – today's a big step.

End of retreat, beginning of the postulancy. Today I find out what activities I'll be doing for the rest of my introduction here.

I knock on the door to Brother Richard's office. I suppress the memory of our initial meeting. I've avoided him since; retreat made it easy.

'Come in!'

'Hi – you wanted to see me?'

'Yes.'

He should tell his face. He's looking at me like I'm roadkill.

'So, you're a law student?'

'Uh, yes – technically.'

'And I can see from your application that you're interested in the advocacy work we do. But, within that, you're especially interested in our research collaborations.'

'Yeah, earth jurisprudence.'

'And what is earth jurisprudence? In your understanding?'

'Er, well – I don't know loads. But isn't it the idea that the rest of nature needs to be more than just an afterthought? In the way we regulate ourselves. As humanity. Because we're just part of the bigger whole?'

He doesn't respond. I keep going.

'So, it's, like, a way of evaluating and reimagining our systems. The economy. Law. A way to figure out if they're really fit for anything.'

He doesn't nod, doesn't smile. Just a little encouragement would be enough.

'It's a theory to help shift the focus. So that things are more balanced.' I'm pouring words into a bottomless pit. 'A way to create frameworks where human laws or rights don't automatically trump non-human rights. Which is actually how humanity lived for centuries, right? And how Indigenous groups still function. If they can.'

'And you've heard of Thomas Berry?'

'Yeah. Earth jurisprudence was his idea.'

Brother Richard's eyes narrow slightly. 'Thomas Berry articulated a particular line of thought. The ideas are ancient. They don't belong to a single group, let alone an individual.'

I mentally kick myself. I know that. I get the nuance. There's just something about talking to Brother Richard that sets me on edge. I can't think straight. I wasn't scoring highly to begin with. I don't know how to recover. 'I've read a couple of books by Thomas Berry.'

'Do you cook?'

'Sorry?'

'Food – do you cook?'

'I mean, I can. I guess I haven't done it that much recently – in college it's catered. So, we all just go to hall. And at home, I don't know, Mum does most of it.'

'But you can peel veg competently? Boil pasta?'

I don't know if he's joking. 'Yeah.'

'Good. I'm assigning you to help Brother Hamish in the kitchen. He'll talk you through your duties.' He moves across the room, opening the door for me to leave.

I can't. I'm too shocked.

'I don't underst—'

'Ben, why are you here?'

'What . . . ?'

He sighs. 'Are you interested in becoming a monk or an academic? Because it seems to me you were pretty well placed to study earth jurisprudence in Oxford.'

'It's not on the syllabus.'

'Do a research master's. Do a PhD.'

I feel winded. This man is acidic. Abrasive. I'm never going to win his approval. It's obvious – he's already decided. I'll never be good enough in his eyes.

He won't let me belong here.

And suddenly I'm incensed – who does he think he is?

'All right, fine. You know what? You're right. I don't know exactly why I'm here but that doesn't mean you get to just write me off!'

'Are you looking for your dream job? Is that it?'

'No!'

'Are you looking for an easy life on some picture-perfect island? The good life?'

'No!'

'What are you looking for?'

'God! All right! I'm looking for . . . I just want to . . . I just think there's more. There's a way to know more. About God. And life. I want a meaningful life. Before it's gone – I'm gone! And I wanted to . . . I *still* want to try and concentrate on that. Instead of being constantly bombarded by petty shit!'

I'm swearing at a monk.

I'm shouting and swearing at a monk who already thinks the worst about me.

Perfect.

He stares me down. His face is inscrutable. 'You'll work in the kitchen, Ben. That's my best and final offer. Take it or pack your bags. Your choice. You're free to go at any time.'

I sigh. 'Fine. Kitchen it is.'

I turn and leave. I resist the urge to slam the door on my way out.

twenty-two

BEN

Three Years Ago

When I got to the address Jono had given me, there was no church in sight.

I checked his message again, stamping my feet to warm them up. The cold came out of nowhere and I hadn't brought a coat – mainly because Mum told me I'd need one. Why I felt the need to be at war with her was a mystery. But I couldn't stop myself. The more she tried to look after me, the harder I fought her. And the more I fought her, the more she worried and tried to look after me. Vicious circle.

Increasingly vicious.

'Hi, you look frozen!' Jono approached me from the nearby car park, locking his car at a distance. 'It's this way.'

We entered some sort of community centre that sat in the middle of a fairly large park. Making my way across to it, I'd seen football pitches, playgrounds, open fields. Joggers lapped a tree-lined cycle path that wrapped around the perimeter. Lots of dog-walkers. Parents with pushchairs. Kids on scooters, too. Basically, a nice space that plenty of people seemed to use. But nothing obviously associated with religion.

'How's it going?' Jono led us through the main entrance, down one corridor, then another.

'Yeah, all right.' It had become my standard answer. Not too dishonest. Not too revealing. 'How does this work, then?'

'What was your church like?'

'Oh, you know – pretty big. Stage, lighting. Music –'

'From bands led by boys with guitars and really healthy hair . . .'

'Ha! Pretty much.'

'And, let me guess' – he grinned – 'teaching from middle-aged men with lots of heterosexual family anecdotes thrown in for free?'

'Exactly.' I smiled.

He shrugged, smiling more to himself than me. 'Well, that's one way of doing it. OK.' He pushed open a door. 'This is us.'

The room was small – it would be hard for it to hold more than about twenty people. It seemed like it maybe functioned as a crèche during the week: one wall had kids' paintings hanging all over it.

A couple of little girls, probably sisters, sat colouring at a small table, their heads close together. A toddler was struggling away from a woman who sat on the floor near the girls. A few adult-sized chairs were arranged in a semi-circle, turned to include the kids' area. Some were occupied, but not all. Three of the adults in the group had shunned the seats, opting to kneel or sit cross-legged on the floor instead.

'So' – Jono paused in the doorway, whispering – 'we have the meeting first and then catch up with each other afterwards. We don't usually sing. Someone might, but it's not like a regular thing. Someone might play some music on their phone for the group if they think that's the right thing to do. But we just . . .' He shrugged again. 'It's kind of hard to explain. We basically sit and listen. And speak if we feel we have something to say. If not, we're just here.'

'We sit? In silence?'

'Yeah, and listen. Where do you want to be? By the door, I'm guessing?'

I laughed. It was clear that Jono was more perceptive than most. 'Yep, definitely by the door.'

We took our seats as an older woman struggled to her feet. A boy who looked about twelve – a grandson maybe – gave her his arm. Her grey curls had a pink tinge. The folds of her tie-dyed cardigan cascaded onto the floor as she straightened. She looked like she'd been a hippy before the movement started. When she spoke, her voice rasped.

'Hello, everyone, and welcome to our visitors.' She nodded in my direction. Her gaze shifted to another man at the far end of the semi-circle. 'We'll do introductions at the end, but my name is Helen. The next hour is for us to spend enjoying God's company, sharing anything relevant. Feel free to move about or leave the room if necessary, but please try to avoid distracting others where possible. As always, we begin with the Lord's Prayer.'

This was a mistake.

I already felt awkward. Spending an hour in silence was the last thing I needed. I could hardly shut my thoughts down for five minutes.

The collective prayer evaporated, over far too quickly. My mind was shouting. It was only a matter of time before everyone figured out I was an imposter, incapable of whatever this was.

I held my breath.

The toddler wailed. People shifted in their seats. The boy next to Helen whispered to her briefly. A man let loose an irritating cough at regular intervals. The girls scribbled away. Clearly, silence would be a relative experience. It was impossible for the room to go completely quiet, but no one seemed fussed.

I felt the tension in my shoulders ease a bit.

Maybe I wouldn't be outed as a fraud.

Jono was leaning forwards, his head in his hands. I copied his posture, trying not to bounce my leg. Sitting still was half the battle. But now that I'd found an OK position, the noise in my mind kicked up a level.

So far, no one was saying anything. My hands itched to pull out my phone.

The thing Helen had said about 'enjoying God's company' didn't sit well with me. I didn't want to think about why, but my mind went down that rabbit hole anyway.

I'd always thought of God as a Someone. Not just an idea, or energy, or source. So conceptually it wasn't a big deal. I could enjoy God's company as much as anyone's – like hanging out with Harri.

In theory.

But if that was the case, maybe the real issue was I didn't want to be anywhere near God right now. I didn't like God right now.

God, I hate you.

Was that a prayer? Was it true?

I don't hate you, exactly. I hate that I can't trust you anymore. You were supposed to be a good shepherd but you led us right into a shitstorm.

This had to stop.

Coming here had been a mistake. I made a move to leave, but caught sight of a man standing up. It was the other guest. He seemed awkward, unsure about what to do next.

'I have something to share. I think.' He looked at Helen and she nodded. People shuffled, rearranging themselves to give him their attention. 'I'm Rob. I'm in town for work this week, so just passing through. This could be for everyone generally, but maybe it's specific. So. Anyway.'

He clasped his hands together and bit his thumbnail. Not a natural public speaker, even to a group this small. It was painful to watch. I put my head back in my hands, looking at the floor.

'I was thinking about the story of Jacob wrestling the Angel of the Lord. Do people know it? Jacob wrestled with the Angel of the Lord for a whole night. Possibly we all know the story? But anyway, the fight changed him. He got a bad limp from it. But then when the sun was coming up, the Angel gave him a new name and let him go. He found his identity. And now, for billions of us, Jews, Christians – he's a patriarch for us. So. Anyway. Having real faith in God is a struggle. Relationship with God is a struggle. But it won't break you. It will mould you. The real you. Because God knows who you are and can, sort of, bring that out.'

Somehow, he'd found his stride.

His conviction made him almost eloquent.

I had to look up. Everything he'd said felt relevant. How could he do that – pinpoint the one bit of the Bible that basically paraphrased exactly what I was feeling? And then find the hope in it, when all I'd ever seen in that story was conflict?

He was biting his nails again. The room was quiet. That, or my heart was loud – thumping in my chest like an internal assault.

'I have something to add.' The woman holding the toddler had her phone in one hand. 'It's a psalm – I think for the same person. Psalm one hundred and three, verses thirteen to eighteen. This translation is from the Good News Bible. Sorry, can you?'

She passed the phone to the boy sitting next to Helen. He read in an unsteady monotone: *'As a father is kind to his children, so the Lord is kind to those who honour him.'*

My chest exploded.

Every thought went straight to Dad – his firm, steady care. All the lost love I would never get back.

'*He knows what we are made of; he remembers that we are dust. As for us, our life is like grass. We grow and flourish like a wild flower; then the wind blows on it, and it is gone – no one sees it again.*'

I was shaking, fists clenched.

'*But for those who honour the Lord, his love lasts forever, and his goodness endures for all generations of those who are true to his covenant and faithfully obey his commands.*' He stopped. 'Was that it?'

'Yes. Thank you.'

It felt like someone had pulled a hood over my face. I couldn't see. I couldn't breathe. I was on my feet in one move. The chair fell down behind me. I was through the door, down the empty corridor before my brain could re-engage. I heard footsteps behind me. A hand on my shoulder.

'Are you –'

I grabbed him, slamming him against the wall. 'You told them about me!' I shoved him, pressing on his collarbone. 'Fuck you! You set me up!'

'Get your hands off me. Right now.' Jono's voice was low. Commanding.

I dropped my grip, stumbling backwards. Something guttural came up from the pit of my stomach. I retched repeatedly, trying to get it out. Until I realised it wasn't sick. This wasn't sick – these were sobs. Huge, unhinged sobs, shaking my whole body. I bent over double. I fell to my knees, forehead on the manky carpet. I fought the urge to curl up, right there, like a foetus, on the floor.

If I never moved again, it wouldn't matter.

'Ben?' Jono knelt down next to me.

I knew he was there but I couldn't acknowledge him.

'Ben?'

I sat up a bit.

Slowly.

I could see his jeans, his hands on his knees. I couldn't look at him.

'Let's get out of here, OK? Come on.'

He hauled me to my feet. I followed him blindly, back out into the cold.

'Here.' He nudged me towards his car. 'Get in for a minute.' He opened the passenger side for me. He slammed the door shut behind me. He went round and sat in the driver's seat. He put in the key, turned up the heater.

I watched it all like I was underwater. The feeling wasn't a million miles away from being stoned. I knew time was passing. I knew I should probably say something. Or do something. But I couldn't get my body and mind to align. I was like a caged animal: trapped in the shock of the moment. It was easily the most unnerving thing that had happened to me. Not horrific, like finding out about Dad. But disorienting.

Eventually, I calmed down enough to speak.

'They were talking about me. It really felt like they were talking about me. But you swear you didn't say anything?'

'I didn't. I would never do that.'

I believed him. A different person and I would've had doubts. But Jono – he didn't strike me as manipulative.

'Am I being . . .' I didn't trust my judgement. 'You think that was for me?'

'I mean, I don't know for sure. But, yeah, I'd say so.'

'Why?'

He looked at me. He hesitated.

'It's OK, I'm asking – I want to know what you think.'

He laughed a little. 'I'm gonna sound like such an idiot.'

'Do it. Just say it.'

'Jesus loves you, Ben.'

I burst out laughing. 'A classic line.'

'I know. Never gets old.'

'Jesus loves me.' I smiled, looking out the window. It all came flooding back – songs from children's church, cards from my grandparents. It was hard to reconcile with this experience. This was more like a cosmic punch in the gut.

'Think about it, though. If God is real, she has to know all about us.'

'She?'

He rolled his eyes. 'Pronouns are a bitch. He/she/they. But if God knows us, and if we can talk to God, maybe sometimes things get passed along. So that we know we're seen.'

I sighed, suddenly exhausted. 'I'm not sure I want to be seen right now.'

'Probably you don't want to be judged. But seen – I should know. Before I came out, I felt invisible. But if you're seen, you can be accepted.'

We were quiet. This was the most intense conversation I'd had in a while. My deep chats were normally with Harriet, but God had been totally off-limits with her since Dad died. It was kind of nice, being back on familiar ground. As much as it hurt to think about God, I wasn't ready to leap with Harri into atheism.

For me, the question wasn't one of existence. I couldn't write off what I'd already experienced. If only I could – I'd have fewer questions. The problem was the disconnect. It was the betrayal. It was everything being so wildly fucked up. What was this all-powerful God of love doing?

And not just for me, but for all of us? Everyone and everything in pain.

'Jesus loves me, huh?' I had to laugh again. To be fair, Jono had balls – coming out with that. 'Funny way of showing it.'

'Shit happens.'

I didn't know he swore. It was reassuring somehow. Like, for all his faith, he was still in touch with reality.

'It does!' He looked at me. 'Horrible shit happens. But does that mean God doesn't care? Or isn't on it? I don't think so. I think eventually love wins.'

I sighed again. I had hit a wall. My capacity to think this hard or feel this much was completely used up. But there was one more thing that absolutely needed saying.

'Listen, Jono.' I felt nothing but shame. 'Back there, the way I grabbed you – I owe you the biggest apology. I was way, way over the line. I'm so sorry.'

'You were triggered. I get it.' He clenched the steering wheel. 'But don't you *ever* touch me like that again.'

I looked at him. Putting two and two together. Coming up with four. 'Someone's done that to you before, haven't they?'

He didn't look at me. He turned away, looking out of the side window. When he turned back, his answer wasn't an answer. 'Ben, are you talking to anyone? A professional?'

I shook my head.

'I can recommend a place.'

I nodded. 'I'll think about it.'

'I'm sorry, too, by the way.' He smiled – the thin, sad smile again. 'I didn't mean for things to get traumatic.'

'That's life, right? Not your fault. I actually would like to come back.' My mouth was more honest than my head. I realised I meant it as the words came out. 'Maybe next week? If I'm still allowed after that shit-show.'

He smiled – a real smile. A grin. 'Of course. Open invitation, remember?'

'You're a seriously good person, Jono.' He squirmed, but I wasn't going to let it go. I knew the cost of leaving nice things unsaid. 'I mean it.' It was my turn to risk sounding like a cliché. 'I reckon Jesus is really proud of you.'

He looked at me – uncertain. Like maybe I was taking the piss.

'Really.'

He was silent.

He blinked a few times, staring straight ahead. He nodded, clearing his throat. Trying to let it in.

'Jono, I know I'm a mess but trust me – you're definitely one of the good ones.'

'All right, all right.' He smiled, shaking his head and turning on the ignition. 'Enough. Let's get you home.'

twenty-three

_____

HARRIET

'So, I've been thinking. I'm going to apply to do maths next year. At university. Instead of art.'

I make the announcement between mouthfuls, sitting round the dinner table with my parents. It's Thursday and they're tired. We're eating an assortment of leftovers – snatching time together before we go our separate ways: Mum to her work emails; Dad lost to TV. It seems as good a moment as any. They might not have the energy for an inquisition.

'Well, that's new!' Mum's fork stops mid-trajectory, hovering over her plate, then waving over to Dad. 'Did you have something to do with this?'

'If I did, I'm flattered!' His smile is broad – undisguised relief breaking over his features. 'Seen the light, then?'

I wrinkle my nose at him, part of me wincing at just how over-joyed he is. Did he really hate the idea of me doing art that much? 'Not exactly. I just think it could be more stable. In the future.'

'As I always said, you can paint in your spare time.'

'You've *never* said that . . . ?'

'To your mother. Seemed pointless to upset you when you were so convinced. But I'll admit now, I did worry.'

'Oh.'

It's a revelation. I don't know what to do with it.

As much as I appreciate this new affirmation, I don't love discovering the inner workings of my dad's mind. All along, I've been living with a subtext I was clueless about. I knew fine art wouldn't have been his first choice for me. I didn't realise it actually bothered him.

Mum is suspiciously quiet. She's almost squinting at me, as if she can't quite make out my face – like she's looking at me through a fog.

'Is this about Ben?'

'Mum!'

'Honestly, Mags – she makes a sensible choice, and you find a way to make it about a boy!'

Mum smiles, shaking her head. She's practically laughing – her sixth sense firing on all cylinders. She pats Dad's hand, wordlessly teasing him. He shrugs, turning his gaze to me too. His eyes are asking for reassurance – confirmation that I'm as rational as he's always hoped.

'It's not! It's not about Ben.'

Is that true? I'm not entirely sure.

'OK, so, maybe that whole thing got me thinking . . . with him maybe not being in London next year after all. But I'm finding art really tough at the moment, so maybe it's not the great fit I thought. Whereas maths – it's not like maths is easy, but at least I know where to start and there are right answers and it makes sense if you follow the rules.'

They exchange glances: silently debating, deciding between themselves who will tackle me first. Dad isn't going to step up to this one. He doesn't believe in it enough to try to talk me round.

'Harriet, it's great that you're exploring your options. Just make sure you think it through properly. You shouldn't let all your choices revolve around –' Mum's lecture is cut short by the doorbell. I leap up from the table.

'Sorry, gotta go – going for a run with Justin. I'll let you know when I'm on my way back.'

I hear them – the beginnings of a low-level argument rumbling as I flee. I fly through the front door so quickly, I nearly knock Justin over – colliding with him on the porch like skittles in a bowling alley. He grins, steadying me with both his hands on my shoulders.

'Wow, you're keen.'

'You're literally saving me right now. That whole dinner conversation with my parents was about to get really awkward.'

'See, now I'm curious.'

He hasn't let go of me yet. I can't help noticing the weight of his palms, part of me contrasting his touch with Ben's. It's a split-second comparison, but it's enough to unnerve me. I shrug him off as subtly as possible. He takes the hint, stepping sideways, giving me more room.

'Oh, it was just . . .' I don't want to get into the details. I barely mention Ben when I'm with Justin. There's something novel about having someone look at me and see a whole person, instead of the wounded half of an inseparable duo. It makes me feel more centred. Less like an amputee. It's a complete illusion, but I'm not ready to give that up. 'I was just getting a bit of a grilling about next year.'

'Well, happy to help.'

'So, what route were you thinking?'

We've been adding in more runs each week – not just the Saturday morning parkrun. At first, he always initiated but now I'm totally on board: there's something therapeutic about pounding the pavement.

'The university? We could do the lake? Or sports ground? Lake *and* sports ground?'

I smile. 'Keen, but not *that* keen. Lake?'

We stretch and head off at a pace that should be comfortable. Justin is guaranteed to start talking, and I can normally keep up and chat – my cardio is improving all the time. But, tonight, something feels a bit off.

'Here's a question.' He launches in, predictably, as soon as we're into a settled rhythm. 'The party next week, are you going?'

'Big yes. Annie's on the sixth-form committee this year and she's done most of the organising. So, it's basically mandatory for me.'

'But it's not really your thing?'

I don't know how to explain myself – it's been a while since I've done the 'getting-to-know-you' routine. 'I'm more of a one-to-one kind of person. A roomful of people I only half-know who are all in their cliques . . . that's a bit of a nightmare.'

'So, you need a wingman?'

'Basically. And Annie will be too busy making sure the venue doesn't get trashed. Plus, she's great at the social butterfly thing anyway.'

'Who's your fallback?'

Running side by side has its advantages: it's easier to dodge a question when we're both staring ahead. 'Are you volunteering?'

'Yeah, of course!'

I glance at him – his smile couldn't be wider.

'Really?'

'Why not?'

'I don't know, I think I had you down as someone who'd be more in the middle of things. Not so much on the sidelines.'

'Depends who's on the sidelines.'

He does a pretty good job of sounding nonchalant, but the comment still registers. Something sinks in the pit of my stomach – the feeling in sync with the warning flare that shoots across my mind. I slow down.

He stops running too. 'Everything OK?'

Justin is so unguarded. Spending time with him is a breath of fresh air. I can't believe how essential that feels now, when a few weeks ago I hardly knew he existed.

I know I should say something. I know I need to clarify where we're at. But I don't want to ruin anything. I don't want to be on my own.

'It's nothing – I've actually just been feeling a bit queasy.'

'Did you say you ate before we left?'

'Yeah, I came straight from dinner – that's not great, is it?'

'Not the best. Is it like a stitch? A cramp about here?' He gestures, frowning with concern.

'Yeah. Sorry, maybe I should head back.' I don't really mean it as a question – more of an indirect goodbye. The nuance seems to be lost on him.

'Or we could do something else. Cinema?'

I look at him. He's waiting – patiently, confidently. He doesn't seem like someone who's just suggested a first date. I'm overreacting. I'm reading way too much into this whole situation.

We just get on. Of course we can hang out.

Besides, Ben and I have done a hundred and one date-like things that apparently have meant absolutely nothing to him. So, obviously, I'm not great at reading the signs.

'Yeah, OK – let's see what's on. No romance, though. Something funny.'

He smiles. 'Got it.' He pulls out his phone, searching for options.

This is probably not the best idea I've ever gone along with. The list of things I haven't told Annie is getting longer and more complex by the minute. But the thought of sitting cosily in a dark room for a couple of hours, immersed in a comedy with someone who makes me feel less alone?

Honestly, all I feel is relief.

twenty-four

HARRIET

May, Last Year

Modern Art Oxford was vaguely familiar – I'd been to the gallery years before with my parents. But moving through the Jenny Saville exhibition was like sleepwalking through a vivid dream. This time, there were no distractions or escape routes. All my usual habits were redundant: without my phone, I couldn't take photos, look up extra bio details, cross-reference her influences.

I had to just look.

I had to allow myself to really see.

I was used to looking at nudes. I had been taking life-drawing classes for months, trying to master the physical form – one of art's enduring obsessions. But the thing about the body, the thing I was realising more fully in the middle of all the mess, was – even though everyone has one – examining it can make people ridiculously uncomfortable.

Her art made me uncomfortable.

It was so brutally clear-sighted. Bruised, sagging, dimpled flesh. Huge in scale – all these uncontainable women, exploding from the canvas, refusing to fit in and be small, smooth and filtered.

It sparked something in me.

Questions of power and representation, palette and portrayal all swirled in my mind as I walked fairly aimlessly through the space. What about my experience – the identities I embodied? Fighting to be seen and embraced on terms free from centuries of rancid toxicity. Too often vilified, minimised, traumatised, objectified, home to a hundred generations of ancestral lineage – but uniquely mine to live and love in.

I could feel the momentum of my thoughts snowballing, the first seeds of an art project beginning to take root. It was a familiar feeling – a feeling I lived for. I just didn't expect to experience it here and now. I could *never* have imagined the circumstances would have such a gift to give.

Ben did that.

He joined the dots for me.

My steps quickened, my pulse picking up – I was practically dancing between the works. I was like a sponge, absorbing the layers of her vibrant, viscous painting style – letting it all soak in and re-energise me.

I was like a famished wanderer, feeding off the energy from her line drawings: I hadn't seen her work in pencil before. I'd always thought of it as a pretty bland tool, but experiencing the hectic, overlapping lines of her drawing style was like living through time travel – all moments alive at once.

I jumped out of my skin when a hand touched my back.

'Whoa! Just me. Did you have a good time?' Ben was back from seeing Charlotte already; I was so deep in flow everything else had evaporated.

I couldn't stop myself – I threw my arms around his neck and clung on with all my might; there were no words for how much I appreciated him.

He was surprisingly muscular.

The thought caught me off-guard.

Maybe it was the angle, the way I was leaning into him? Maybe it was the exhibition? The focus on physicality. Maybe that explained it – my acute awareness: his body against my body, his skin on my skin.

He wrapped his arms around me, briefly, letting go again almost immediately.

I felt the moment slide, descending into awkwardness.

We had touched more in the last twenty-four hours than probably our entire lives. That seemed relevant, somehow – like a tripwire had been set off, exploding an invisible boundary line.

I let go too. 'How was it with Charlotte?'

He frowned slightly, shaking his head. It was obviously off-limits. I didn't push it.

'Can I just quickly go to the shop?'

He nodded, still mute.

I felt self-conscious as he trailed behind me, waiting for me to select postcards for future reference. He wasn't impatient, but clearly something was bothering him. He was quiet – too quiet, not the good kind of peaceful. More like he was nearing a black hole in his mind, about to disappear into an unreachable space. There was no point asking if he was OK. He'd tell me at some point. Rushing him was always counterproductive.

Back outside, the afternoon was long gone; the air was marginally cooler as evening took hold. We walked towards his college in silence, the occasional tap of my arm steering me in the right direction.

Everything was different.

Whatever had happened – whatever was said in his conversation with Charlotte – Ben had come back to me a different person.

But it wasn't just him.

It was ludicrous and alarming and completely new, but each time he touched me – just his hand on my arm – it went all the way through me. I could barely concentrate on putting one foot in front of the other, feeling clumsy with confusion, feeling awkward every time I accidentally bumped into him.

The walk was short; we were opposite his college in no time. I stepped off the kerb.

'Harri, watch out!'

It was massive, bright red and right there.

I didn't see.

A horn blared. Ben yanked me backwards. A double-decker tour bus: pulling away from its stop, gaining momentum as it headed straight for me.

'What the *fuck* is wrong with you?!' He rounded on me – fists clenched, his face contorted. 'Shit, Harriet!'

I gasped, winded.

'How could you do that?!'

The driver sped past us, beeping again for good measure. Buses and bikes surged along the busy street. People pushed past us on the pavement. Everyone kept moving. Everyone except us. It was as if neither of us could find the way forwards. Ben had never shouted at me before. Not once – for all his issues and our bickering over the years. He'd never lost it. Not with me.

I collapsed under his fury like a house of cards.

'It was an accident.'

He winced at the word.

'I was distracted. I'm so sorry.'

I was usually so careful, paranoid even, after everything with Uncle David. Starting to cross the road without looking was pure stupidity in action. It was unacceptable at the best of times, but especially with Ben right there next to me.

Nothing had happened. It was over in an instant. But we both knew it could easily have been worse.

Ben took a deep breath. He gripped my hand, marching me to the other side of the street like a toddler who couldn't be trusted. We walked under a colossal bell tower and into the sanctuary of the quad, its impenetrable outer walls dampening the noise of the traffic behind us.

I couldn't think straight – too many things were going on at once. Artistic inspiration still buzzing in my veins. My carelessness so drastically letting Ben down. The weirdness of feeling like I was noticing him for the very first time. It was too much – too much adrenaline, too much stimulation.

Ben released me, pushing his hands deep into his pockets again.

'Listen' – his voice shook a little – 'you *have* to take care of yourself. I won't always be around to do it.' He sighed, running a hand over his curls. 'That's what Dad used to say to me. All the time.'

I nodded, speechless.

He looked away, towards the fountain in the centre of the quad. 'I could really do with going to chapel. Evensong is starting now.'

'OK.' I tried to sound emotionally stable. 'I can head back to your room and wait for you there?'

He paused. 'Or you could come with me?'

I hadn't been to a church service since Uncle David's funeral. But it wasn't about me. 'Sure. Am I OK to go in like this?' I gestured to my flip-flops, my bare legs and arms.

'You look . . .' His smile was small, almost shy. He let the sentence fall away, incomplete. 'I don't think there's a dress code.' He shrugged. 'There's no time to change anyway. We can always sit at the back.'

The chapel was more than a cosy prayer room: a monumental cathedral was nestled in the far corner of the quad. As we walked around the outskirts to reach it, the quiet between us was slightly lighter. The prospect of evensong seemed to revive

Ben a little – beginning to put him in a better frame of mind. The bells pealing across the quad shattered some of the tension in the air.

But I couldn't shake it off.

Not his anger or the shock of the bus. Us. The idea of us. I tried to regroup, silently flailing around in my mind. Trying to ignore the unnerving knot in my stomach that tightened each time I glanced his way. Trying to suppress the new scenarios fluttering through my imagination. It was as if the bottom had fallen out of my sanity, my thoughts in frantic overdrive.

Ben stopped abruptly – halting under the archways near the entrance to the cathedral.

He was quiet.

'I can't believe I swore at you like that.' His hands twitched in his pockets; he stared at the stone slabs on the floor. 'There's no excuse. Absolutely no excuse. But that was . . . I was –'

'Scared.'

'Terrified! Completely terrified.' He looked up at the ornately carved ceiling, like a sailor consulting the stars for guidance. His hands stayed in his pockets but he stepped towards me, filling my personal space. He looked at me. He studied me – his eyes travelling slowly, covering every part of my face.

'I can't lose you. You do know that?'

The moment felt like paralysis. I couldn't form words, despite the questions coming at me, thick and fast: What was this? Was something happening between us? Did he feel it too – the ripples disturbing our coexistence?

I couldn't say it.

It was too much to process, let alone ask out loud. I lowered my gaze to his chest instead, trying not to think about how good it felt to be so close to him.

He stood there a little longer, hesitant on the threshold of the church. The sounds of the service in progress rang out through the open door – the organ, the choir, the liturgy underway.

He turned, severing our connection. He looked over his shoulder at the gathered faithful in their seats. 'Shall we go in?'

Before I could answer, he disappeared through the door.

twenty-five

HARRIET

I arrive at the sixth-form party alone.

This is not my idea of a good time.

The committee hires the same upstairs room of the same backstreet venue every time – a tradition going back so far, its founders are probably about to retire. The basic rationale is the same: cheap rates and management that turns a blind eye. It's not exactly unsafe, but it still feels uncomfortable.

I hang back, hovering near the doorway and assessing my options. Even before I fully enter the room, the music starts to beat my mind into submission – berating me for being uptight, accusing me of being unsexy, telling me who to be and how to think. It's an endless string of sing-along insecurities that I don't want to own.

Does no one else listen to lyrics?

The tunes bleed together, each one harder to take than the last. It's like some form of twisted hypnotherapy – casually eroding my self-esteem. Am I really the only one affected by the roar of subliminal messaging? It's like a physical pulse pumping through me, changing the tempo of my mood – putting a downer on whatever spark I might otherwise have had. I can't dance to this.

This is not Annie's playlist – that's all I know.

I look for her – peering through the heaving throng. She's on the other side of the room, effortlessly engaging everyone around her. She spots me. She smiles and waves enthusiastically, blowing me a kiss, before turning back to her conversation.

I manoeuvre further into the crowd – cautiously navigating between bodies that bump into me at random. I'm trying to avoid detection, quietly making my way around the edges of other people's friendship groups. But arms are flung across me. A voice screeches in my ear.

'Harriet!'

I give a quick squeeze back, then stumble out of the embrace – distancing myself from the face imprinting on my cheek. 'Hi, Felicity. Hi, Dylan, how's it going?' I keep moving; the trick is to smile and keep moving.

'Dance with us!'

I shrug an apology, waving my cup-free hands and pointing towards the bar. 'Sorry! Maybe later.'

The floor is already sticky – drinks sloshing over the sides of plastic cups, sugary liquid caking laminate tiles. Officially, no one is drinking. Officially, the party is just for our year group. But half the faces are unfamiliar to me – and not just because I keep a small circle.

Word always gets out; it's part of the reason I feel so endlessly awkward. It's hard to relax with loitering strangers – their eyes evaluating, their phones capturing. The quickest way to not feel vulnerable would be to drink myself into indifference – but then I'd be more vulnerable than ever.

But it's OK; I can do this. I'm here for Annie. Show my face. Stay for a bit. Go home as early as possible.

'Harriet!'

I turn – and the relief is immeasurable. 'Justin!' My smile is completely involuntary, my face muscles mirroring his huge grin. He pushes through to where I'm stranded, breaking away from his group.

'Best night of your life?'

'Absolutely – can't you tell?'

'I was worried you'd changed your mind.'

'No, just stalling.'

The music is so loud, we have to lean in – shouting into each other's ears. Someone stumbles; the drunken shove knocks Justin into me. He smiles and points back the way I've come. 'Do you want to get some air?'

We weave back out of the crush – it's so much easier, moving as a pair. People part like the Red Sea – making way for us. I sense double-takes, curious glances. It occurs to me that we look like we're leaving together.

'Better?'

I can breathe again – back on the fringes in the foyer. We lean over the banister, watching people come up and down the stairs, flitting between the dance floor and the toilets below.

'I do like parties!' I'm not sure why I'm acting like he's judging me.

'Just not crap ones. That's fair.'

'Right.' I smile – laughing at myself. 'Were you having fun? I don't want to ruin your night.'

'You're not ruining anything.'

'I was so relieved to see you!'

'Ha, no worries. You did seem like you were drowning there. The way you dodged Felicity –'

'Oh no, you saw me?!' I cover my face with both hands.

'Well, I wasn't spying on you or anything – but I did see you arrive. I was looking for you.'

I peek out at him from between my fingers. It's there again – that feeling: the suspicion that he might be communicating more than what his words are saying. I scramble for a neutral topic, but he speaks up before I've landed on anything suitable.

'You look great, by the way.'

'Ah, thanks! Although, I think I've probably been setting the bar quite low with my exercise outfits.'

He smiles, and I think he might protest but I don't let him interrupt. 'While I remember, I can't do parkrun for the next couple of weekends. Or any runs in the week, actually.'

'Shame! How come? Are you away for half-term?'

'Yeah.' My heart rate climbs. I remind myself to keep breathing. 'I'm visiting a friend in Scotland.'

'Sounds fun.' He hesitates. 'I'll miss you.'

This is it.

This is the gap where I should say something – fill the lengthening pause between us with the truth he deserves to hear, whether it's relevant or not.

'Justin –'

It's too late.

He kisses me.

And I want to say it came out of the blue, and I didn't think we were heading here and I'm so sorry, but most of that's dishonest, and I'm too caught up in the feeling of his lips, his mouth, his tongue – which I guess means I'm kissing him back. Oh, shit!

I pull away.

'Justin, I didn't mean to – I don't –'

'Oh, my God.' He's frozen somewhere between horrified and humiliated. It's the worst expression I've ever seen on his face, and I hate that I'm responsible for it. 'I thought. Because. No? So, I guess I should just –'

'No, please wait!' I've grabbed his arm – I'm clinging to him like I'm sinking. 'Can I explain?'

He hesitates again, almost willing to hear me out. He's like the embodiment of decency and I can't believe I've hurt him. What do I say to that?

'It's complicated, but –'

'Actually, I can't. I'm sorry.' He shakes his head, apologising for no good reason. 'I need to go. I'm gonna go.'

He darts back into the party. Justin more or less sprints away from me, and I'm about to follow him, as soon as the room stops spinning and the churn in my stomach settles.

But then I see her.

And she's furious.

'Annie! Annie, please – this isn't what it looks like.'

She's running down the stairs – taking them two at a time, barging past the people bottle-necked at the entrance to the toilets. I run in too, a few steps behind her – just in time to see the stall door at the far end slam shut. Walking towards it is like being on death row; I can feel myself shaking.

We have an audience. Make-up brushes pause mid-stroke; quizzical looks are fired in my direction – bouncing off smeared mirrors under fluorescent lights. The music from upstairs is blaring – clearly audible, the bass thumping through the floor. But it won't drown out her inevitable shouting and soon everyone will know what a horrible friend I am.

'Annie?' I knock on the door.

'Leave me alone!'

I almost want to. It would be easier. At least if she ghosts me, I won't have to hear what she thinks of me.

'Annie, please come out. Or let me in. I'm so sorry.'

I can't tell if she's crying. I can't hear her moving.

'I should've told you that we started going for runs together. And the cinema – once. But I didn't want to make a big deal out of it because really nothing happened.'

The door flies open. She is literally tearing her hair out, fingers splayed across her scalp. 'Are you *hearing* yourself?! Nothing happened?! I *saw you.* He *kissed* you!'

She steps towards me with every sentence, backing me up against the sinks.

'I know – but that was a total first.' I squirm away from her, setting off a hand-dryer. 'It was just a huge misunderstanding. I feel awful; I'm so sorry. I didn't mean for it to happen.'

'Oh, please!' Her sarcasm hits me like a slap across the face.

'I didn't! This wasn't what I wanted at all.'

'Right.' She stares at me, her face flushed, strands of hair sticking to the side of her cheek. She's waiting for me to say something but I don't know what. I've lost the thread of the argument. I'm not the only one unable to follow along: people push past us on their way into the cubicles; they lean across us for the soap and the hand towels – rapidly losing interest in our drawn-out drama.

'I should've told you.'

'Argh, Harriet!' I feel like she might actually slap me. 'Yes! That would've been nice – a good friend would've done at least that. But it's not like he's my boyfriend.'

'So –'

'You *never* own up to *anything!* You "didn't mean it"; you "didn't want it". Things just happen. Or don't happen. It's bullshit! I'm so sick of it! You're choosing! You're always choosing! And you always choose whatever's easiest for you. You don't think about what that means for anyone else!'

'Annie, that's not fair!' I try to stay calm but it's like someone has reached into my ribcage and is forcibly squeezing my heart – I feel it constrict, tightening, pounding.

'Really? How about Charlotte?'

That's random – it takes me a second to place the name. 'Ben's girlfriend?'

'Yeah, his ex-girlfriend, thanks to you!'

'I –'

'You get in the way! You get in the way of other people being happy – people who know what they want and are just trying to get on with things. And the worst thing is, you're not honest about it! You never admit anything! You're never like, "This is happening; I want this." You're always hiding or in denial.'

'I –'

She's unstoppable: psychoanalysis at speed – high on adrenaline and seeing red.

'No! You're a fraud, Harriet! You make all this supposedly great art about having a voice. You talk a huge talk on canvas, but it's totally fake – in real life, you're pathetic!'

I'm stunned.

Her eyes flicker, like she's just registering that she actually said all of that to my face. She sighs – looking around her, coming out of a spell.

'I have to go back up.'

I nod. She knows I'm not coming.

'Just, please! Get it together!'

I've been holding my breath. I only realise it as she sweeps past me and I'm left rooted to the spot, running out of oxygen and more alone than I could ever have imagined.

I pull out my phone; I'm in survival mode. We haven't talked – he said the signal might be patchy; he said he'd be on retreat. We haven't even messaged – not in weeks and weeks, absolutely ages, the longest silence I can remember between us.

It doesn't ring.

'This is Ben Wilkins. Leave a message. I'll –'

I redial.

'Dad?' I'm whispering – my voice is as small as I feel. I push my way towards an exit. It will be a miracle if he can hear me over all the background noise. 'Can you come and pick me up?'

'Harriet, of course! I'm leaving now.'

twenty-six

HARRIET

May, Last Year

Charlotte was there.

When we got back to Ben's room after evensong, she was sitting on one of the sofas – her back to us, mid-conversation with Ben's roommate, their voices low. She'd sunk deep into the chair; I could barely see the top of her head, just her hair shoved up in a messy bun. It was Ben's roommate who acknowledged us first.

'Here they are!'

'Harri, this is Freddie – think you saw him when you got here yesterday.' Ben started to do introductions.

Charlotte jumped to her feet, quickly wiping a hand under her eyes. 'Hi, I'm Charlotte – Ben's girlfriend.' She leant on the last word, a fixed smile on her face.

'Of course! Great to finally meet you.' I meant it. The mystery surrounding her had grown out of all proportion, especially given Ben's total transformation when he came to get me from the gallery – the strange power she seemed to wield over his mood. 'Ben talks about you all the time.'

Her smile relaxed a little. 'And you.' She came over to where Ben stood next to me, slipping her arm around his waist. 'I thought we were all going to informal?'

We had missed the first sitting of dinner while Ben centred himself, shrugging off the shock of the bus and regaining his balance, quietly reciting the liturgy of the day while I looked on. That left us with formal hall – the second sitting, a more ceremonial event.

'Yeah, I ducked into chapel at the last minute. Sorry.'

'Oh. That's OK.'

'Did you eat already?'

'No, I waited for you.'

Ben's smile was so full of gratitude it was almost an insult to my company, even though he had spent near enough the whole day with me.

'Harri just needs to get changed.'

He was talking about me – not to me – pulling Charlotte closer, transfixed. The movement was subtle but I couldn't stop studying them: the way they gravitated towards each other, the ways their bodies touched.

There had been girls around in the past but seeing him as one half of a relatively stable couple was a revelation, a real-life spot the difference. All the gaps in my relationship with him were highlighted and underlined.

It hollowed me out.

I found myself aching for things I had never thought to miss.

It took me a minute to realise everyone was waiting for me.

'OK, just a second.'

I retreated into Ben's bedroom, rifling through the limited selection of clothes I'd escaped home with. Heading back from the cathedral, Ben had filled me in on the pushback against sloppy undergraduates – the threats to turn away diners who showed up looking too laid-back. I plucked out the best I could do, changing swiftly.

I re-emerged. My stomach flipped.

They were kissing.

Ben and Charlotte were kissing in the empty lounge.

My eyes ricocheted around the room, trying to land on something neutral. This was madness. Of course he loved his girlfriend! Of course he wanted her in ways he didn't want me. When had this become so difficult to deal with? Why was I now torpedoed by panic at the sight of him with someone else?

I forced myself to stay still, resisting the urge to flee the scene, trying not to embarrass myself by drawing attention to my presence.

They were interrupted anyway.

'Break it up, kids – we're late.' Freddie reappeared, tossing a wad of black fabric in my direction. 'Think fast!'

'What's this?'

'A gown.' Ben looked my way again, and I noticed the robes they had all slipped on while I changed. He smiled at me, obviously elated, but also a little apologetic. I knew he could read my discomfort. I hoped he didn't know why. How could I begrudge him happiness with his girlfriend?

I smiled back, shaking my head slightly – the fastest way to tell him the things I couldn't say out loud with an audience:

I'm fine.

Stop worrying.

We're good.

A few white lies to keep the peace. Ben smiled again, reassured. He didn't look back as Freddie herded us out. As we ran down the stairs and across the quads, it was Charlotte's hand Ben was holding.

Everyone called the dining space 'hall' – casually, like it was just another room: large but otherwise ordinary. Even Ben seemed to buy into the fiction that being served a three-course meal every night by staff in uniform was normal. We joined the tail end of a slow-moving queue, people flashing their IDs as they filed through the tall double doors. I was ushered in, too – Ben's guest.

The sight on the other side of the doors made me pause mid-step.

It could've been another cathedral. Stained-glass windows haloed the entire room. The high walls looked like sandstone, with more dark wood panelling covering the lower half. A crowd of portraits dominated every available space: kings and cardinals, prime ministers and professors – a long line of college notables stretching down to the doors I'd just walked through. Nearly five hundred years of success stared at me as I walked up the aisle to my seat.

It should've been intimidating, but the whole room glowed – cosy despite its scale. There were golden lamps on the long tables, spotlights over the portraits – everything electric but with the soft imitation of candlelight, a magical aura, a nod to centuries past.

'Don't sit yet.'

I had followed in the slipstream of everyone else, but found myself next to Freddie, on the opposite side of the table to Ben and Charlotte. We'd met two more of Ben's friends in the queue and it was Paige, on my other side, who was whispering instructions to me.

'We have to wait for high table. And grace.'

She nodded towards an elevated platform at the far end of the hall. Another long table was set out at a right angle to us, like the bridal party at a wedding reception. A group emerged from a door in the shadows and took their places. We continued to wait. A girl approached a lectern. Someone banged on the table, like they were calling a court to order. The room hushed.

'*Nōs miserī hominēs et egēnī, prō cibīs quōs nōbis ad corporis subsidium . . .*'

It took all my self-control not to laugh out loud. Where had I landed? Was she actually *speaking Latin?*

I caught Ben's eye.

It was like batting him a ball; he got the giggles almost immediately, his shoulders silently shaking. By the time grace was over, we were both close to tears.

'You!' He collapsed in his seat, when we were finally allowed to sit. 'I can't take you anywhere.'

'What? I said nothing!'

'It's definitely another world, but it's amazing what you can get used to. How long are you staying?' Paige was the friendliest of Ben's friends, and I instantly loved her for it.

'I have to leave first thing tomorrow.' I could've stopped there, but her warmth made me want to keep talking. 'It was very spur of the moment – I needed to get away from some stuff. Some really awful boy-drama.'

The room had come alive around us; conversation and laughter enveloped us, amplified by the space. She smiled sympathetically. 'Ah, that sucks, I'm sorry. Tim, my boyfriend' – she motioned to the person on the other side of Charlotte – 'he heard from one of our other friends that Ben skipped a tute to go and get you, so we all knew it was serious.'

'A tute?'

'Sorry, tutorial. Apparently, Ben said there was a family emergency.'

'I had no idea. Is that a bad thing? For him?'

'Oh, it's OK.' She put her hand on my arm, fleetingly. Everything about Paige was giving me an older sister vibe; the gesture was comforting yet totally dismissive. 'He'll just have to make it up next week somehow. I just meant I get whatever's going on is a big deal. And also' – her voice dropped to a whisper – 'he'd walk through fire for you. And back again. Like, any day. Drives Charlotte insane, but I think it's really so sweet.'

I sat back, shocked.

Obviously, I knew I could rely on him. But was it that blatant? To everyone?

Just friends. Just friends. I repeated it internally, like a mantra – trying to reclaim the thing that used to feel true. I felt myself flounder, drowning in brand-new doubts. It was a relief when someone else caught her attention and Paige turned away.

I looked across to Charlotte, talking with Ben, half-obscured by the lanterns in the centre of the table. She couldn't have overheard Paige. It was impossible – the table was too wide. She must have sensed me staring. Her eyes flicked across to me, then to Ben, then back to me.

Her smile was quick and small.

I was exposed all over again. Only this time, instead of photos, it was my inner secrets – things I barely knew about myself – that were apparently public knowledge.

Charlotte shifted, pressing her upper body into Ben's. Their arms jostled intimately with each mouthful. She stayed that way – avoiding me, glued to him – for the entire meal.

I lost him for the evening.

Ben wanted to take Charlotte out – a peace offering for being absent with me for so much of the day. It wasn't my plan to wait up for him, but my mind was too full for an early night.

'You still awake?'

The knock on the bedroom door was quiet. I paused the stand-up I'd been watching, unsure if I'd heard anything.

He knocked again.

'Yep, come in.' I flicked on a lamp, closing the laptop.

The room had darkened around me while I'd thrown myself into onscreen distractions, strictly avoiding my profiles and feeds. It still felt weird to be phoneless, but I'd successfully occupied the evening anyway – streaming boxsets in bed.

'I just wanted to check you're doing all right with going home tomorrow?' Ben stood with the door ajar, his back against the wall. He seemed tired – his face was closed off, his arms crossed over his chest.

'Yeah, I guess so.'

The prospect of being ejected from this dream-world into a reality where people were bitching incessantly about my body – it filled every pore of me with dread. But at least I'd had a breather, gained some perspective. The fog of powerlessness – that was shifting. I had the beginnings of a way forwards.

It still felt exhausting. 'I'll think about it tomorrow.'

He nodded. 'If you need me to check your phone for you before you leave – scope out the damage. Anything. And let me know how it all goes, all right? Don't just message – call me. So I can hear if you're really OK.'

'I will. Thank you.'

It felt like the end of the conversation, but he didn't move.

'So, now we've covered my issues – what's going on with you?'

'Am I that transparent?'

'Yes. And can you just come in already? You're creeping me out, lurking in the doorway.'

His laugh was a half-groan. He sat at the far end of the bed, putting his head in his hands.

'Talk.'

'Charlotte thinks I'm in love with you. She actually said that! This afternoon!'

It was a collision of clichés – my heart in my mouth, the penny dropping. This was it: the source of his odd behaviour.

The reason he'd come back so quiet and on edge after seeing her. The reason he'd suddenly put a stop to all physical contact – veering from a hug a minute to having his hands permanently rammed in his pockets.

'What did you say?' I held my breath. I couldn't help it.

'I told her the truth!' He threw his hands in the air, exasperated. 'I told her you're my best friend and I can't even *begin* to imagine my life without you. But that's a whole other thing.'

I fought to keep my face blank. Twenty-four hours ago, I would've said exactly the same thing. Even twelve hours ago, those words wouldn't have crushed me.

'I mean, of course I love you! We're practically family.' His frustration was palpable. 'You're like my favourite sister!'

The s-word tipped me over the edge. My fingers drummed the laptop. I pushed it to one side. I drew my legs up, away from him, hugging my knees. My limbs were signalling things I didn't want to say.

'Wait.' He looked at me. 'Why are you pissed at me?'

'I'm not.'

'You are.'

'I'm not!'

'Harriet.'

'Favourite *sister?*'

'Well, what would you say?'

'I don't know.' I hid my face in my knees for a moment. When I looked up again, he was still waiting for an answer. 'Something that's less . . . Something more . . . factually accurate.'

He laughed, raising an eyebrow – an invitation to say more. I didn't take it.

'All right, well, when you come up with your preferred descriptor, you just let me know.' A massive yawn overtook him. He stretched, the bottom of his T-shirt lifting a little.

Just noticing felt bizarre. It was electrifying and unsettling – the random impulse to run a slow finger over the skin made visible by the movement. I clasped my hands together instead.

'Anyway, I'm about to drop so I guess I'll say goodnight.' He scooted up the bed. His hug was relaxed, like – from his perspective – his confession had cleared the air. 'Sleep well. Ten o'clock train, OK?'

He stood up to leave, headed for another night on the sofa in the next room.

'Or maybe you could stay?' I heard myself. The words had entirely bypassed my brain.

It was excruciating.

He was a deer in headlights, and I couldn't undo it. I just had to wait it out, dying a little with the long, silent seconds.

'Harri . . . ?' I didn't know my name could hold so much affection. And confusion. 'What are you asking me?'

'I just – everything's been so intense. The photos, seeing your life here, the exhibition, the thing with the bus . . . And I have to go back and deal with everything. Please. You smell safe.'

He burst out laughing, panic falling off him like a discarded coat. 'I smell safe?! That's such a strangely nice compliment.'

He came back to the bed. He nudged me over as I slipped down onto the pillow, lying next to me fully dressed. He turned off the light.

'You know I can't stay long? I'm not winning any prizes for boyfriend of the year.'

The single bed felt impossibly narrow. Ben's warmth radiated towards me – tangible proof that I wasn't dreaming. A back-alley street light seeped through the thin curtains, its pale illumination tinging everything. I could see the contours of his face in profile: his closed eyes, the rise and fall of his nose, his mouth. For all his talk of being exhausted, I knew he was wide awake. He was too still to be asleep. Too self-conscious.

I wanted this. Him.

I wanted us.

'Ben, can I ask you something random?' I sent a cautious probe out into the unknown.

He smiled, eyes still closed. 'Yeah, go on.'

'Do you believe in soulmates?'

His pause was thoughtful. 'Maybe. But after they're gone – what then?'

Sadness settled on us. Ben's grief had changed over time, shifting from a storm to a kind of quiet snowfall that would sweep in unannounced, cloaking everything.

I had to touch him. I let my arm snake itself across his chest, my body curling towards him.

He hesitated. He rested his arm over mine. 'How about you? What do you think?'

'I think so. Or at least' – I concentrated, steadying my voice – 'I think you can have someone in your life who knows you so well it's like they really see all of you. Which should be terrifying but it's OK because you know they'll always be there for you, no matter what.'

The semi-darkness made his silence easier to take. I knew he was reflecting, mulling over my little monologue.

'That's prayer.'

'Huh?'

'For me – what you just described, that's what talking to God is like. Floating butt-naked in a sea of insight and coming up clean, every time.'

I had to smile. 'Poetic. They should put that in the liturgy.' It was an unexpected twist, but I found myself more curious about his faith than I had been in years. 'How do you do it? Still believe?'

He shrugged; his muscles flexed beneath me. 'It hurts knowing there are answers I'm never going to get. But when I did that retreat – to the monastery – it was like God got a lot bigger. It wasn't about me using faith to explain everything. More that feeling of coming home. A bit rational. A bit not. I don't know; I'm not great at describing it.'

'No, you're fine. It's actually good to hear.' I released my grip on him, rolling onto my back and staring at the ceiling. Delving into my childhood beliefs was like opening a trunk stuffed with memorabilia: bittersweet – confronting things so full of lost meaning. 'I guess I've shut down a lot of those conversations, but I think I do get it. It's head and heart, isn't it? *Love the Lord your God with all your heart, all your soul, all your mind, all your strength.*'

I was quoting scripture to him – unearthed spontaneously from an unused part of my memory.

'Exactly! That's exactly it. So, I try. And I fuck up, but I do try. Good work, by the way! You must've really dredged that one up.'

'I still remember it all. It just doesn't fit for me anymore.'

'Yeah. I understand.'

We were quiet – neither of us rushing to flood such a complicated space.

'So' – he touched my hip, suddenly playful – 'how's my smell working out for you?' The grin was audible in his voice.

'I like it. You smell nice.'

'Ha! Wait until I start farting in my sleep!'

'Ben!' I dug my fingers into his ribs, shamelessly tickling him. 'That's so gross.'

'Ah, noo!' He squirmed around, laughing – such an easy target. 'You *literally* asked for it!'

I kept tickling him; it was so freeing – both of us giggling like little kids under the covers, a world away from anything I'd experienced with anyone else. No politics, no fear, no second-guessing whether being here together was a good idea. Just us. Just closeness and sudden joy – the best definition of messing around. It echoed in every part of me: his ridiculously out-of-control laughter and the fun of being the cause.

'Does that mean you'll sleep here with me?'

I shattered the lightness.

He stilled my hands abruptly, holding them away from him with a surprisingly strong grasp. He rolled onto his back again, staring straight ahead. I could feel his mind whirring; it was like sensing a tremor underground.

'Ben, you don't have to. Obviously, I'll be fine.'

He swung his legs out of the bed, sitting up with his back to me.

I couldn't see his face. I couldn't read his posture.

He crossed the room, hunting through a pile of laundry shoved up against the wall. I watched him, unsure exactly where this performance was going. He pulled out a change of clothes. He pulled off his T-shirt. I tried not to stare. I tried and totally failed. He stopped. He left the room.

When he came back, he was quiet – still elsewhere in his mind. He climbed back into bed; it was a minute or two before he turned to me.

'I hate sleeping on sofas.'

'I know.'

'Reminds me of being homeless.'

'I do know this.'

He wasn't looking in my direction anymore; he was preoccupied – away with his thoughts. When he raised his arm, I almost missed that it was for me – for me to come closer.

'If I stay, I'll have to tell Charlotte I spent the night with you.'

'Isn't that just cruel?'

'You think?'

'Well, does this change anything?' I hoped against hope he wouldn't feel my heart taking on a life of its own – stupidly high on the slim possibility that this could be us turning a corner.

'I don't think so. But she would. You really don't think I owe it to her? Because it matters to her?'

I tried to be objective. As an outsider – whether I wanted to be or not. What had I noticed?

The way he kissed her like every good thing could be communicated without words. The way an inner light went on in him when she looked at him with approval. The absence of any kind of hunger at all in his arms wrapped around me, in his legs caught up in mine – like he was holding someone secure and familiar. The human equivalent of a favourite teddy bear.

The realisation hurt – a throb of physical pain.

'I think you really like her. And if you tell her, it will finish things. She will one hundred per cent break up with you over this, Ben. Guaranteed.'

He sighed. But he didn't move.

'I wish you could've met her properly. She really is great. I just . . .' He sighed again. 'Recently, I just create all this anxious stress in her. It's so toxic.' He rested his chin on my forehead, pensive. 'Maybe, at a certain point, if all you're doing is making someone feel insecure . . . maybe it's time to call it quits?'

'Maybe.'

'Anyway! This isn't your problem. I'm always putting my problems on you! Even when you have your own!'

'It's OK.' I felt him shake his head, beginning to protest. 'It really is OK; I don't mind. It's what we do – we look after each other.'

He went quiet.

'Thanks, Harri.' He sounded emotional.

He cleared his throat, retracting from the tangle we had become. 'Sleep well.' A small smile returned to his voice as he turned onto his side, his back towards me. 'Kick me if I steal all the covers, all right?'

twenty-seven

BEN

I'm ridiculously excited.

It's crept up on me. Now that I'm standing at the pier, waiting for her boat to finish docking, I can't believe how long Harriet and I have gone without any contact.

Time's flown.

I've been too focused to feel homesick recently.

Helping Brother Hamish in the kitchen has transformed the way I think about basically everything. Watching him do anything is a total eye-opener. Nothing is insignificant. It's not just food prep; we're sustaining life. It's not just washing dishes; we're bringing order to chaos. The connections he makes between the physical and the spiritual – it's such an education.

He's teaching me to walk impossible tightropes. Redefining everything. Strength is being selfless but not exploited. Courage is being overlooked but still sure of your worth. He's disciplined and quiet and, like, a hundred years old. Sometimes he barely says three sentences to me all day. But he's made serving a high art. And his gratitude rubs off.

Up until now, I haven't looked back.

But sharing it with Harriet is like results day. I'm hopeful, but you never know. I hope she won't hate it. Or ridicule it – I don't think she would. But it matters so much more to me now. I've started something significant. I hope she can see what that means.

I can't rely on the weather to make a good first impression. It does its own thing.

I told Harriet to bring layers. I told her she needs a good waterproof, proper walking boots, sunglasses. All the seasons can come in a day. The midges are irritating. The gales off the Atlantic are unforgiving. I warned her about every last thing I could think of that might make her uncomfortable. I just want her to have the best chance of appreciating it all.

But we'll see.

This is taking forever. What are they doing? The ferry painstakingly angles itself against the pier. Apparently, it's one of the hardest places to dock in the Hebrides. It's unsheltered. Exposed to the whims of the weather – boats are cancelled all the time. But, come on! Get on with it, already. Waiting is making me nervous. I centre my breathing. I pray through my breath like I do when I'm chopping vegetables.

And then she's here! Carefully descending down the gangplank. Glancing up to look for me.

It's surreal.

It's exactly like one of those films she would make me sit through while she does her braids. She runs at me, grinning, then shrieking with laughter. Her bag drops at my feet and she's in my arms.

The hit is phenomenal.

I'm immediately sky high. I can differentiate all the scents that make her Harriet: hair oils, moisturiser, the smell of her skin. The feeling of muscle memory as our bodies reconnect is overwhelming.

'Ben, what a coincidence! I heard a rumour you were here . . .'

I'm too choked up to speak. I just bury my face against the side of her head. I'm blind-sided. I was *not* prepared for this. It's not a reunion, it's a tsunami. The wave of emotion doesn't have a name. Happiness? Nostalgia? I mumble something even I can't understand. I don't care if we stand here all afternoon. I'm not letting go any time soon.

She laughs. 'What did you say?'

'I don't even know! I think I've really missed you.'

Maybe she can sense that I'm suddenly unhinged. She lets the stillness last. Propping me up. Holding me together. I'm so grateful I could cry.

'I've really missed you too. So much.'

It has to end at some point.

She steps back to look at me. I loosen my arms round her by the smallest possible degree. Still holding on. Reluctant to release her. She strokes my face. Her thumb brushes my lip. 'Is this you trying to be more Christ-like?!'

I forget that my beard is new for her. I don't laugh because I can't breathe.

'OK, that's offensive – sorry.'

'It's not. It's not that.'

Her fingers are still tracing my jaw. Part of me remembers this is normal for us. Throwaway hugs. Casual kisses. But it feels like a foreign language.

'You caught me off-guard. People don't caress my face here.'

'Yeah, well' – she smiles, lowering her hand – 'that would be inappropriate.'

'It's just an extra layer. Because of the wind. You'll wish you had one after a few days. Do you like it?'

'Does that matter?'

I nod.

'I could definitely get used to it. It's fun! It feels nice.'

I finally let go of her – still reeling. Unbalanced. As if I'm the one fresh off the ferry. I'm so intoxicated, I have to laugh. 'So, anyway . . .' I try to sort myself out. 'Hello, Harriet.'

'Hello, Ben.'

I don't know what I tell her as I show her around the monastery. It's a total blur. Everyone wants to meet her. I've mentioned her more than I thought. The monks queue up to introduce themselves, like she's a visiting celebrity. Brother Richard is noticeably absent. I try not to let it spoil things, but it's obvious. Hard to ignore.

The afternoon vanishes and I have to get back to the kitchen. It feels like a good omen when that doesn't seem to bother her. She even comes to chapel at the end of the day – observing from a seat near the door, but still present. Open-minded. It's the kindest thing she could do for me. I completely love her for it.

It's hard to sleep at first – knowing she's just down the corridor. But the adrenaline dump wins out in the end. I sleep like a log and wake up excited. It takes my brain a few minutes to remember why. For the first time in weeks, morning prayer feels inconvenient. I can't wait to take her to my favourite bay. Brother Hamish is giving me some time off, and we escape first thing after breakfast.

'This is . . . !' She looks around her with amazement when we arrive.

'I know.'

The shoreline bends, sheltering us in private seclusion. Apart from the little rock clusters sprawled along the beach, the golden sand is undisturbed. There's a brilliance to the water that's completely compelling. And the sky – it's almost inconceivable just how much sky there is. Unbroken. It distorts all sense of dimension. Feeling close and far away, simultaneously. Today, clouds are shaped like mountains. And there's no one else in sight.

'Wow. Do you come here a lot?'

'I did to begin with. In the first couple of weeks. Not so much at the moment, now that I'm working in the kitchen.'

'How's that going for you? Do you like it?'

I have to laugh; she knows me too well. 'Obviously not at first. But now, I can't believe I thought it was trivial. I'd read all these essays about looking after the earth but it wasn't until I started cooking with Brother Hamish and met all his connections – all the local suppliers. And it clicked. We're so interdependent. The full circle. The earth looks after us. And literally, the *earth* – he's been introducing me to people who've been developing all this expertise, all this knowledge about soil health, and seed diversity, and nutrients.'

It's a chain reaction. One thought triggering the next.

'Because it's a completely uphill struggle here – trying to farm anything plant-based. You'd think: *it's beautiful, there's so much nature everywhere it must be environmentally friendly*, or whatever. But to actually live off this land? Viably? Sustainably? There's so much to figure out. And a lot of that capacity's been lost. The livestock farmers have been doing what they can, but a lot of food's just delivered in from the mainland. Most of the fish gets sent off to Spain. Because of the economics.'

I can't stop talking.

'But now people are asking if that whole globalised model is really inevitable – and it's not just here, but smallholders all over the world. So, that's the whole point of advocacy at the monastery. Learning from and amplifying those voices. It's about collaboration. And practical action – to rediscover and reintroduce different crop varieties. Things that grew here before everything got so profit-driven and industrialised. I mean, there are so many totally different ways to think about value. It's completely mind-bending. I have so, so much to unlearn. I had no idea.'

Each time I think I've finished, there's something else to say.

'And then to be able to set that in a spiritual context, and not be constantly fighting the spiritual–secular divide. Not being fragmented all the time. It's amazing! It's the best thing! It's like I've been walking around on a foreign planet with my space helmet nailed on. But now I can take all that crap off. And just breathe.'

I've been talking at her. A total stream of consciousness, staring down the coast. I glance at her. She's so quiet, I check she's listening. She's looking at me, an odd expression on her face.

'What?' I smile. 'Am I being too intense?'

'No. No, it's – this might not be the right thing to say.'

'Try me.'

'I love . . .' She pauses, looking around like she's searching for a landmark. She looks at me. I notice a freckle near the bridge of her nose. 'I love seeing you like this. So excited. It's a lot like you were when your dad was alive.' She rushes past those words, quick to apologise. 'I'm sorry; I'm not trying to make you sad.'

But it's not sad. It's as if she's handed me a present. I don't know how to thank her for it. Other than to keep talking. Not let it get awkward.

'That doesn't make me sad. I think about him a lot here. But it doesn't make me sad.'

'He'd love it, wouldn't he?'

'Definitely. The things they say – all these little sayings: "God in the unexpected"; "the land bears witness". I can imagine him coming out with a lot of it.'

'What does it mean?'

'Which one?'

'Either. Both.'

I laugh. I'm not sure I'm in the mood to dive into a theology class. 'Oh, I don't know – I have brain-ache from all the contemplating. What do you think?'

She stops walking, looking around her. She watches the waves roll in and out. And repeat. And repeat. 'I guess maybe that we don't know as much about everything as we think we do? And maybe that we're short-sighted. Humanity. When, really, if we're stupid enough to destroy each other and poison the planet, it will just regenerate without us.'

It's a pretty depressing interpretation.

I look at her – there's something missing. 'Wait, where's your camera?'

She freezes as if I've put a gun to her head. 'I didn't bring it.'

'What?! Do you remember that summer you dragged me across all of London taking photos of the pavement?'

'Ah! I'd forgotten about that!'

'Chewing gum. Paving slabs. Drain covers. "Interesting" cracks –'

She's laughing – it was definitely one of her more random artistic fascinations.

'Hours, you had me out there for! Every day! And then you come to the Hebrides, to this' – I sweep my arms across the landscape – 'and leave your camera at home?!' I'm teasing her, but it's genuinely confusing.

She smiles. She doesn't explain.

I've been engrossed in all the things I want to share. Enjoying her attention – her questions. The way she's interested in my answers. I know this isn't her comfort zone, surrounded by religion. But she's come out guns blazing. Embracing it. Making such an effort with everyone and everything. Having her here is already better than I could've imagined.

So, I almost missed it.

Now I'm peering backstage. Seeing behind the show.

She's sad. Really, really sad.

'Harri, what's going on?'

She takes a few deep breaths. When she finally looks at me, I can see she's trying not to cry. 'I got into a huge fight with Annie. Really bad. I went along with something I'm not proud of. She called me a pathetic fraud.'

'Whoa! She doesn't pull her punches.'

'You think she's right, though?'

'No! Of course I don't think you're pathetic. Or a fraud. And I bet she doesn't either. But –'

'There's a "but"?!'

I have to tread carefully. I know that much. 'For whatever reason . . .' I pause. Waiting. She's not going to say more. 'For whatever reason, it sounds like she's just frustrated with you. Maybe you need to be straight with her? Annie's really upfront. And you're a bit cryptic.'

'You find me cryptic?!'

I'm surprised that she's surprised.

'Harri, I'm *always* guessing! I've just known you long enough to guess right sometimes. But I'm not a mind reader! Half the time, I have no clue what's going on with you.'

She's quiet – clearly having some kind of lightbulb moment. The fact that I don't get why kind of proves the point. 'You usually find a way to tell me the important stuff, so I generally just wait and hope. But Annie strikes me as more impatient. So, maybe you need to speak up for yourself a bit more?'

She nods slowly. Digesting something that seems harder to hear than I expect.

'Look, you don't have to tell me what happened. You know I've done things I regret. Whatever it is, I'm pretty sure you'll be able to fix it. But what can you do about it from here?'

'Not much.'

'So, forget it. For now, at least? Just be here. With me. And a camera.' I still don't get the connection between fighting with

Annie and leaving her faithful film camera behind, but, if she's really going to make the most of being here, she needs to take photos – that much is obvious to me. 'You can borrow one, actually. Brother Martin runs a photography course for guests. I'll introduce you. If you want?'

'Thank you, Ben.' Her hug is ferocious – an actual bear hug. Tight. A little bit wild. She's not quite OK. Almost, but not quite.

'Do you want to yell at the sea?'

'What?!' She laughs, unsure, like I'm borderline insane.

'It helps.'

'Just shout? At the sea?'

'The sea. The sky. The world, you know – whatever.'

'Just stand there and yell?'

'Who's judging?' The bay is empty. We're alone with the wildlife.

She giggles. It's as if I've dared her to streak naked across a football pitch. Something sparkles, inspiration in her eyes.

'Go for it. I'll wait here.'

I sit. I lie back on my elbows, watching her walk towards the seashore. Her footprints mark the smooth surface of the sand. A lonely trail to the water's edge. The clouds and the coast dwarf her. It's funny seeing her from a distance like this. A distinct person. An isolated speck against the horizon. The perspective is different.

She's someone else.

Not just 'Harri'. Someone beyond me. Engulfed by the extreme beauty that surrounds us. Separated from me by an unfamiliar expanse. It's like changing filters. Or removing a frame. She becomes more. More than all my memories. Not just an extension of me. This must be how other people experience her. People who remember meeting her for the first time.

I can't tear my eyes off her. The whole point of waiting here was to give her space. But I can't look away. I'm in a trance.

She's self-conscious at first, holding back.

Then something shifts.

She finds her lungs, really going for it. Total abandon. Screaming at the ocean. Emptying everything out. Screaming, shouting, doubling over at the waist. The anger is raw and endless. Difficult to witness. Going on for so long, I start to worry. I'm about to get up and go over to her – just to double check she's OK. But something shifts again.

And it's a resurrection.

Rage turns to relief. The sun cuts through and it's poetry in motion. She's dancing in the break of the waves. Fearlessly tapped into some internal beat. Splashing. Jumping in and out of the surf. Vulnerable. Free. Cartwheeling across the sand until she falls to her knees. Laughing – I can hear it on the wind. She stays there, the water inching towards her.

The only girl in the world.

So stunning it hurts.

I shield my eyes, looking into the light as she eventually makes her way back to where I'm stretched out. She drops down beside me. We lie there, propping ourselves up on the edge of the dunes. Together. Looking out at the enormity of the sea.

'Better?'

She smiles at me. My heart starts pounding for reasons my mind won't explain.

'Yes.' She rests her head on my chest. Automatically. Like occupying that spot is her God-given birthright. Like she's come home at the end of a long day. 'You always make everything better, Ben.'

And I don't answer.

I don't know what to say.

Because nothing I feel makes sense.

twenty-eight

HARRIET

I'm trying to write my personal statement for my university applications.

I've been trying every single evening since arriving. The week is disappearing fast. Once today is done, I only have two nights left – and then I'm gone and half-term is over, and I'm back to school. I need to get this written. I've been procrastinating, deleting all my attempts. But we have to submit the drafts when I get back. I'm running out of time.

I've had the awkward conversation with Ms Harrington, trying to explain why art isn't an option for me anymore. I completely delighted my maths teacher, who gave me a run-down of the best universities since I missed most of the open days; I'd purely focused on art schools. I've been doing my research – collecting statistics on rankings, trawling the internet for commentary and reviews, listening to podcasts and careers interviews. I feel like I have the basic landscape mapped out. I just need to explain how I see myself fitting into it.

I thought it would be easy to write here.

When Ben explained the silences, I thought I'd have the perfect window to get my head down and concentrate on pulling it all together, spelling out exactly why studying maths at university is the smart choice for me. After the last chapel service of the day, everyone observes the Great Silence. No talking, no screens in communal areas, no noise from nine in the evening until six in the morning, unless it's an emergency.

Like most things here, I thought it would be weird but I've actually found it liberating. Knowing I get to be alone with my thoughts at the end of each day has been reassuring. It's like a pressure-valve set to timed release. I get the daily chance to sift through thoughts that would otherwise overwhelm me. I get to sleep in peace.

Only, I've been having trouble sleeping and none of my thoughts are about maths.

Everything is different here.

Ben is different here.

On the journey up to Scotland, I was completely prepared to hate it. But when I stepped off the ferry and saw him waiting there – I don't know. It wasn't some crazy, abstract idea anymore. It's a reality – a beautiful, curious reality. And it suits him. He's so centred, so inspired. Listening to him talk about the things he's learning and experiencing, it's like watching new birth happen. It's hard to be cynical in the face of so much wonder.

I've loved being here.

The sense of scale once you arrive is beyond anything I anticipated from looking at maps on my phone. Islands are further apart than I imagined, and I'm only here for a fraction of time – not long enough to go to the Outer Hebrides. We day-tripped to the closest Western island instead, wandering and eating. And learning more about Hebridean culture – the deep traditions of crofting and the pain of the Clearances, barely scratching the surface but still being awed by the histories people hold in their blood and land and language.

I loved coming back and going to a midweek ceilidh, being welcomed by an intergenerational community unashamedly

proud of their traditions. I think my dancing may have dese-
crated the art, but twirling around with Ben and laughing so
hard I got hiccups, then hitching a lift home together from new
friends in the thick cloud-covered darkness of an island without
street lights – it's special; I'll admit it.

I even love the monks.

There's a dignity and kindness that's impossible to disre-
spect. No one has made me feel like my lack of faith makes me
inferior. No one seems interested in trying to re-convert me. It's
like the point of being here is just to be here. We cross paths at
different times throughout the day. Unless they're in retreat, the
monks join the guests for communal meals. There are five of us
visitors. A couple of people are here for a kind of spiritual therapy, like Ben was on his first visit. The others just want a rest. We
must be intrusive, but the hospitality feels so sincere.

There's definitely something radical about the monks – it's
undeniable, and a little unnerving. But the rhythms they live
by feel soothing to me, like the constant sound of the sea. Ben
has his schedule, but they've lightened his duties this week to let
him spend time with me. We've fallen into a kind of hybrid life,
a working holiday: I know when I'll see him and when I won't.
And, when I'm not with him, I carry on exploring. The camera
changes everything; I take it everywhere. I see because it sees.
And what I find is breathtaking.

The only place I don't take photos is in the chapel. I was
asked not to, but since I've been joining some of the services I've
begun to understand why. It's something I can't describe. And
I don't know why, but to take photos feels crude and invasive
– almost morally wrong. There's something private and mysterious happening in those moments. Maybe also mundane and
monotonous after a while – I don't know.

But when I've been there, when I've sat there and listened, and watched Ben – really seen him in that space – it's like he's drifting away from me to a place of angels and miracles, myths and fairy tales, a place where healings happen and broken things are reset. And I can't follow because the current doesn't reach me. It doesn't sweep me there. It just leaves me stranded and shipwrecked and deathly afraid.

And then I sit here, in this room at night. And wonder.

I take in the simplicity around me – the lamp shedding light on my blank screen; the wooden chair I'm sitting on, the desk next to the bed; the silence that is so complete it almost has a physical presence – I look around, and I wonder:

How do I survive this?

He has no idea I'm in love with him – I get that now, after our conversation at the beach on my first full day. But finding the right time to tell him, when he's clearly so content here – it's impossible. It's unthinkable.

Where does that leave me?

What do I do if he doesn't come back?

Is maths really the answer? Trading in the risks of creativity for a retreat into predictability – seriously? Because, at some point, even maths stops adding up. There are unsolvable equations, indivisible numbers, conjectures still unproved.

What if there are no guarantees? What if there is no stability?

I don't know how to outrun this fear, this feeling that there are no more safe places – not anymore, not for me.

I need one. I have to find one.

And I'm running out of time.

I think I imagined the knock at the door – it's almost midnight; I'm dozing, in and out of consciousness. But I didn't – that's definitely a knock at the door.

I open it and Ben is in my doorway, smiling like it's Christmas morning. He points over his shoulder down the corridor, then up towards the ceiling. It's a ridiculous game of charades and when I laugh, he laughs too, quickly covering my mouth with his hand. He peers over my shoulder, spotting my open laptop, and dives into the room.

Come with me. I need to show you something.

He stands back to let me read the text he's typed. I can feel his eyes on me. I'm suddenly aware that he's fully dressed and I'm not wearing very much. We share the thought telepathically – I'm sure I see him blush as he hunches over the desk again.

Bring your coat!

I go to the wardrobe to get it, ramming on my shoes, and when I turn around he's stripped the pillowcase off my bed. He motions for me to turn again and, for reasons entirely unknown, I find I'm being blindfolded. I hear him snatch my key from the desk; he takes my hand, steering me out of the room and locking up behind me.

It's truly the oddest thing – and with anyone else, I'd be screaming right about now. But instead I register that we've left the building, we're in the courtyard, now down an outside path of some kind, round the edge of a wall. Even with my coat, the air is cool – colder than it's been on other nights. We seem to be coming to a standstill. There's an element of precision to the spot he makes me stand on, even tilting my chin up a little. He takes off the blindfold.

It's astonishing.

Stars.

But not stars like I've seen them at home – a scattering of dots, straining against the semi-darkness like dull sequins on the pavement. This is indescribable. A glittering crowd, too many to absorb. This is like standing at the end of the world, like we've tiptoed into outer space – within arm's reach of galaxies. Clouds of stars, luminous dust and radiant pinpricks, constellations charged with uncontainable life. It's humbling and awe-inspiring and slightly terrifying to feel so small.

I look at him in disbelief.

He grins and nods, turning back to the vastness like it's called his name.

The sky has his full attention. We aren't touching. He doesn't hold my hand or put his arm round me. But being invited to share this with him is more than enough. I feel like I've been woken to live a dream. Seeing this is an unspeakable gift, the most magical thing anyone has ever done for me. I'm glad I didn't have time to grab the camera – there's no way a photograph could ever hold everything this night sky is showing us. It's immense and limitless, real and here. Light from millennia finally catching up with us – the past and present coexisting together. I'll remember it forever.

I don't know how long we stand there.

An eternity.

A second.

But when it's time to go back in, we feel it in our bones. We turn, almost in unison, lingering a little like the last notes of a song. The sounds of our footsteps crunch through the silence until we're back indoors and the carpet muffles the motion. He stops outside my door, handing me the pillowcase and my key.

If it wasn't the Great Silence, I would try to say thank you.

If we weren't at a monastery, I'd want him to come in.

But it is the Great Silence, and we are at a monastery. So, I open the door, and he hesitates, and I hesitate. He laughs a little – quietly, breathlessly.

And I smile and close the door.

twenty-nine

BEN

I had a hunch the sky would be alive tonight.

I really wanted her to see how spectacular the stars can be here but, until now, we've had thick cloud cover. I didn't mention it. I wanted it to be a surprise. And I wasn't sure if it would work out. It took hours for the visibility to really clear. We were out later than I'd anticipated – I'm just so glad she was awake.

I'm buzzing. I'm absolutely buzzing. If I sleep, it will be a miracle.

I do sleep.

But the dream feels so real.

In the dream, we're back in Oxford. In my bed. In the dream, it's a totally different story. We're not sleeping. Not talking, either. She lets me touch her. I can't stop. She's so responsive. Our mouths travel everywhere, all-consuming. Her body is the greatest adventure. Her skin. Her shape. Her hands all over me. And I don't remember how our clothes come off, but then Harriet's on top of me. And I'm deep inside her.

And her smile makes me feel superhuman.

I wake up.

I'm thrown from sleep like in those falling dreams where you never hit the ground. I hear someone groaning, wounded in the darkness. I realise it's me. I'm soaked in sweat. I'm painfully hard. My heart is leaping out of my mouth. If I'm still breathing, I can't tell – my chest is so tight.

For a split second, I honestly worry I'm having a heart attack.

Then my mind kicks in. My inner critic translates what my body is shouting at me. A singular insight. Just one thought:

Ben.

You're an imbecile.

A total and complete imbecile.

I groan again. My arms are too empty. I clutch the pillow. The thought of jerking off is unbearable. Too depressing. I writhe out of bed, stumbling into the en suite. I fall into the coldest of cold showers. It's beyond cruel – the fact that she's right down the hallway, but a million miles from knowing how I feel. I would punch the wall, but I've broken my knuckles before and I don't want to do it again.

Everything aches.

My room is haunted.

I'd give anything and more to climb back into that fantasy. To feel so seen and connected. For it to be real.

It's not.

I have to talk to someone.

Obviously, I can't go and hammer on Harriet's door. Where would I start? What would I say? *Sorry to wake you but you were absolutely epic in my dreams. And I'm totally confused and in danger of ruining the best friendship I've ever had, but you're even more amazing in real life and I'm still majorly turned on – so, how about it?!*

It's actually seriously tempting. Only, I care too much to be that reckless.

And who else is there to share this with? The Great Silence won't end for at least another hour. Somehow, I don't think this is what the monks had in mind when they said it's OK to break the silence in an emergency.

No, it's just me.

And God.

If this counts as praying, it's a plea and a confession:

Please – you have to help me! I'm so completely screwed.

*

'Ben, oh my God –' She looks over her shoulder, checking whether she's offended anyone. 'You look awful!'

We're heading to the chapel before breakfast. It's become our routine. Part of me hoped she would skip it this morning, even though it's so nice that she's willing to join us.

'Thanks.' I try to smile.

'You're welcome; I mean it.'

It doesn't help that I can't look at her. She touches me. I try not to flinch.

'Seriously, are you ill?' She reaches for my face. I pretty much leap out of the way. 'OK, now you're really scaring me.'

She grips both my shoulders, making me face her. Everyone is filing inside. A couple of the monks glance our way. In another few minutes, we'll be late.

She studies me. And I know this isn't fair to her.

I know all the reasons I've given her to worry about me in the past.

The times she did this exact same thing. Looking me over. Trying to figure out how high or drunk or stoned or depressed I was. Trying to protect me. From myself. From the consequences of the worst version of me. The times she covered for me, even though we both knew it was a terrible idea. The times she lied for me because I wouldn't admit the truth. I couldn't admit I needed help.

I muster up every last scrap of courage I have. All my self-control.

And I hug her.

I let her feel that I'm here. And I'm safe. That, despite appearances, I'm basically all right. This is not the same as back then.

'Really, I'm fine.'

'Promise?'

'I promise.'

She sighs, sort of collapsing into me, her stress slowly evaporating.

Holding her is agony.

'All right, well – you do look really bad. So, I don't know! Maybe it's time to consider shaving the beard, OK?!'

It's a relief to laugh.

thirty

HARRIET

Something is seriously up with Ben.

He's so twitchy – so on edge and haggard. I haven't seen him like that in I don't know how long, and we haven't had a chance to talk properly. He was quiet over breakfast – barely making eye contact, his head in his cereal, eyes glued to the table. And the second the meal was over, he raced off to the kitchen – mumbling something incomprehensible and immediately sprinting away like the whole building was on fire.

Really weird.

Whatever it is, it will have to wait. I have plans of my own this morning: Brother Martin is showing me how to develop film – another incredible experience I couldn't have guessed would be part of this trip. I make my way to the small art studio off a lounge in the communal area. For a community under vows of poverty, there's a surprising amount of warmth and homeliness to all of the interiors I've been in – just lots of clean, natural materials and an absence of clutter.

Like someone has really thought about what to own.

I find Brother Martin perched on a table, absorbed in a book. My first guess is the Bible, but on closer inspection it's photography. We've spoken quite a few times since my arrival and I liked him immediately. It's hard to tell how old he is: I've only ever seen him in his habit and those robes make everyone look ancient. In reality, he can't be much older than mid-thirties

– younger than a lot of the other brothers, older than Ben. He looks up as I approach, smiling, glancing over my shoulder.

'Ben isn't coming?'

'He's on kitchen duty this morning.'

'Oh. OK.' He puts the book to one side, jumping down from the desk and handing me a clipboard. 'So, there are extra safeguarding measures we need to follow, then. I have to ask you to sign this consent form – saying you're happy to use the darkroom. And you'll have to also tick here and here to say "unaccompanied". And this one says you understand there's CCTV.' He keeps flipping through the papers, sheet after sheet. 'This part is the privacy notice – how long we keep the footage for and why and all that. And this is for you. Put it somewhere discreet.'

He hands me a flat disc – the size of a key fob, but thicker. I turn it over in my palms. 'Sorry, what is this?'

'It's a silent alarm. It's set up to send an alert to the monastery office and also externally if, at any point, you feel . . . uncomfortable. And you should know I have one, too.'

It hadn't occurred to me to feel threatened. But now I *am* uncomfortable. The insinuation sits awkwardly between us.

'Is this really necessary?'

'Necessary, I'm not sure about. But we do think it's appropriate. To be clear, we've never needed any of this. We just want to be safe. For everyone. Do you still want to go ahead?'

'Of course!' I sign the forms – all six of them. 'I'm happy to, if you are?'

He smiles, countersigning the paperwork and filing it away. 'I was really excited when Ben told me I'd have another artist here.' He hits a switch on the wall – the *in use* sign illuminates above a door to our right. 'Is photography your main focus?'

'Not really.' I follow him into the darkroom. A heavy fire door swings shut behind us. 'It's more the way I document things. In the beginning. And then I sometimes move through to drawing, but generally end up with abstracts. Paintings.' The uneasiness dissolves and innocence re-emerges; I love these kinds of conversations. 'But I like film because the photos are more about what I feel in the moment than what I see. And that works well as the foundation for abstracts – interpreting the emotional connection to a visual.'

'Ben says your work is – well, there were a lot of positive adjectives, I can't remember them all. "Mesmerising" was definitely one.'

'He's always had a huge amount of faith in me.' The sadness in my voice is not subtle – even to a virtual stranger it's glaringly obvious, a conversational roadblock.

'Anyway, welcome!' Brother Martin changes the subject with an upbeat pivot. 'Let me talk you through the equipment first and then we'll get going.'

I feel like I've landed on Mars – the room is flooded with a reddish glow from a dim 'safelight', ensuring we can see without disrupting the development process. An enlarger projects light through the small film negatives onto photographic paper, transforming them into a bigger image. A focus finder makes sure the projections aren't blurred. Brother Martin walks me through a series of trays – the developer, stop and fix – each filled with a different mix of chemicals to bathe the photos in before they're washed off and pegged up to dry.

Opening up the camera to begin shining light on the negatives feels like the point of no return, but he lets me practise on some of his before I get to my own. I'm concentrating, fully present – I'm hardly aware of the fact that I'm grinning as the first images come through, forming from the blank.

'It's great, isn't it? Different to digital. Although I like them both, personally.'

'It's so good! Ben said you run photography courses here?'

'Aye.' He nods enthusiastically, keeping one eye on the prints. 'I was – well, I still *am* a professional photographer. I used to do weddings, mainly, but after my life vows that became a wee bit too painful, if I'm honest. So I trained in art therapy and I run photography courses for guests, locals – anyone, really. Lots of spiritual metaphors in the darkroom process so, depending on the audience, that's part of what I teach.'

I start on the first of my own images. Brother Martin adjusts the photo with a pair of print tongs, nudging it to make sure the solution is spread evenly across the paper. We watch it crystallising, slowly taking shape.

'I really had no idea there was so much going on here. Sorry, that's probably really insulting?'

'No.' He shrugs. 'I wouldn't say so. Our spiritual disciplines are a large part of our lives. And they're the part that's unfamiliar, so it makes sense for people to focus on that. We do have more vocations than some other religious orders – although, we're maybe less defined by our work than perhaps we would be outside of the community.'

'But you do earn money?'

He moves the image to the next tray for me, nodding. 'We decided we'd charge for some things – otherwise we'd completely undermine the other businesses here like the hotel, the restaurant. We're not-for-profit, we're an employer and we're self-sufficient.'

'But you personally don't own anything? How does that work? Is that, like, a socialist thing?'

'Ha! How long have you got?'

I feel like I'm being inappropriately nosy, but there's something about the safelight – it makes me feel like I can say anything.

He doesn't seem to mind. 'Really, there are all kinds of principles that govern how we deal with money. But it's basically just a tool to indicate what we value. It shows our care or appreciation – for people, nature, whatever we invest in.'

It's so fascinating – the level of thought that goes into every detail of this way of life. I can't decide whether that feels empowering or restrictive: having guiding principles for absolutely everything.

'Don't you ever just want to, I don't know, splurge on something stupid?'

He grins. 'Oh, aye! But it's not like we're being really noble. It's just having responsibilities. We have social care bills for the older brothers, buildings to maintain – all the everyday concerns. We're not that different to any other family or organisation.'

'Apart from the vows.'

I rinse off my first photo – a picture from Ben's favourite bay. We've walked there almost daily since the time I yelled at the universe.

Brother Martin pauses. I brace myself – I can feel where the conversation is going.

'Do you know how it works? The discernment process?'

'Not really. I haven't wanted to hear about it. From Ben.'

I peg up the finished photo; we stand back to admire it in silence. We start on more prints – the process has its own rhythm, and I'm getting into the groove. It's easier to enjoy the transitions; I'm less concerned about messing up the end result.

'Maybe you could tell me a little bit more?'

I'm not sure I want to hear it all, but at this point not knowing is even worse.

'Well, the first thing to say is it's a very slow process. Always. It can only be extended – never shortened.'

'How come?'

'Becoming a monk is a new life – a radically different way of life. You can't rush it. A wee bit like a pregnancy. Healthy development just takes time.'

'How much time?'

'The novitiate is a year, minimum. With Ben, if he comes back to us after Christmas for the rest of the academic year – and then factoring in time to finish his degree – I guess we're looking at two or three years? After that, initial vows are for three years – with the possibility of three extensions, of a year each. People leave in all those stages, for all sorts of reasons. But if they don't, then it's life vows.'

I dip the next photos into the developer tray – fixing my gaze on the blank squares, steeling myself for the question I don't really want to ask. 'And that's like the equivalent of a marriage, right?'

'With a far lower divorce rate. Life is for life.'

His response should hurt.

But I'm distracted – two of the images are completely unfamiliar. My face appears, my upper body gradually emerging. Ben is next to me, laughing as he holds me close. I can tell Brother Martin used to be a wedding photographer – my expression has 'first dance' written all over it. I'm oblivious to the camera in both shots, but in the second Ben grins into the lens.

'These are from the ceilidh.'

'I saw the camera and I saw the moment. I couldn't help myself. I hope you don't mind?'

'No, of course not. They're so beautiful.' I'm crumbling. 'Thank you.'

'Harriet' – his voice is soft – 'no one becomes a monk without personal sacrifices, but there are huge knock-on effects – we know that. To be honest, it's probably easier for us. We get to live the life we feel we were created for. We have a sense of purpose that can make up for the losses. And we get to choose. But this life asks a lot of the people closest to us who have to take the fall-out.'

I nod. I've basically stopped functioning. Brother Martin takes over, moving the photographs on while I stand back, trying to recover.

He keeps talking.

'The church has a bad track record on psychological safety. I'm so aware of that. We can be crude and careless, at best. At worst, we're abusive and evil. I promise we're trying to do things differently. To do things well – and to learn from past mistakes. That's why the selection process is so rigorous.'

I nod again but, really, I want to run away. I've been playing along – I see that now. Pretending I could join in, as if I had a right to be so happy here. Imagining this could be real life when, for me at least, it will only ever be a holiday.

'We're not perfect. Not even close. But I want you to know, we do see you. And we'll do our best to be careful. I don't know what that will look like, but you have my word – you're a factor in this. A big factor.'

'How come *everyone* can see how I feel? Apart from Ben?!'

It's not like Brother Martin would have the answer to that, but the question just bursts out of me anyway – uncontainable.

He pegs up the photos; I feel mocked by my own smile.

'I don't know, Harriet. But just because he likes what we do here – that doesn't mean he'll become a monk. There are so many ways to be part of our community. Otherwise, our lives would be completely impoverished – we'd be without interfaith dialogue and women and families.'

I've abandoned the photographs; Brother Martin keeps going with the process, talking as he moves around the room. 'Lots of people follow our rule of life without ever taking vows. Some people even commit to us as companions – so they're an integral part of our spiritual community from their own context, whatever that is. The monks – we're just the tip of the iceberg. Only a handful of people who come here to explore the calling ever go on to make initial vows, let alone life.'

I know what he's doing. It's nice of him to try to explain – maybe even give me hope. But I need him to stop. Just stop.

'Please! I really appreciate it. All of it – everything you're saying. But I've known Ben my entire life. He lives in the extremes. This could really work out for him. Couldn't it?'

'I can't –'

'I know, it's a process and you can't say for sure. But there's a possibility, isn't there? A strong possibility that he'll be one of the few?'

He pegs up the last of the prints.

'I think so. He's mature for his age – maybe from all his struggles. He has a phenomenal capacity for devotion, as you already know. And he questions *everything*. Relentlessly! A true seeker. So' – he nods thoughtfully – 'there's a strong possibility. He could become a really exceptional monk.'

We study the photos – moments strung out on a line, fragments of life frozen and held fast, even as they slip away. I can't believe this is really happening.

'But, Harriet – we'll see. Please try to trust the process. We've got to wait and see.'

thirty-one

BEN

I ambush Father Graeme straight after breakfast. I'm supposed to be heading to the kitchen, but I chase him down instead.

I don't manage to catch him before he disappears into his cell. I'm banging on the door like a maniac.

'Ben! Is everything OK?'

'No, nothing's OK! Everything is not OK!' I barge through the door, inviting myself in. I remember it's rude and backtrack into the corridor. 'I had a dream. About Harriet – my friend who's here at the moment.'

I don't know why I'm explaining who she is. Maybe if I keep referring to her as my friend, she'll fit back into that box.

'What kind of dream?'

'The kind of dream I've *never* had about Harriet.' I'm blushing hard. I start to pace. Agitated. So embarrassed.

'Ah.'

The ground refuses to swallow me whole. He motions for me to come in and sit down instead.

'And you're concerned this has some significance? In terms of your feelings for her?'

'It's not just the dream. Seeing her here . . .' I slump into the chair he's offered me, covering my face with my hands. 'My ex-girlfriend – she did say. She told me, repeatedly, actually. She said I'm in love with Harriet. She said I've been in love with her for so long I couldn't see it. And I tried to be nice about it but I did pretty much call her paranoid.'

He chuckles. 'I imagine that explains the "ex" part.'

'But now, I mean, she was so, so right. And I'm *such* an *idiot!* How could I not know that about myself?! And what do I do with it?'

'Are those questions directed at me?' He seems mildly amused.

'Well, yeah – I guess so! I really don't know what to do!'

'Hmm. All right. Walk with me, Ben.' He stands up, waiting for me to follow.

'I'm supposed to be in the kitchen.'

'That's fine; we can stop off and tell Hamish we're heading out. Come on.' He hauls me to my feet. 'Let's get some air.'

I think the small talk is for my benefit. I think Father Graeme is trying to distract me. It's not working. I just feel claustrophobic. Even the openness of the grassy dunes isn't enough to help me breathe.

'You know, the machair is so valuable for biodiversity. A very special habitat.' He points to the ground, then out towards the coast. 'It's the wind-blown shell sand – it's changed the porosity of the soil, and we end up with a richness that's home to wildflowers, bees, butterflies. Quite distinctive.'

I nod. I didn't know that. I try to care.

'It's dwindled considerably in the decades I've been here. And I'm a newcomer, relatively speaking. Sometimes, I do wonder . . .' He stops, looking around. 'Did we do the right thing – coming here? We thought so, at the time. We've tried to blend in. To do the things that were welcomed. But then that's brought "development" – more holiday homes, more tourists. At an environmental cost. So, who knows?'

My face is blank. If he's asking me to justify his entire existence, now is not a good time. I'm a little preoccupied.

He bursts out laughing. 'The point I'm *trying* to make, Ben, is – to some extent – we're all stumbling in the dark when it comes to figuring out what God wants for us. Who can say for sure whether any choice is a good choice? But we're guided by our narratives, aren't we? So, let's think together. Let's think about Abraham.'

'Really?!' I have to interrupt. 'I tell you that I'm at a monastery having sexual fantasies about my childhood best friend, and you want to talk about nature and the patriarchs? *Really?*'

He grins. 'Humour me. What did Abraham desperately want in his life, more than anything?'

I think about the conversations I had with Father Graeme when I was eighteen. The rancid grief he waded into with me. The tools he gave me to pull myself back to safety.

'All right, OK . . .' I think through the story. 'He wanted a child. With Sarah.'

'Right, Isaac, the promised heir – his greatest love, the key to his status in the community and his legacy. And after this miracle child arrived, what did God ask Abraham to do?'

'Sacrifice him.'

'And did he?'

'No, he was about to but God stopped him at the last minute.'

'Right. So, what did God really want from him?'

I've reached a dead end.

He shrugs too. 'Well, I always hesitate to answer my own questions. What I think I know today, I often unlearn tomorrow. But today my best guess is: trust. I think God wanted Abraham's trust.'

'So, it was like a test?'

He smiles. 'You students! Don't get me started on the education system – so fixated with exams. Maybe a test, but I like to think God's tests are more about us being shown the great things we're capable of. Not earning anything from God. Not being ranked and graded and in competition with each other. But I digress.'

His digressions are infamous – the brothers tease him for it, constantly. 'Trust.' I bring him back round to his original point.

'Right. Being willing to let go of anything and everything for God, if asked – it demonstrates that we trust God's love to give us security and well-being, more than the things we've given up.'

I get where he's going, and I don't like it.

'I'm not sure I can do that. With Harriet, I mean. This is not some abstract, future possibility anymore. She's literally right here. She has been for years. And I've been too stupid and slow to see it. If there's even a possibility that she wants to be with me, how can I give her up?'

'Ben, this is the way of the cross. This is what Jesus did for us. It's the call we answer, the example we follow. Whether you're a monk or not. I think of it like a divine exchange. All that we are for all of God. Nothing held back, in either direction.'

'That's a massively high bar.'

'Yes. And, of course, we struggle to live up to it on our side. But it's our freedom, I think. The way I understand it is this: if our deepest trust is rooted in anything else – our money, our possessions, our relationships, our health and abilities – then, I believe, we risk living lives that are captive to the fear of loss. And I think, more than anything, God wants us to be free. So, the call keeps coming. *Let go. I'm enough. Fall. I'll catch you.* That's faith. We give up what we can't keep to gain what we cannot lose. And we trust that whatever comes back to us, from that place of total surrender, is God's gift to us – God's best for us. You won't be left empty-handed.'

I exhale, slowly.

It's a persuasive argument. I can relate to the idea that clutching things kills them. Strangling a good thing out of fear? That's not appealing. I don't want to live like that. And I recognise that fear in me. After everything with Dad. But there are degrees. There's a difference between strangling and holding. There's a difference between holding and letting go. Can't God just compromise? Why do I have to lose everything? To be so all-in?

'You're coming at it from the wrong direction, Ben. Look at it from the other way around. Not the losses. The gains.'

I don't know how he does that. He has a way of hearing my thoughts.

'Think about the things you love. The things that make life meaningful to you. All the good gifts – whatever that is for you. Are you doing that?'

I nod. The list is instantly long. Brother Hamish's gratitude exercises have made me an expert at pinpointing all the good things in my life.

'Then think about the giver. If there's a giver, and the gifts are so good, what must the giver be like? And now think about your choice. You can grab the gifts and run – God isn't stingy; you won't be stopped at the door. Or you can put everything down and have the giver, first and always. Not grabbing anything. Resting in the security of knowing and being loved by the source of generosity. And *then* receive the gifts that the giver chooses for you – gifts from Someone who knows who you are, knows what you love.'

I do get what he's saying. Kind of. But I don't know what it means – in concrete terms. What am I letting go of?

'So, you're saying that if I trust God totally it means giving up everything to be here, including Harriet?'

'Possibly. But then – and this has been true for many, many other young men I've counselled – it could be giving up the dream of this life to embrace a more mainstream faith. Leaving all this behind' – he sweeps his arms to the sky, the free expanse – 'to trust God in the joys and complexities of having a partner. A secular career. Maybe fatherhood.'

'Seriously!' I can't believe we've come full circle. 'So, basically, that was a massively long sermon with no straight answer!'

'Indeed.'

The man is a nightmare!

He erupts with laughter. 'I don't know what your gift is, Ben. And I'm sorry to say it, but I don't think there's a shortcut for you to discover it. The community will support you, if it's our place to do that. But you have to walk a path to really know where it leads.'

That sounds exactly like the kind of mantra a sage on a remote island would give me. When, really, what I want is a quick fix. An actual solution. A way to shut down the confusion. But I guess there's a reason I trusted him with this.

Maybe a quick fix isn't what I need.

'You're like a Rubik's cube, you know that? Just when the things you say start to line up, there's a twist and I'm stuck again.'

'That's not me. That's the beautiful mystery of God.'

'Beautiful mystery, huh? Is that what we're calling it?'

He chuckles again – but it's a knowing laugh. 'Or the unique torture, depending on the day.'

It does feel like torture. I feel like I'm being dissected. Torn apart, limb from limb. All my ideas about myself are being deconstructed. And I have no idea what form they'll take when they're eventually put back together.

'You're not going to tell me what to do, are you?'

'Absolutely not!' He laughs like I've told a side-splitting joke. 'How could I possibly do that? I'm a monk, not a Magic 8 Ball! You can't just shake me until you get the option you want.'

He really seems to find the idea of dictating answers to be completely ludicrous. And then I remember he doesn't work like that. I remember why he's always made faith look so attractive. Why there's a whole community willing to make vows of obedience under his leadership.

I sigh again. The lack of sleep is catching up with me. I rub my face. Harriet's right; I do need a shave. 'Well, all right. But do you have any practical advice? Anything at all?'

God, I miss my dad.

'Yes. I *can* tell you that you need to be honest. Whatever you do, do it with integrity. People mistake monastic life for an escape. It's not. Here, of all places, you can't escape yourself – as I think you're beginning to realise. There are no distractions. There's silence and your soul. And repression will destroy you. So, my advice would be – if you tell her, if you don't, whatever that looks like – try your hardest to make sure you can live with it.'

It's good advice.

I have no idea what I'm going to do with it, but it's good advice.

'If it helps, we've all been there – in one way or another.'

I smile for the first time all morning. 'It does. A bit. Thank you, though. For all of it – talking to me. Listening. I do feel a bit better. Just slightly.'

He laughs, clapping me on the back. 'You're welcome, Ben. Any time.'

thirty-two

HARRIET

When Ben comes to meet me after I've finished in the darkroom, everything in me wants to throw my arms around his neck and hold on forever. Something in his body language stops me – I can't say what, exactly. A barrier. A hesitancy.

We're not right.

Yesterday we were easy together – when we came up with our plan to go and visit some kind of bird sanctuary, precisely because we're not bird lovers.

To be honest, there's a limited range of things to do here and it's one of the few things we haven't already done. We know next to nothing about birds – we can't identify different species; we can't distinguish different songs. Beyond the sight of blackbirds and sounds of pigeons, it's all a blur at home – let alone here, where rare species are flourishing.

Ben is trying to learn more. It's all part of his goal to heal the disconnect: painstakingly trying to assimilate a vocabulary, banishing the ignorance, one fact at a time. Learning to see, then love, then protect.

We were enthusiastic about it yesterday.

I had visions of us huddled over the same pair of binoculars, closing the physical distance that seems to have grown between us. We don't hug and kiss like we used to and I miss it! I still miss him – even when I'm standing right next to him.

Yesterday, it was a great idea.

Today it feels like neither of us can remember why we're trudging along this grassy track in the drizzle – struggling to find our way to the heart of the nature reserve, contending with unreliable phone signal and maps that vanish without warning, despondent and off-key.

Something's changed.

I feel it. Ben's somewhere else, mentally. And all I can think about is my earlier conversation with Brother Martin.

'Ben, are you sure you're OK?'

He smiles. 'I would say yes, but you're like a human lie detector. I just have things to think through. About being here.'

'Can I ask you something about that?'

He looks alarmed for a moment – so far, we haven't really talked about his choices. Not directly. 'OK. Go ahead.'

'Do you feel like you belong here?'

He exhales, frowning slightly but I don't think he's cross. Just concentrating. 'That's a really tough question. I feel welcome. But no, I guess not really. Not yet.'

'Because you're new?'

'Sort of. And there are layers. Not exactly inner circles, but nuances. Gaels, Scots, English. The mainlanders, the islanders – all the labels. It's a bit political at times, you know? The whole question of who gets to call this place home.'

We finally locate some signage – clues that we're heading in the right direction for the information room. We wander along unmarked routes, hoping the well-worn paths of other people's journeys will eventually lead us where we want to go.

'But the identity of the community – belonging to that, it must help hold everyone together?'

'Yeah, it seems to. At the end of the day, it all comes back to God and the vows.'

I don't know whether to push him. Talking to Ben about things he's not ready to hear – it's like shouting at a tornado. Futile. And a little bit dangerous.

I do it. What do I have to lose?

'The vows – I mean, they're pretty drastic, Ben.'

He sighs. 'I know.' He's calm – calmer than I expected. 'Honestly, I'm not sure I'll even be allowed to get to that stage. You haven't met Brother Richard. He's the novice guardian, so he's someone I need to impress. And he's so unimpressed with me!'

'Really? Why?!'

'I don't know. But he finds me completely unacceptable. It's not just up to him – whether I'll get invited back after Christmas. But who knows? Maybe he's right. Maybe I don't belong here.'

He stops walking. We stand there – isolated, together. There's an openness to the landscape everywhere we go – visibility stretching onwards in every direction, land and sea colliding in the distance. The fields around us are noisy with geese squawking and squabbling as they feed.

'I feel like I don't belong anywhere.' My confession surprises me – this was supposed to be about him. And it wasn't my agenda, I didn't mean to engineer this, but he automatically hugs me.

It's brief.

So fleeting – it's over before I can hold him back. He's indecisive – like he can't decide the best way to show he feels my pain: touching my arm, taking my hand, then dropping it just as quickly. He starts to pace.

'Isn't that just school, though? Once you start really choosing for yourself, things might feel like a better fit?' There's something slightly desperate in his voice – like he needs to believe what he's saying almost as much as I do.

I nod – I don't want to disappoint him. But he doesn't drop the subject. He's looking at me too intently.

'How's that all going, anyway? Art school applications. I haven't even asked! Is your portfolio done?'

I've got to tell him – it's unavoidable. 'I'm not applying to art schools anymore.'

'You're not applying to Central Saint Martins?'

'Or any of them.'

'In London?'

'At all. I'm going to do a maths degree.'

He raises an eyebrow. 'Since when?'

'Since now.'

'I don't get it.'

'I just changed my mind.'

'Why?'

'Well . . .' I don't know how to respond. 'You know, I don't think I have to explain myself to you. I can be whatever I want.' He's interrogating me on things I don't fully understand. I walk away from him. I've spotted a viewing platform and I make a break for it, like it will shield me from the coming onslaught. It doesn't.

'*Whatever* you want – how does that work? Surely you can only be you. Or die pretending.'

'I'm not pretending to be good at maths.'

'I know that – that's not what I'm saying. You're amazing at maths. But you're an artist.'

'I can be more than one thing.' I'm louder than I want to be – a wildness creeping into my voice.

'I know that too! Why are you having a go at me?! You're the one who's suddenly saying it's one or the other. No art foundation applications? At all? Seriously, what are you thinking? Stop with the weird vagueness.'

I study the view. I'm not sure what I'm supposed to be seeing but it gives me something to focus on. 'Maths is useful. It's constructive. It has a purpose.'

'Art has a purpose! Harriet, you're so gifted! That's not just for you. That's also for the people who look at what you make and feel less alone in the world. And get through the day because you made it more beautiful.'

'But you don't know if that will happen!' I try to suppress the hysteria bubbling beneath the surface. 'There's absolutely no guarantee that anyone is *ever* going to feel like that about a single thing that I create! Whereas if I do maths, I know I can get a real job that actually needs doing.'

'I don't even – who am I talking to right now?! Harri' – he spins me round to face him – 'being an artist has always been your dream. Always! And now you have a chance to study art. Full-time. For four years. Without having to pay anything upfront. Wherever you want. And you're not even going to *try*? Why are you suddenly so afraid?'

He's too close. Too close to me. Too close to the truth.

'I'm not afraid! Maybe I'm just not OK with being completely and utterly irrational about big life choices, like you are!'

'Wow.' He shakes his head – disbelief written all over his face. 'Look, I'm sorry if taking some risks to do something I believe in makes me seem like such a monster to you! But not all of us can just sell out overnight!'

'Argh, you're unbelievable!' I flee the viewing platform, back to the path, shouting over my shoulder – a kind of loud whisper; I don't want to disturb the birds. 'I'm not selling out! I just changed my mind. You changed The Plan. I changed my mind! It happens.'

He follows me, jogging to catch up. He touches me.

It's different.

Not my hand, or my arm, or my shoulder. He grabs my waist – pulling me to a halt right in front of him.

'Don't do that! Don't put this on me. This is about you!'

He's too much. Too insistent. Too demanding. Just too much.

I try to push him away but the gesture stalls, getting stuck halfway. I end up leaning against him, stroking his chest instead.

He lets go. He stumbles away from me, running his hands over his curls.

We look at each other: a metre gap between us – full of silence and static and the sounds of birds and sea.

'Harriet.' He's quiet but still exasperated – staring at me, looking at me like I'm a total stranger. 'Obviously, it's up to you. Maths or art or whatever. But be honest! What do you actually want to do for the next four years?'

thirty-three

BEN

I'm such a hypocrite.

As soon as the words leave my mouth, I know I can't answer that question either.

I want to be here.

With her.

It's impossible.

I've completely stressed her out. She bites her bottom lip. Rubbing her neck. Massaging the tension in her shoulders. She's so hot it's unfair. Obviously, I'm frustrated with her. And I think that's legitimate. But, at the same time, it's also just about sex. All the sex we're not having.

'Well?' I should probably back off but I'm too wound up.

She's saved from answering me. My phone comes to life – a stream of notifications. Messages. Missed calls. I must've been in a dead zone. The numbers are all from the monastery. From the main office phone. From Father Graeme's phone. Minutes apart. I open the messages:

Call me back as soon as you see this.

I play the voicemail. It's urgent.

'Harri, we have to go.'

'What? Why?'

'They need us back at the monastery. Right now. Some problem to do with the weather.'

I scan the horizon, as if I know what I'm looking for. The skies are dramatic. Clouds are gathering – dark bruises in the distance. That doesn't seem so unusual. But what do I know? We power-walk in silence. I'm not in a rush to pick up where we left off. My mind is swimming. I have too many issues of my own to obsess over Harriet's choices. But, also, what the hell? Nothing makes sense.

We're within sight of the monastery buildings when she finally speaks.

'Ben, I'm sorry for what I said. About you being totally irrational. I didn't mean it.'

I don't know why she's doing that – backtracking. After she's finally been open with me. OK, it was fairly brutal. But still. Better than nothing. I think she's trying to keep the peace. But my peace is in shreds anyway. I don't need her to be nice.

'You did.'

I stop. I have to. I'm so struck by the realisation, I have to stand still. I really do love her. Even now. Even at her most ludicrously annoying. Even when she's being cagey and petty and less than the person I know she is.

I love her.

'On some level, you meant it. But that's fine, Harri. I can take it. We don't have to fall out forever because we think differently.' We're back at the entrance to the monastery courtyard. We should go in and find Father Graeme. See what's going on. I'm not ready yet. There are things I need to say. 'For the record, I absolutely meant what I said, too. I do think you're selling out.'

'It's not about money.'

'I'm not talking about money either. I mean what you owe to yourself. You're giving up on yourself before you've even started. And I don't get it. At all.'

'OK. Fine.' She heads inside the gates before I have a chance to finish. 'Let's just go and find out what's happening.'

We don't get far. Father Graeme comes striding towards us. I half-register two of the other guests standing behind him. With suitcases. 'Harriet, good, you're back.'

'What's going on?'

He looks at me. I've seen that face before – not on him, but it's universal. The breaking bad news face.

'We've had a severe weather warning. It's serious. It's looking like we'll be isolated for a few days – the ferries are disrupted and flights are out of the question.'

Harriet is quicker to catch on than I am. 'But I have more time! I'm supposed to have more time here.'

'I'm sorry, if we don't get you back to the mainland now, we have no guarantees we'll be able to do so ahead of your return to school next week. It's the same for all the guests due to leave this weekend.'

'I can miss the start of term – a couple of days won't matter.'

'Harriet, you have to go home. Now. The ferry is in forty minutes. Obviously, this will affect your onward travel plans. We can either put you up in Oban until your scheduled travel connections. Or we can refund the cost of new tickets, if you'd rather just get home. We can discuss it on the way to the ferry, OK? I'll take you and the others. For now, I need you to pack. Quickly.'

I've been listening to the conversation. To the words. But there's a time delay. The sounds and meaning are out of sync. It takes a minute to compute. The situation. The fact that she's leaving. Suddenly. Right now.

I burst out laughing. It just keeps coming.

Not because it's funny. Not because I'm glad she's going. Just because I'm wired and it's ironic.

They both stare at me. Her jaw drops. Her eyes narrow. She spins away from me, marching off towards her room.

Father Graeme catches my arm as I start to follow her. 'Ben, you need to be quick. For everyone's safety – five minutes.'

'I'm sorry – Harriet, I'm really sorry.'

'You think this is *funny?*' She's seriously pissed off. Possibly the maddest I've seen her. Throwing clothes into her suitcase. Pushing past me to grab her laptop. I can't believe this is it. If I'd known she'd be snatched away like this, there's no way I'd have spent the last hour arguing with her about what she should do at university.

'I don't think it's funny. It's been so amazing to spend time with you here –'

'So amazing you're *glad* it's over two days early.'

She's half-right. I'm relieved. But it's way more complicated than she thinks. 'I'm not happy you're leaving early. But it's a monastery. It's not like you could stay.'

She stops lashing around the room. The whirlwind dies down and she stares at me. 'And that doesn't *bother* you?! You really don't care about me! You don't care about me at all.'

'Stop saying that! How can you look me in the face and say that?! After *everything!* That's not even remotely true and you know it!'

The long night. The tensions and fights of this morning. It all accumulates. I haven't handled this well, but I don't deserve that. She blinks slowly. She turns and zips up her bag, deflecting. When she answers, it's like she's talking to a child. 'Then *why* are you *here?*'

'I can't answer that in a couple of sentences before you get on a ferry! That was the whole point of you coming here! I thought you saw. I thought you got it. At least a little bit.'

She's quiet. 'I did. I do.'

'So, what do you want me to say?'

I feel breathless just looking at her. Our five minutes must be gone by now, but I can't rush this. She's wrestling with something. I can see it. And a thought occurs to me. It's massively egotistical. But:

Is it possible she's in love with me?

My mind starts racing. Sifting through the evidence.

She was so strange with me when we went out for dinner before I left. But, then again, she was also really drunk. She's found the whole idea of me becoming a monk so upsetting – beyond anything I anticipated. But this is religion taking me away from her. She's easily the most tactile person I know. No one touches me as much as Harriet. But does that mean anything?

She cares.

I've always known that.

But there are so many reasons to care about someone.

I need her to help me. If she just wants me back because I've always been there, I don't think I can do that anymore. But if it's something else. Something more. That's a totally different question. I can't keep guessing. I need her to tell me how she feels. And we don't have all day.

'Harriet' – I take both her hands in mine – 'what do you want from me?'

For a second, I'm hopeful. We're on a knife edge. There's a look in her eyes. But then it's gone – blown out like a candle. She's closing down. She shrugs helplessly. Starting to cry. Again.

It's not enough. Not even close.

I sigh, pulling her into a hug. I may as well – she'll haunt me anyway. I can't believe how often I used to do this. Hold her. And not think anything of it. No wonder this is so difficult. I'm not being transparent either.

'All right. Safe travels.' I sound cold. I don't mean to.

I'm just so gutted.

She recoils, hurt. She picks up her bag and slips out of the room. Gone.

And that's it.

No more glances over meals or seeing her in the pews. No more evening conversations, mulling over the day. No scenic walks. No private jokes. No fighting the urge to kiss her every time she reaches out for me.

I curl up on her bed. The sheets still smell like her. I'm devastated. And angry – at myself. For wasting time.

I stay there.

Skipping meals. Ducking out of my duties. A key scratches in the lock – someone coming to clean the room. I tell them to fuck off. The regret is immediate. I call out a lame 'Sorry.' But I don't get up. I'm too weighed down to open the door and apologise. They don't come in. I'm left alone. Hiding. From everything and everyone. For hours – her room grows dark around me.

Until the bells ring for evening prayer.

I drag myself to chapel.

thirty-four

HARRIET

There is no way I'm staying in Scotland a minute longer than I have to.

Even if it means crawling on my hands and knees down the highways and motorways all day and all night, I am going home.

I'm going straight home.

I'm so mad at Ben! The list of offences is long, and expanding all the time – I'm stewing as I sit cramped on the coach making the hideous trek back down south. I'm mad at him for calling me out. For insisting on telling me things about myself that I don't want to hear. For instinctively understanding almost everything about me – apart from the one thing that really matters.

And how many times is he going to ambush me?

I'm not like him! I can't think on my feet the way he does. There's always a waterfall of emotions in my mind, cascading and cascading – always. But the journey of words from my thoughts out of my mouth – it's treacherous. It's full of pitfalls, and things get lost, and I can never hold them together the way I want to. I'm not eloquent. Not out loud. That's why I paint. That's why I like maths. Outside of my own head, it's hard to make the words line up the way they should.

What was I supposed to say?

Ben, I've been in love with you for at least eighteen months, if not my entire existence, and the thought of you disappearing from my life into a religious black hole makes me want to walk to the water's edge and just keep walking?

Or, how about:

Anyone with half a brain can see that being here is possibly the best thing that's happened to you in the longest time, but I want you to give it all up immediately and come home with me because I miss you?

He's put me in a completely impossible situation!

And then it's somehow my fault – I'm the pathetic fraud who can't speak up for herself in real life? How is that fair?!

I don't know who I'm addressing – silently throwing rhetorical questions around the ether. My music is up loud and I'm shut off from the world, dulling the savage heartache and the tedium of travel with all the technology I didn't think to miss at the monastery. It's not like I didn't have access to it. I guess I just didn't need the distraction. Now I do. Now I'll take anything. I even check my emails – despite the fact that the only emails I ever get are from school or online shopping receipts.

That's when I see it.

How long has it been sitting there? The notification got buried in a string of social media alerts. Sent two hours ago – from Br Richard Fraser. Who's that? The name rings a bell. Did I meet him?

No, apparently not:

Dear Harriet,

I apologise for not having the opportunity to meet you during your stay. My name is Richard, I'm the novice guardian – meaning I oversee the various selection stages that applicants pass through in order to join our community. I understand from Ben's form that you may be willing to provide a character reference? If you are happy to do so, please could you follow the link to complete the attached form as soon as possible. There is no obligation, but I'd be grateful if you could please confirm your intentions either way so that we can be sure we have all the information to hand when we begin our final deliberations.

Best wishes, Br Richard

I should think about this.

I should take a minute to reflect – I'm not in a good place. This is not good timing. It's about as perfect as a monster storm sweeping in and throwing me off the island when I should've had more time. It's just as ironic, just as *funny* – maybe it's fate.

Because I would bet all the money in the world I'm not the only one keeping secrets.

How much do they know about Ben? At the monastery. Really?

They know he was coming back from a bad place when he first stayed with them. They know he spiralled after Uncle David died. That the drugs got out of hand, and he didn't care – about himself, about the girls who wanted to be with him. Just about his grades – irrationally: stubbornly sure that if he was successful academically, Uncle David would've been proud.

They know he had anger issues – toxic rage, alarming, frightening.

And that he hit rock bottom – fast and hard – before coming back up almost as quickly.

But do they know the tipping point: how it all happened – what he actually *did*?

I doubt it.

A character reference is important. If I'm going to respond, I should think about this. But I'm tired. I'm tired from all the travel. I'm weary of feeling so wrung out all the time – the worst aspects of myself: sad and scared, terrified of being alone. I'm tired of being accused of things that are only half justified. And, above all, I'm sick and tired of thinking about Ben.

So, I don't think. I type. I don't bother with the link to the form. I just hit reply to Brother Richard and I pour out everything I know.

I tell him the whole truth.

The full story.

And send.

I don't go straight home.

Somehow, the rest of the journey has sped by. I think I must've slept. The email was a weight off my mind – like tossing a coin into a fountain. It's out of my hands. It's in the lap of the gods now.

I hobble off the coach at the train station in the centre of town, and I do intend to get the bus home. But instead I find I'm at Clara's building door. I ring the intercom. I've travelled through the night, arriving back mid-Friday morning, so the chances of her being available are fairly slim. She could be anywhere.

'Hello?'

She's at home. And hearing her voice, I'm angry all over again.

'It's me. I need to talk to you.'

'Uh-huh.' She buzzes me in.

When I get to the flat, she's waiting for me – regal and unassailable, completely unfazed. 'I wondered when you'd show up.'

It's annoying. 'Why did you send him there?! Who sends someone on a monastic retreat for their eighteenth birthday?!'

'Nice to see you too. Come in, then. Tea?' She holds the door open for me and I fling my bag on the floor.

'I'm serious, Clara – you've ruined my life!'

She looks at me and I feel about twelve years old – hormonal and moody, picking fights with my second mother. Clara has no time for melodrama, but she's all for the truth. I think she can see that I mean it.

'And do you think this is easy for me? This isn't the answer to my prayers either, Harriet. You think I want to be alone in old age? You think I don't want grandchildren someday? Open your eyes. You're not the only one he's leaving.'

The thought hasn't even occurred to me. I've been too consumed with my own pain – exclusively attentive to my own injuries. The weight of what she must be feeling hits me between the eyes – forcefully, like the onset of a headache.

'Auntie!' I'm wailing, a lost child. 'What do we do?!'

I haven't called her that in years. Her smile is nostalgic. She doesn't answer, moving through to the kitchen where the radio is talking to us quietly in the background. 'Help me with this.'

The ritual is familiar. I chop the rough skin off the ginger she's handed me. I go to the bottom left cupboard for the grater while she boils water on the hob. Locating the tea strainer, the mugs – it's all second nature. There's always been something intuitive about the way Clara's kitchens are organised.

'You know, for a while our biggest fear was that he'd get you pregnant? David and I – we were completely paranoid.' Laughter shakes her shoulders. She wipes away a tear.

'What?!' I have to laugh too. 'Seriously?'

'Of course! He's *three* years older than you. And you spent all your summers together, roaming around London doing God only knows what!' She chuckles, shaking her head, stirring sugar into the bubbling water.

'Is that why you were always making us keep doors open?!'

She grins. 'Can you *imagine* how that would've gone down with your parents? They entrusted you to us, for weeks on end. My God, I wore out my knees praying over you two! And, of course, we couldn't mention it to him – the last thing we wanted was to put ideas in his head.'

'I kind of wish you had.'

'No, don't you do that.'

'What?'

Clara hands me a tea – stern and affectionate in a way that's totally unique to her. 'He might not be showing it in the way you want, but don't you start pretending you have no idea how much you mean to him. Harriet! You saved him. After David died.'

She collapses into a chair alongside the little table pushed up against the wall. She's instantly aged – suddenly staggering under the burden of memory.

I sit with her. The ginger hits my nostrils first, then the back of my throat. It cleanses me – a deep internal detox. I stir the liquid and watch it swirl, pale gold in my light cream mug.

'I don't know about that.'

'Well, I do. I tell you – watching the lights go out in your only child . . . Seeing the world, the unfairness, seeing that crush this life you've brought into existence and tried your hardest to keep whole . . .' She sniffs, sipping her tea. 'And I know we owe Jono a lot. He's been a good friend to Ben. But I honestly believe there was a point where you were his only reason to keep going.'

Her words are sword strokes, piercing my soul. She's pruning away the weeds: the self-pity and the rage. I can't look at her – I stare into my drink, watching it blur and refocus as I blink back tears. She's right. Of course she's right. I still can't believe he's willing to contemplate leaving me – that he can survive, maybe even thrive, without me – but she's right. It's not because he doesn't care.

'He doesn't need me like that. Not anymore.'

'And that's a really good thing. Hard. But good. Look, you don't have to explain to me the fear of being outgrown. I'm his mother.' She chuckles, rolling her eyes. 'It comes with the territory. But if you just need him to need you, for the sake of your ego – that's not being in love, Harriet. That's being insecure.'

'Ouch!'

Really – how do I attract all this straight-talking tough love? Annie and Ben and Clara – they should all get together and compare notes. But there's more than a grain of truth in her assessment. There's something harsh and stark – it starts to rub, niggling at the back of my mind.

'How was he – when you were there?' She ignores my plea for sympathy.

'Good. He seemed really well. Mostly.'

'So, there you go. You need a villain? I can be your villain; I don't mind. But really it was David's idea.'

'Uncle David wanted him to go to the monastery?'

She nods; her smile is small. 'He thought we're losing sight of our nature, in dominant culture – our real human nature. Too individualistic. Too materialistic. Too divorced from ourselves as social animals existing as part of the natural world.' She ticks the list off on her fingers. 'You know how he got about these things.'

I see him – clearly. More vividly than I have in years. I can imagine Uncle David – laying his cutlery to one side at the dinner table, lacing his fingers together and embarking on a quiet rant. Never strident, not like Ben and Clara. But just as passionate, in his own way.

'And David had so many issues with the masculinity narrative. It really bothered him. I think he just wanted Ben to have an open mind. See different ways of being. They were actually supposed to go together. That was the plan. You know how close they were.'

I can't believe what I'm hearing – the implications. The fact that Ben being where he is might possibly have been his dad's dying wish.

'It was supposed to be a surprise. To celebrate Ben turning eighteen. Mark the beginning of adulthood with a positive rite of passage. Ben doesn't know that. Yet. I will tell him – I think he can handle it now.'

She's talking but I've stopped listening; the niggle is morphing into a full-blown roar – a drill, boring a hole through my mind. I can feel the panic rising in my chest.

'What?' She looks at me. 'What is it?'

'I've done something completely awful!'

'What did you do?'

'I was just so mad! I was so upset about the whole thing, and we had this super intense argument, and then I suddenly had to go, and he was weird about it, and the email was sitting there in my inbox.'

'What email?'

'They asked me for a reference. Clara, I told them every-thing! *Every*thing.'

She's silent. Her pause lasts forever. The radio keeps mutter-ing – whispering in the background. Her hands grip her mug too tightly. 'Well, I mentioned it too – in passing. Or, actually, not really. I alluded to it, I suppose. But it's the past. History, isn't it? So, I thought it wouldn't do any good to . . .' She trails off, her eyes finding mine. 'Everything?'

'Clara, I've completely betrayed him! He'll *never* forgive me!'

When she puts her hand on mine, it's worse than being yelled at or told off. The gesture is so simple, so full of pure, sad resignation. 'Oh, Harriet!' She's quiet; my own remorse echoes in her voice. 'You don't know that. He's . . . Maybe . . . Well, you don't know that for sure.'

For once, she sounds full of doubt.

thirty-five

BEN

'It has to come from him. This isn't enough.'

'Graeme! What more can there be?'

'I don't know. That's the point.'

I'm hovering outside the door to Brother Richard's office. Eavesdropping.

The monastery is a goldfish bowl. I get that now. Everyone sees everything. The proximity is intrusive, even when people try to give you space. They all know I'm 'out of sorts'. I've tried to pull myself together. Apart from the afternoon she left, I've shown up to everything that's expected of me. For sure, I've been quiet. Inside my own head. But I've kept a lid on the swearing. I've tried to reciprocate the kindness everyone's been showing me. I thought I was doing OK. Until I was summoned.

'He'll need time to process. We can't do this today.'

That's Brother Hamish. Why is he involved?

'Is this a full community matter?' Brother Richard again.

'No. Surely not? Some of the brothers have barely met him! Hamish – what do you think?'

'Perhaps just the representatives? I don't know. We need to think it through, Father Graeme. We have no procedure for this. We don't want to shame him. But, also, there has to be accountability.'

What are they talking about? I knock on the door.

It's opened for me. Brother Hamish ushers me in with a slight bow. He returns to where the others are standing. Lined up. Like a firing squad. For at least a minute, no one looks at me directly. They were in full flow before I knocked. Now, it seems like they don't know where to start.

'Look, I know I've been sulking but –'

'No, Ben. It's not that.' Father Graeme moves across the room to meet me in the doorway. 'You're entitled to your emotions. It's a complicated time for you and we understand. This is . . .' He looks over his shoulder to the others. 'Well, this is something else.'

Brother Richard interrupts. 'We've received a reference. The allegations are serious. And previously undisclosed.'

'Do you know what we're referring to?' Father Graeme's voice is quiet. Tinged with sadness.

I've never fainted. I feel like I'm about to. The room is a hundred degrees. No air. I'm suffocating.

'Ben? Do you know what we're talking about?'

I nod. I can't speak.

'We want to understand. From your perspective. We want to understand what happened. And why you . . . withheld this information from us. We need to ask you to take some time, and then come back to us. We haven't worked out the process yet, but we want you to have a fair hearing. We just want to understand. Can you do that for us, Ben? Can you explain?'

I nod. I'm not convinced I can, but I can't exactly refuse to try. Not now. Not when they already know one version of the truth.

'OK, good.' He puts his arm round my shoulders. I try not to break down. 'We'll carry on as normal until then, OK? Same duties. Everything.'

'Three days.' Brother Richard is firm – the others look at him, surprised. I know the decision is unilateral. It doesn't surprise me. He can't wait to get rid of me. He's always wanted me gone. 'We're not dragging this out. We need your answer in three days.'

The wind is howling. It whips round the side of the building, but the wall shelters me. I listen to it. Dazed. My feet walked me out of Brother Richard's office on autopilot. I ended up here – collapsed on a bench in the monastery garden. A metre away from where Harriet and I watched the stars. A lifetime ago.

They want answers.

They want to hear it from me. I don't know if I can give them what they're looking for. Of course I remember. It's seared into my subconscious. But it's not chronological. It's not factual. I was too off my face for my memory to hold all the details. It's visceral. It's trapped in my limbs. I feel it. The waking nightmare that never leaves. The knowledge of what my body is capable of.

What I'm capable of.

It was the winter we were living with Harriet's family. The first one after Dad died. Short days. Long nights. The darkness was almost tangible. Whatever I thought I'd found at Jono's church didn't last. I kept going back but the silence was deafening.

I remember it was Harriet's idea to go to the gig. I didn't want to. I didn't want to do anything except sit around stoned. She dragged me out. She said we should celebrate. I'd just got my offer from Oxford. It meant something to everyone else. I was just numb.

I think she brought Jono for back-up. Maybe Mum told her to. Maybe Maggie and George didn't trust me with her.

There are gaps.

I'm stoned. At the bar. Getting served on fake ID. Jono comes over. Tries to talk me out of drinking whatever alcohol I'm downing. The music is terrible. The venue is shit. There are too many people. I'm claustrophobic. I'm angry they're all alive. What the fuck are they doing – all of them, alive? These strangers I don't give a flying fuck about. Why are they all here?

More gaps.

I'm outside, throwing up on the pavement. Harriet is with me. I think Jono is somewhere inside. Her face. I do remember her face. She's under an old street light. Not one of those LED ones – the amber kind. It makes her skin glow. And she's worried. I know she's really terrified. She says she's going to get Jono. She says, 'We need to go home.' And, 'Wait there, don't move. You're not allowed back in – remember?'

I don't remember.

I don't know why I'm not allowed back in.

I try to follow her. The bouncer stops me. He blocks my path with his arm. I look at him – I'm completely enraged. 'Not tonight,' he says. 'You're done for tonight. Go home and sober up.'

Who the fuck does he think he is?

But he's huge. Seriously massive. He gives me a shove. Elbows me to one side. I stumble. Humiliated. His radio crackles and he steps away from the door, back into the venue. A fire door. It swings shut behind him.

I'm alone on the street.

Someone walks towards me. We're a similar build. Roughly the same age. I'm a little taller. And he's alone. Just walking. Somewhere.

When I punch him, he staggers. Time is weird. I should see him regain his balance. I should see him swing back at me. I don't see it. I feel it. The blow to my torso is a detonator. A match to a keg of raw pain.

It's not a film. When my fists connect, there are no sounds. There's hardly any feeling. Even though I know I'm being beaten up too. I'm completely out of it. It's just movement. Frenetic. Frenzied.

Fists. Knees.

He blocks. He falls. And I kick him. And kick him. And kick him. I crouch over him, raining down punches. He rolls. My fist slams the tarmac. The pain registers but only briefly. It's blind rage and mental paralysis. Everything and nothing. Totally senseless. But the obvious conclusion.

I must've known I'd end up there. Surely.

When I started off down that road – self-medicating with the drugs and denying everything else, part of me had to know this is where it would lead.

It was all me – I did it. My choice.

More gaps.

So many gaps.

They want answers.

I only have questions.

I know the things I was told later on.

It was Jono who pulled me off him. It was Harriet who called the ambulance. And the police. He was in hospital for three days. No one pressed charges. So, technically, I'm not a violent criminal. They told me he recovered – is that true?

Does anyone really recover after being brutally assaulted by a random stranger?

And what if there'd been knives involved? Would I be dead? A murderer? Or both?

And *why* did no one press charges? Not him or his family. Not the police. They were told about 'my circumstances' – but is that really relevant?

Is it only relevant because I also speak with the 'right' kind of accent? I have the 'right' socio-economic background?

If my skin was a few shades darker – less racially ambiguous – would the dead dad story be enough to keep me out of prison?

If I had ended up in the criminal justice system, would all those statistics about ex-offenders be true for me too?

If the school didn't want my Oxford acceptance on their record, would I have been expelled?

If I hadn't got into treatment immediately, would I have finished my exams – let alone gone to university?

And what about that – my recovery?

What if Jono hadn't had the knowledge and connections, from his complex family history, to immediately stage a professional intervention?

What if Harriet hadn't begged – literally got down on her knees – and begged me to get help, would I have listened to anyone else?

What if Maggie and George hadn't had the money to privately fast-track me through every conceivable form of therapy?

Rehab. Anger management. Bereavement counselling. Family therapy. All running in parallel and on time. All my issues caught and worked on in that critical window when I could still turn it around.

Basically, why me?

Why did I get a second chance? Why did I have a safety net – when so many other people don't?

How is that right? How is that fair?

And, also –

I know it's my fault. I know it's my history. My actions. I'm one hundred per cent in the wrong. It's my past catching up with me. I guess I deserve that. But –

How could she?

Obviously, it was Harriet. How could she expose me like this? This *way*?

Completely out of the blue. No warning. Not even a hint. Just turn around and undermine me so totally, when she's always been on my side?

When she was the one taking me out for Chinese after every single therapy session – so I could decompress before going home to Mum. When she was the one sitting with me through withdrawals and flashbacks – reading up on how to support me, knowing I was a train-wreck but believing I could get better.

She stayed with me in the shadows. I know that was tough on her. Maybe too much to ask. But for her to turn around – now – and use it against me like this?

Why?

Why would she do that? What was she thinking?

I mean, what the *actual* fuck?

thirty-six

HARRIET

I'm trying to retrace my steps.

It's early – a little after eight in the morning; the winter sunlight is weak through the windows and I'm sitting in the quiet of my studio bay in the abandoned art block. I've barely slept all weekend; the guilt has made it impossible. And, of course, Ben's phone is switched off. None of my follow-up emails to Brother Richard have been answered, either. They're busy. Busy figuring out what to do with the loaded gun I've handed them. Deciding whether to exile Ben – whether to cast him out, send him away from everything he's been working towards. Back to me.

What have I done?

So, I'm here. Surrounded by my mediocre, lacklustre art projects – the drawings that feel flat, the paintings that are full of muddle and discord. Because where else can I go? This is my equivalent of a chapel – my place of introspection. And I have *got* to get a grip. I've got to find the moment, the crossroads, the point where I became someone who would do something like this. The miscalculation.

How did it come to this?

How did I end up feeling so scared at the thought of him not being in my life that I would actually sabotage his plans?

What he did was awful.

But this is unforgivable too.

'Harriet?'

I jump.

'What are you doing here?' Ms Harrington puts her folders down on my desk, taking a moment to survey my walls. 'I like this one.' She points to a drawing I've just pinned up: an incomplete sketch I started in Scotland. 'It seems very free. It has a nice tempo, doesn't it? Fluid.'

'Thanks.'

'You remember I said at the start of term that it wasn't time to panic?' She pulls up a stool, sitting next to me. 'And we're not quite there yet. But I'm concerned that your work isn't developing as much as I'd like to see at this point. You still have your A levels to finish, even if you're not doing art next year. I'd love to see you finish strong. Hmm?'

I nod – clutching my hands together in my lap, willing myself not to cry. Not to be that person, crying in public over a boy – falling apart because he's gone.

'Talk to me. What's your process?'

'How do you mean – when I'm painting?'

'Painting, drawing – whatever. How do you do the work?'

I feel my body relaxing as my mind switches track. 'I guess there's normally something that interests me on some level – like a pattern, or an emotion, or maybe a concept. Something to break down and rebuild on my own terms. And, I don't know, I normally just go with it.'

'I can see that. Sometimes. Here' – she points to the sketch – 'but not here. Why is that? This is confident. This is not. Why are you second-guessing yourself here, and not here?'

'You'll think I'm pathetic.'

'Pathetic or not, you have an A level to complete. So, break it down for me, OK? I'm not having you fail on my watch.'

'I have a friend, and he's always been around' – I will myself to keep speaking – 'but he's not anymore. And a lot of my ideas in the past, I guess he's had some major input into them. Like, last year – the body project I won that prize for – he took me to the Saville exhibition. And it's more than the ideas or the fact that he thinks I'm good at art . . .'

This is excruciating. The struggle to articulate the loss I feel is overwhelming – humiliating. Why does it matter? Why can't I be the way I'm supposed to be? Independent and self-sufficient. Full of my own self-belief.

I can't explain it. I don't have the words.

I borrow Ben's.

'I'm afraid. I actually told him recently that I'm not going to do art next year. And he asked me why I'm suddenly afraid. Which I hated hearing – but only because it's so accurate. I am really afraid to do it without him. And I know he doesn't get that. Because he thinks I'm really confident. But it's more like he puts all my insecurities on mute. He makes me feel at home. In myself. So, I'll try *anything* – I can be creative and loose and fluid, because I don't have anything to prove.'

I can't tell if I'm making my point clearly. I look for the right image to illustrate what I mean.

'Kind of like a kite – you know? Flying, but grounded – I know I'm not going to get lost in the wind. It's just fun and exhilarating and an amazing view. I don't know how to be like that without him. Anchoring me.'

There it is.

Finally. The simple, unflattering truth.

I completely rely on him.

I wait for her to tell me to pull myself together. I'm braced for the harsh rebuke.

'You know Lee Krasner was married to the painter Jackson Pollock?'

'Yeah.'

'She asked him – when she was really pushing the boundaries and scaring herself – apparently, she asked him if what she was creating was good. And he reassured her. He made her keep going with it.'

'I didn't know that.'

'Harriet, we all need encouragement. We all need support. But, also, leaving home is part of growing up – isn't it? So, maybe it's time to find your own way forwards.'

She suddenly leaps to her feet, excited in a way that's unexpectedly childish.

'Argh, it's perfect!' She pulls out her phone, typing something, scrolling.

'What?'

'What classes do you have today?'

'I have –'

'Actually, I don't care. This is what you're doing. You need to get to the Krasner retrospective. In London. Today.'

'I have school!'

'Pah! What was the last exhibition you went to?'

'Choucair.'

'I thought Choucair would be good for you, with the maths connection. But, actually, I think you need to learn to embrace a bit of chaos.' She's pacing around, waving her hands with feeling. 'General rule: if it's personal, it's universal. This is what I'm always trying to teach you kids!'

I genuinely think she's about to start jumping up and down – she's jet-propelled, full of energy.

'This is why I nag you about going to see other people's art! Yes, technique. Yes, context. But mostly empathy, resilience. Get out of your own heads. Love, loneliness, insecurity – someone's been where you are and made it through. And made it beautiful. Or provocative. Or captivating. Doesn't matter whether they're from your generation or ethnicity or gender or century, even. They can still help you move forwards as a person and an artist, if you pay enough attention.'

She marches back over to where I'm sitting, pointing a commanding finger at me. 'Go and see Krasner – and I want you to look for the shift in her work. You'll see it.'

She stops, suddenly deflated. 'I guess we need to ask for parental consent. Drat.'

I've caught her vision – I don't want a day trapped in class-rooms either. Besides, I have double art anyway, so I'm hardly missing much.

'My mum might say yes?'

There's an eternity between each ring and then we're thwarted by her voicemail. Calling back doesn't get us any further – I know she'll probably be tied up for most of the morning.

'How about your dad?'

It's a gamble. He's more likely to be available – and more likely to say no. But now that the idea has been floated, I'm desperate to see it through. He picks up on the first try. She puts him on speaker – we lean over the phone like co-conspirators.

'Hello, Mr Johnson? This is Ms Harrington – Harriet's art teacher.'

'Oh hello, is everything all right – is she OK?'

'She's fine. But' – she looks at me, a sly grin on her face – 'I've been concerned for some time now that Harriet's not been achieving her full potential on the course this year, and I hoped you might consent to her visiting an exhibition today at the Barbican. To move her forwards at what is quite a critical juncture, coming into the new half-term.'

She pauses – she pulls a face at me in the silence, like she can't believe her blagging. I hold my breath.

'You've noticed too?'

'Uh-huh.' She looks at me and shrugs, playing along.

'I have to say, it's always concerned me – her fixation with art. Because, well, if I'm honest, I guess it doesn't make a whole lot of sense to me. But now that it seems to have fallen off the radar for her a little bit, if anything, it's actually worse. I mean, I worry more. Because she doesn't seem quite herself, if that makes sense?'

Hearing his thoughts gives me goosebumps – I feel my skin prickle, emotion in my pores. I'm listening in on a private confession I never dreamt I'd hear. My dad. Advocating for my art.

'So, yes – that's fine by me. Do you need me to put it in writing?'

'An email would be perfect, yes!' Ms Harrington beams at me – giving me a double thumbs-up.

'And maybe get her to call me when she gets there?'

'I will do, of course.'

I zone out as they sort out the details and hang up. All I know is I'm free – a totally unexpected release. Free to find a way back to myself. A pilgrimage of my own.

*

There's an otherworldly calm to the gallery space – tucked away from the bustle of the streets in the upper floors of the Barbican.

The building itself is a Brutalist wonderland – a concrete monstrosity or architectural gem, depending on your perspective. I've grown to love it, outside and in. The nooks and corridors – the way the interconnected levels sprawl. Libraries and cafés, auditoriums and restaurants – cultural incubators at every turn. But I don't come very often; I've never been here with Ben.

One of the few London landmarks that isn't tainted with bitter-sweet déjà vu.

As soon as I start walking through the exhibition, I can feel the tension in my body evaporating. It's quiet. Monday is the perfect day for this – almost deserted, people back at work and school. I'm in the company of elderly art enthusiasts and parents with babies in body-carriers. I can take my time. When I linger over the wall text, I don't have to shift to accommodate other onlookers. When I get right up close to see the brushstrokes on a canvas, the only thing I need to worry about is setting off the security alarms.

I follow the curator's chronology – walking with Krasner, seeing her style develop. Her Little Images are vibrant – mosaics full of the things I'm naturally drawn to: rich colour, geometric shapes, balanced compositions that make me feel like life is a treasure hunt.

I keep moving – weaving in and out of the rooms on the upper floor of the exhibition space. The diversity of her styles is eye-opening. I had her pegged as an abstract expressionist, but her struggle through different schools to become a pioneer is encouraging – seeing her break with realism into cubism, then into abstraction. The way she didn't allow herself to be pinned down; she pursued new avenues – complete departures from her previous work.

Is this the shift I'm supposed to be looking for?

Ms Harrington said I would know it when I saw it.

I keep wandering – following the rooms, following her story: her professional trajectory, the turbulence in her marriage. Life shaped by art; art shaped by life.

I stumble across the painting Ms Harrington mentioned. The one that pushed the boundaries – the one Pollock told her to keep exploring. *Fraught with foreboding*, the wall text says. Krasner called it *Prophecy*; it's hung with a trio of canvases – three other paintings rarely seen together. Seething and violent and erotic. With a backstory that shatters me – just reading it.

How did she survive it?

Alone in Paris. A phone call from the other side of the world. The news that her husband, her creative ally, struggling with alcoholism, had crashed his car. Hearing he'd died in the collision, killing another passenger too. Finding out that the only survivor was the woman he'd been having an affair with.

How did she keep breathing?

How did she keep *painting*?

I'm led downstairs – following the crumbs of the curator's trail. Captivated – in awe of this woman's strength. And then I see it. The shift. It's unmissable.

Up to this point the canvases have been fairly large and full of colour.

But this – this is something else. The canvases are massive. Impossibly big – at least two metres high and over four metres wide. Colossal. And as for the colours – it's a different story to absolutely everything that's come before. Suddenly the primary colours are gone – banished from her palette. The new vocabulary is muted. Dark and earthy. Two tones across the whole canvas. Bleak, but still alive.

I read the wall text.

It makes so much sense. This is grief – these are the shades of a painter struggling with insomnia, unable to sleep and unwilling to paint bright colours under artificial light. The shift is so total – so dramatic and misunderstood – that it cost her a solo exhibition, cancelled overnight.

And the size.

It's the size that really stuns me. I stand in front of them. I move from end to end. And back again. Exploring.

There are more in the series – I study them all.

Where did this scale come from? This overnight transformation?

I go back to the notes.

And it all clicks.

I get the point Ms Harrington is making. I know why she wanted me to see this. *In 1957, Krasner decided that she would take over Pollock's barn.* The best work venue – large and full of natural light. These canvases are the result. Born out of his absence.

This is her filling the space that Pollock had previously occupied. Literally. Metaphorically and creatively, too – living the options she didn't have when he was alive. Expanding in a way that wasn't open to her before.

This is art she could only make without him.

Because she had more room.

I sit. I find my way to a bench positioned in front of another canvas – the colour is seeping back into the works at this stage. This is all red – crimson or maybe magenta – a rich red dancing in between creamy whites. It's gigantic, pulsing with the will to live. It's called *Another Storm*. I have to smile – the theme of weather is pursuing me; the cosmos has a dark sense of humour.

I didn't ask for this – to have Ben ripped out of my hands without warning.

But maybe I need it.

Maybe I need space from Ben.

Maybe he needs space from me.

What we have – what we are to each other – it's a complicated thing. An unnamed intimacy. An accidental coupling forged by life and death and other people's histories. I do love him. Being with him would be a dream come true. But I don't want to fall into a relationship with him because I'm clinging to the familiar, afraid to move forwards. And I don't want him to stay with me because I bulldozed over his options and forced my way in.

It will *never* work out like that. For either of us.

Obviously.

It's incredible how much a painting can show me. A visual image – translating inner turmoil into clarity. I need this. I know there are people who think art is irrelevant, or nice to have – a plaything on the side of life, self-indulgent and non-essential. But for me, it's everything. It saves me. Every time.

Of course I need to do art next year.

It's a no-brainer.

I could stay here forever – all day in front of this one canvas. And sitting here, overshadowed by the greatness of someone else's genius, feeling part of a larger story, seeing the fingerprints of artists who've gone before me and left a legacy for me to step into – I understand what Ben is doing.

What he wants.

I understand what it feels like to want to pursue something enigmatic. Wanting to follow an enlightening impulse to its end conclusion – even at the risk of failure and ruin. To chase the spark of life, even as it fizzles and scorches and burns.

To choose faith.

Ben loves God like I love art: centrally and always, at the very core of his being. The one thing – the *only* thing – he can't live without. He's already given up job offers in the City and a six-figure salary within reach, left his friends and the prestige of his college, risked falling out with his only remaining blood family – how much more evidence do I need?

In a conflict with his faith, I don't win.

The immense canvas – it puts everything into perspective.

Ben doesn't know if he'll become a monk – just like I don't know if I'll ever be a full-time artist. But I know he has to try.

If it's not too late – if I haven't already ruined everything for him – I have to stop with all the clutching, and fighting, and crying, and resisting.

I have to let him go.

thirty-seven

BEN

I've lived the longest three days of my life.

They said everything would continue as normal – but it hasn't. It couldn't. Every time someone looks at me, I wonder how they'd see me if they knew. Sharing the kitchen with Brother Hamish, I read judgement into his silence. I don't know how much Harriet said. They won't show me. They want to keep things neutral. They want to hear my version of events, as I remember it. Not in response to allegations.

Just my experience.

All the brothers gathered again after breakfast this morning. To prepare. Everyone has been asked to pray for me. Only eight people know why. They've convened a special committee – four brothers who know me and four who don't. Only the ones who know me have seen the reference: Father Graeme, Brother Richard, Brother Hamish and Brother Martin. The other four will hear it from me. The rest of the community don't know. I guess they'll be told after they kick me out.

They asked for my input – to see if it seemed fair. The complex dance of their internal democracy makes me feel like I'm on trial. I guess I am. But if anything, I think they're going above and beyond. In their shoes, I'd have packed me off the island by now.

I knock on the closed chapel door.

It's opened by Father Graeme. He doesn't smile. 'Come in, Ben. Welcome.'

There are two chairs facing each other in front of the altar. Father Graeme sits in one and points me towards the other. The other seven brothers line the pews behind him. I feel like a guest on a daytime chat-show. One of those programmes where the interviewees end up screaming at each other. And the audience jeers as lives fall apart on stage.

'So, Ben' – Father Graeme is straight down to business – 'you indicated that you know what the reference is about. So, let's hear your thoughts on it, please.'

I exhale. I don't know what to do with my hands. I start to crack my knuckles. But that probably makes me look like a thug. I hold on to the arms of the chair. I try to be direct.

'You know I had various issues after Dad died. That's never been a secret. I didn't tell you that I beat someone up in the street. And hospitalised him. Unprovoked. It was . . .' I exhale again; I stick to the facts. 'It was a turning point. I hope I'd never do anything like that again. Or even come close. But I guess, I don't know for sure – and that's why I'm totally clean now. I don't even drink. I don't want to risk it. Being that person.'

'Why didn't you tell us?' Brother Richard calls down from the pews. 'Is it because the charges were dropped? So you didn't have to disclose it when we asked about having a criminal record?'

'No.' Of course he'd think I hid it on a technicality. 'No. I didn't bring it up because I *never* bring it up. Because I'm completely ashamed.' I can't look at them. I fix my eyes on the floor.

There's a pause.

'Are you sorry?'

The question comes from a brother I haven't spoken to. It's so basic, I can't believe I haven't said that already.

I nod. 'And I told him to his face. The police put us in touch.'

We were part of a pilot programme: restorative justice. Putting victims and perpetrators in contact to talk through their experiences. It seemed a lot to ask of him but he said it would help.

The exchange was brief. He said what he needed to. That I was 'fucked up as fuck' and should donate to a charity for victims of violent crime. Pay off my debt to society.

I took every job I could. Sold half the contents of my room. Set up an indefinite direct debit.

It's not enough. This isn't something you absolve with money.

'I'm so sorry. I'll always be sorry. But, I mean, that's *completely* inadequate! What does that change? It's not like I can take it back.' My voice breaks and I know I can't say anything else. That's all I can manage. That's as much as I can say out loud.

The pause returns. It lengthens into silence. I suppose that's to be expected. They leave space for quiet at the best of times. Even more so when there's something this ugly to confront. I sit with my head in my hands. Waiting. For whatever comes next.

'What do you want, Ben?' Father Graeme is quiet, but his voice carries through the hush.

I don't fully understand the question. Is he asking if I still want to be a monk – if I want to be allowed to stay? Is he asking if I would erase my regrets, if I could? What do I want? Where do I start?

'I just want to do better. Now. Going forwards. I just want to be good enough.'

'Good enough for what?'

Peace.

Forgiveness.

Acceptance.

All the things I know I don't deserve. I want to quiet that voice in the back of my head that constantly tells me I'm morally deficient. I'm a bad person. I'm a spiritual failure. The worst kind of man.

I shake my head. It's too much to ask. But he pushes me.

'Good enough for what, Ben?'

'Love.'

He lets the word sit between us. He lets me feel it. The pain. The longing. The hope and hopelessness.

'Ben, you're human. We are all capable of terrible and glorious things.' Father Graeme speaks with his usual measured tone. 'Look around you. Look.'

I look up. I look at the group as they stand, gathering around me.

No one avoids my gaze.

'None of us deserve the love we've found. We haven't earnt it. But we are worth it. And so are you.'

It's Brother Richard who reaches me first.

He puts his hand on my shoulder. He squeezes it, and that little gesture starts an avalanche. I'm collapsing on the inside. More hands reach out. And I can't help it. I'm crying, and I cry and I just keep on crying.

Someone's arm is round me.

Someone gives me tissues.

Someone starts a benediction:

'Therefore, confess your sins to each other, and pray for each other so that you may be healed. The prayer of the righteous is powerful and effective.'

The others join in – they all seem to know the words.

'We pray for you, our brother.'

'We pray for you, our son.'

'We pray for you, God's child.'

Father Graeme stands, joining them, completing the circle around me and finishing the prayer. 'We see you as you are, Ben. The Christ in you. The image of the divine in you. The Spirit in you, who knows all things and understands all things and empowers you in your weakness. We honour and affirm you – Benjamin David Wilkins – God's beloved.'

I'm such a mess, blubbering away. I can feel my head starting to throb. But it's cathartic. Cleansing.

Someone gives me bread, non-alcoholic wine. Communion – a ritual in remembrance, millennia old. It's never felt so relevant. The cross, with its intersections and contradictions. Brutality and forgiveness. Justice and mercy. Death and new beginnings. A mystery.

'Body of Christ, broken for you.'

'Blood of Christ, shed for you.'

'Spirit of Christ, keep you in eternal life.'

They sing as I eat and drink the offerings. In harmony, they sing over me – their voices soar: an incantation. And I don't know how to describe it, but it's like I see it all explode. A swirling supernova. Light refracting through brokenness – sending beams shooting out in every direction. Every dark corner, illuminated. Every weight, dissolved.

A quiet opens up in me. A stillness. A clearing where condemnation used to lurk. The whispers stop. The reminders of wrongs done. The accusation and crushing guilt. The inadequacy. The truth is still there. The truth of what I did. Who I was. But also, the truth of who I am. Who I can become. It's all there. Coexisting. Peacefully.

It won't last.

I'll have to fight to hold on to this sense of freedom. I don't know what that will look like. Maybe more therapy? Maybe I need to –

'A blessing of Moses' – Father Graeme interrupts my thoughts – 'to the tribe of Benjamin – he said, *"Let the beloved of the Lord rest secure in him, for he shields him all day long, and the one the Lord loves rests between his shoulders.*" So, just rest – OK, Ben? I know that's hard for you.'

He has his eyes closed, but he's looking into my soul.

'No more striving. Just rest.'

I'm wiped out.

It's as if I've reached a mountain summit just in time for an incredible sunrise. But now the moment's over, and the climb is catching up with me, and the journey back down needs facing. They all slipped away – giving me space to think. Father Graeme will check in again later. For now, it's me and God. No one wants to get in the way of that.

I'm not sure how long I've been here.

Time is irrelevant. Nebulous. It stretches and bends when you're keeping company with the eternal. I pick up a Bible from the pews. It feels thinner than mine. Mine is falling to pieces. Stuffed with questions. Notes in the margins. Comments on Post-its. On napkins. On whatever I have to hand. Thoughts. Responses. Unanswerable things. It's too far away to go and get from my cell. This will do.

I open it up. And listen. And speak when I'm spoken to. Continuing the conversation that's always been the heartbeat of my life.

We start to talk about Harriet. But it hurts. So I stop.

A cough startles me. It comes out of nowhere. I turn to see Brother Richard has reappeared. He's standing in the chapel entrance. Uncomfortable. Unsure.

'Can I come in?'

I nod. I don't have the energy to send him away. And it's a public space. Maybe he needs to pray too.

He sits down – a little further along in the same pew. Looking at him side-on, I realise it's the first time we've ever been next to each other. Instead of in opposition. His features are softer from the side. Not quite so stern. Not so severe. I figure he's here to reflect, so I leave him to it.

'Ben, I owe you an apology.'

The interruption surprises me. It's so far from anything I expect to hear. But he seems awkward enough as it is. I try to tone down my scepticism.

'OK . . .'

'I haven't been fair to you. When I read your application. And your personality profile. And then you arrived – so full of ideas, challenging everything straight off the bat . . . You remind me so much of a brother we lost. Stephen. That's been a real struggle for me.'

He isn't looking at me. It's not clear if he wants to say more.

'Did I meet him? When I was here before?'

'I think he was away. Otherwise, I'm fairly confident you'd remember him. He's not easy to forget.'

'And he died?'

He shakes his head. He crosses and uncrosses his arms. Fidgeting. Finding the words. 'He left us.'

'He broke his vows?'

'He did.'

It takes a minute for what he's saying to sink in. And I already know the answer but I ask the question anyway. 'Initial?'

'Life. Fifteen years in.' Brother Richard is quiet, studying his hands. 'And I miss him. Maybe that seems trivial to you?'

'No, of course not.'

I don't know what to say. The only thing that springs to mind is what everyone says. And it's trite and annoying. But maybe it means something here. I don't know. I can't think of anything else.

'I'm really sorry for your loss.'

He laughs – a small, bitter sound. 'I suppose it does feel like that. At times. A death. Or maybe a divorce. There isn't really a box for it.'

'Does it need a box? I mean, it's just hard – isn't it? Losing someone you love.'

'It's hard when it's their choice to go. The rejection. We're pack animals, aren't we? No one likes being left behind.'

I look at him – remembering everything I've projected onto him over the weeks since I've arrived. I had no idea. All the things beneath the surface. All the scars and wounds and stories.

'Anyway. I'm not giving you my burdens to carry. I'm just saying, it's not your fault. It's nothing to do with you. I just wanted you to understand the context. Because if you do decide to come back to us after Christmas, Brother Martin will be the novice guardian. I need to take some time. And we've agreed he'd be good in the role. Plus, he's met Harriet.'

'I can come back? I can do the novitiate?' The statement is slipped in so subtly, I have to check.

'Of course! We all think the world of you!' He looks genuinely taken aback – but I really wasn't sure. 'Ben, I'm sorry if we weren't explicit on that. I think we assumed you knew. You'll get your formal invitation soon. And remember – you don't owe us anything. Not yet. Not for a long while. So, think about it. And keep thinking. All the way through. Don't fall into anything because you think you have to.'

Almost all of me wants to do a celebratory dance. I'm living a dream, and it keeps coming true. Every door I push swings open. Nothing is blocking the path.

He laughs again – a touch of incredulity in the sound. 'You really do remind me of Stephen. Very insightful in some ways. But, also, completely blind. Maybe it comes with being so self-critical?'

He stands up, looking at me and shaking his head.

'Take care of yourself, Ben. You're doing just great. And if I had to guess, I'd say you're far more loved than you know.'

The impact is immediate. My whole body starts to shake. It's as if he's aimed at me with an emotional slingshot. Slaying all my giants in a passing hit and run.

He stops in the doorway.

'Can I ask you one more thing?'

I'm not sure I can take it, but I nod anyway.

'Putting you in the kitchen. I know I could've handled the conversation better. But was it – did I do the right thing? Was it helpful?'

I laugh, thinking back to my reaction and how far I've come. 'Yeah, absolutely. You changed my life.'

He beams – the first smile I've seen on him. Ever. He nods and slips away.

It's unbelievable.

I can stay. After everything, I can still come back here.

People are so complicated.

And then – I can't help it – I'm thinking about Harriet again. About how no one likes being left behind. How rejection hurts like hell. And maybe I really *am* more loved than I know. Thinking about our fights. And our tensions. And her dumb, nonsensical choices. And I think I get it. I'm sure I finally get it.

She's in love with me. Wildly, insanely in love with me. And she's scared.

Of all the ways she could've told me, this would not be my first choice.

But I hear her.

Loud and clear.

thirty-eight

HARRIET

Justin isn't answering my messages.

I can't tell what that means. Scrolling back through our history, I realise he never really answered them. He'd just show up or start a new conversation – a few hours or days later. It's hard to read a pattern into the sporadic, spontaneous interactions. So I do the only thing I can think of. I tell him I'll be at the parkrun on Saturday. I know he'd normally go. I give him minimal notice and hope he shows up.

The weather is miserable – rain falling in sheets. I've doubled up with a headscarf and hood. I'm fairly sure anyone with any sense will sit this one out, but as I approach our meeting spot, I let myself believe the person sheltering under the bare branches of the tree is Justin.

'You came?'

'You asked me to.'

'I know. But I didn't know if you'd want to see me. After what happened at the party.'

'You mean when I kissed you. And you kind of kissed me back. And then you slammed on the brakes and I ran away?'

I smile. It's nice to see he's still unguarded. 'Yes, exactly.'

'Did I miss something? Did you tell me?' He flicks rainwater out of his eyes, frowning. 'I miss things sometimes. My brain – I get distracted. It's like an overload sometimes and I don't always notice things the way someone else would – it doesn't always sink in.'

Listening to him blame this on his ADHD is heartbreaking – my conscience can't take it. 'It's not that. At all. I was fairly sure we weren't on the same page. But it was more convenient to pretend it was nothing. That's awful, I know! Criminally selfish. But I was so lonely.'

'You used me?'

'I do really like you. I miss our runs. But if you want to be definitive about it, I guess the answer is yes. I did. I'm sorry.'

He nods, jogging on the spot. 'Is there someone else?'

'Yes.'

'How's that working out?'

'It's not. It's not going to.'

'Because they don't feel the same way?'

'Because we haven't talked about how either of us feels. And I don't think we will. It's too complicated.'

'That's dumb. No offence.' He grins. 'There's nothing more complicated than trying to guess how someone else feels. Look at us! You should say something.'

'I can't. I've tried. Sort of. I was drunk.'

'Doesn't count.'

'All right, I know. But I find it really impossible to just come out with things. I'm not good at spontaneous declarations. I get stuck.'

'This seems fine. This conversation.'

'I thought about it. A lot.'

'All right – so think about it. Don't try to be spontaneous. Figure out what you want to say. And how. And where. And when. And make it happen.'

'Isn't that a bit fake?'

'Why?'

I don't have an answer for that. I guess I just have expectations. I've always assumed I'd be caught up in the moment:

there'd be this point where emotion would overwhelm me, and the words would materialise out of the chemistry in the air. It would be dramatic and magic, perfection taking us both by surprise. Something like that.

Something unreal.

'Harriet, I have strategies. All the time, I use strategies. So that I can be myself and still do things that are hard for me, that other people don't think twice about. If you want to say something, you shouldn't worry about how someone else would do it. Or how *everyone* else would do it. Just do it your way.'

The smile starts in the centre of my soul – a warm glow tingling all the way through me. This changes everything: the fact that I don't have to find the moment.

I can create it.

Justin is smiling, still jogging on the spot. 'Are we done? Everything OK? Can we run now?'

'Yes!' He's a better friend than I probably deserve, but I'm so glad he's still here. 'Yes, let's run.'

I message Annie as soon as I get home.

Things are still frosty between us – she hasn't apologised for the things she said about me; I haven't asked her to. But I need her help to pull this off and I know she'll be on board. Maybe that's what a good friend is: someone you can still count on, even after you've both been out of line.

I get out of the shower to find her response.

I'm all in. What do you need?

*

I call Ben the second I think he might have reliable signal.

I've waited weeks for this but, now that he's on his way home for Christmas, I need to know. I have to find out – on a scale of ten to off-the-charts – exactly how livid he is with me.

I'm pacing around my bedroom, trying not to give myself any more excuses. I close the curtains and turn on the fairy lights. I study the photos of us from the ceilidh, taped up on my mirror – focusing on his smile before it all went wrong. Yes, he might be tired. Yes, he might prefer to talk in person. Yes, I could message him first. But, either way, I have to face this – so I'm just going to get it over with.

It rings.

For the first time in a month and a half, his phone rings. Twice, three times. Voicemail. He *hung up?* He hung up on me?

I don't know what to do with that. It wasn't even on my radar as a possibility. I sink onto the bed – completely floored. My phone slips out my hand; I'm frozen – trying to figure out my next move, all my plans unravelling around me. Everything I want to say won't mean a thing if he's not even willing to speak.

I almost miss it.

The distant buzzing sound is being smothered by my duvet. Ringing – my phone is ringing. I snatch it, fumbling, swiping, forgetting basic functionality.

'Hello, ratbag.' He's laughing. 'Remind me *never* to let you fill out paperwork for me again.'

I can't believe he's laughing.

'Ben, I'm so sorry! I really shat the bed.'

'Wait, are we still talking about the reference – or just now when you decided to call me?'

I have the giggles – how is he being normal with me? I don't know what to respond to first. 'Argh, Ben!'

'Yeah, I know. But it's all right.'

'It's really not! Why aren't you furious with me? I actually thought you hung up on me.'

'Ha, no. Tunnel – I'm on the train. I was mad. Obviously. And now I'm not. It needed saying. A little heads-up would've been good. But, really, don't worry about it.'

'Are you sure?'

'Of course! Harriet, you'd know if I was pissed off with you.'

'Very true.'

He laughs. There's a pause – it feels like he wants to say something but doesn't know where to start. I help him.

'It worked out, didn't it? They invited you back?'

'Yes.'

'Ben, that's really such good news.' I flip back the duvet and climb into bed, cradling the phone to my ear and diving deep under the covers. 'When?'

'Third of January. But it's not that simple.' He sighs, unsettled. 'I really want to stop putting you on the spot. But, Harri, we *have* to talk. About us.' He sounds anxious.

'I know. Do you trust me?'

'Er . . .' I can hear a raised eyebrow in his laughter.

'OK, fine – ignoring recent history!'

'Of course. Always.'

'Great! Because I got a few of us tickets to the Abbey Festival on New Year's Eve. You, me, Jono, Annie, your Oxford friends. The line-up is great. And I just really wanted you to have a proper celebration either way.'

'Ah, that's the nicest idea!' I can hear his excitement – it's exactly the kind of thing he'd want to do but not think to organise. 'How did you manage that?! You're amazing!'

'Why, thank you! So glad you've noticed.' I don't need to see myself to know my smile is radiant. 'And I promise we'll talk – but can it wait until then?'

'Yeah, sure. Sounds good.'

'Great.'

'You sound cosy.'

'I am cosy – I'm in bed.'

The line goes quiet. I poke my head out of the covers, checking I haven't lost him. 'Hello?'

'Still here.'

That's all. He doesn't say anything else. But the pause is utterly revealing – it calms me. The answer to the burning question I've carried around for weeks: replaying my time at the monastery and over-analysing all our interactions. Desperately trying to decode the shifts in our dynamic, uncertainty tearing me up inside like a hurricane in my heart.

This silence says something. I'm almost certain I know where his head is at – what's on his mind and what he's picturing.

I think he feels the same way.

He wants me too.

My gut flips. I have to do a little celebratory jiggle, kicking my feet around under the covers and trying to stay soundless.

'Anyway' – he changes the subject – 'if it's OK with you, I was thinking I'd spend Christmas with my mum. I know we normally come to you. But I really want to cook her a big feast and just . . . hang out. While I can.'

'Wow – that's a really huge step.'

'I know.'

I sit up, hugging my knees. The fact that he feels ready for that without his dad – he must be in a very different place.

'We'll probably be banging down your door by Boxing Day. But I think we can manage one day. Is that all right?'

'That sounds so lovely – she'll be really, really happy.'

'You think?'

'Ben! Of course. You're the only son she's got.'

I wish I could hug him. The love I'm sending him is at least three-dimensional – it can't fully translate down the phone the way I want it to. But, on the flipside, there's something completely wonderful about having his voice right in my ear.

'What are you thinking?'

'Honestly?'

'Yeah.'

'I was thinking . . .' I cover my face even though it's not a video call and he can't see me. 'I was thinking about how much I love the sound of your voice on the phone.'

'Ha! Weirdo.' His laugh is gentle. 'I'll send you a voice note of me reading the dictionary. That's your Christmas present done.'

'Clara told us no presents!'

'I meant for me. I don't need anything. Although maybe just the A section for you – because that's a lot of work.'

'All right, I'll look forward to that.' It's so ridiculously good to laugh with him – but I know it's only a matter of time before this becomes completely unbearable. Maybe for both of us. 'I guess I should probably let you go? Otherwise we'll be here all night.'

'OK. I guess so.' He sighs. He sounds exhausted. 'Night, Harri. See you soon.'

'Night, Ben. Thank you so much for not hating me!'

'Yeah, well. I did try, but . . . you know.'

thirty-nine

BEN

When I open the door on New Year's Eve, part of me falls apart.

I can't believe how beautiful Harriet is.

'Ready?' She kisses my cheek. 'How are you – does it still feel strange?'

She's talking about the reverse culture shock. Living in the centre of town. All the shops. All the stuff. And traffic. And litter. The way the sky doesn't dominate – it's reduced to almost nothing. The way no one gathers three times a day for prayer.

None of that is on my mind right now.

'Harri, you look absolutely like the most stunning person I have ever seen.'

Smooth.

She grins and twirls.

I have no idea how to approach this evening. Mentally. I'm already doing a terrible job of masking how I feel. I'm dying to say more. But I absolutely want to do as she asked. To trust her to lead. She touches my face. I've tamed the beard to a light stubble. She runs her fingers along my jaw. 'You're not so bad yourself.'

She takes my hand as we leave the empty flat. She hugs me from behind as I lock up. And with those small acts, it's decided.

Tonight, we're together.

And I'm the luckiest person in the entire history of the world.

'Ben!' Everyone hugs me. We're all talking at once.

The group energy is off the scale – I'm massively humbled by how happy they all seem to be. Just to see me again. Seeing Jono is always good for the soul. Annie seems surprisingly glad to be here. Oxford feels like a lifetime ago – Tim and Paige and Freddie have all come. Charlotte, too.

As soon as I see her, I want to apologise.

It's been well over a year since we broke up, immediately after Harri came to visit. It wasn't the easiest adjustment, but we were completely civil, all through Oxford second year. Our friendship group stayed the same – we didn't avoid each other. We just kept stumbling over the question of Harriet's place in my life.

It was totally unresolved.

'Hey, is it all right if I just . . .' I nod over to where Charlotte is walking ahead of us.

'Sure, of course!' Harriet smiles and nods.

When I catch up to her, Charlotte's smile is wider than I anticipated. 'So, a monk – I didn't see that one coming!'

'Ha, you and the rest of the world! I think if someone had told my sixteen-year-old self that this is where he'd end up, he would've – I don't know. Not been happy. Put it that way.'

'I definitely had other theories, as you know.'

I'm about to tell her – let her know she was right. All along.

'But,' she continues before I can say anything, 'I guess, well, there's no competing with God, is there? That's pretty next-level!'

I'm torn. This feels vaguely familiar.

In recovery, I had to face the fact that there were people I'd been awful to. I started apologising. It felt awkward and border-line weird: contacting girls I'd silently dropped. Numbers I didn't know I still had. Maybe it could've all been said in a message. A smarter person would've probably done that. I didn't. I made this whole ceremony out of it – coffee with 'I'm sorry' on the side. Why anyone agreed to see me again, I don't know. But some people said yes.

The first conversation ended in tears, but good ones. She was grateful it wasn't all in her mind. Glad that it really was me, and not her. It worked out so well, I was confident for the next one. Probably too confident.

It was a bloodbath.

Everything I said came off as insulting. Degrading. I realised too late that I was ruining her memories. She'd never thought of it as being used. She'd just enjoyed it while it lasted. I quit my apology tour after that. Some truths are chaotic. Out loud, they just cause pain. Maybe it's kindness. Or maybe I'm a coward. But I can't go through that again.

'Thanks for coming, Charlotte.'

She smiles. 'You're welcome.'

Charlotte was right about Harriet. And I've admitted it to myself. Maybe that's enough. Besides, she's here. And she's not blind. It won't be long before she knows.

We walk the short distance from my block to the abbey ruins, crossing over the river to the spot where a huge royal monastery was built nearly a thousand years ago.

We walk under crumbled arches. Former monks' quarters are now grassy mounds. It existed in splendour for·centuries. Until the politics changed. All the monks were banished. The abbot was slashed up. The whole place was trashed. The historical facts aren't new to me, but the connection feels more significant now.

It could be depressing, given its past. But it feels like it's come full circle, back to a place that's vibrant. Alive with celebration. The main stage is illuminated, glowing against the night.

Coloured lights are projected onto ancient brickwork. The spotlights shift. Pink. Green. Orange. Blue. Flooding the musicians. Then swinging out into the gathering crowd.

I'm so happy to be here.

Acutely present. Transcendentally aware. So completely conscious of Harriet next to me, her hand in mine.

The party's still getting started. People mill around – queuing for food and drinks at the pop-up stalls. We stake some ground near the heaters dotted across the site. We sort ourselves out – raiding the vans in shifts for 'gourmet' street food and 'craft' beers. I can't help wondering where everything comes from. I get into an overly long chat about supply chains with a vendor. The impatience of strangers hurries me on.

I want to spend time with everyone. It's so special to catch up. Rotating round. Exchanging news. Then giving up and shouting song lyrics instead. Jumping. Swaying – depending on the song. But in everything – all the time – I find I'm within arm's reach of Harriet.

I can't help it. We're magnetic.

I feel the curiosity of the others. We interact with them from the comfort of our own little nucleus. We've never looked more like a couple. And it probably does need explaining. But the music's good. And the food's good. And the company's the best. So, I go with it. Always one arm round her. Or she's pressed into me. Or we're holding hands. Or I'm leaning in to talk with her over the songs.

And – all the time – she's smiling.

Smiling with old joy and new contentment.

'You're happy.' I'm stating the obvious.

Her smile gets wider. 'So happy! It's just so good to be here with you.'

I don't know what to make of it. Such a radical transformation. She told me she's back on track with her art. Maybe that's what's keeping her balanced. I'd love to think the insane fight we went through at the nature reserve was worth it. Either way, I'm just grateful. Supremely thankful that, whatever happens, we've at least had this. Tonight.

She looks up at me as the band changes and the music shifts. 'Dance with me?'

We drift. Disengaging from the group. Not subtle. Dancing with her is one of my all-time favourite things. Wordless and symbiotic. Like a higher plane of existence. A sphere of just us. The growing audience almost fools me into thinking we're unobserved. Lost in the crowd. Until I feel other hands clamped on my shoulders, a voice in my ear.

'You don't dance like a monk.' Freddie's laughing at me.

I backhand him.

He ducks, laughing even more. 'Just saying!'

He's irritatingly right. I do need a time-out.

'Harri . . .' Given we still haven't talked about everything, it's a difficult sentence to finish.

She looks at me and nods, smiling. 'Let's go back to the others.' She checks her watch. 'I need to catch up with Jono.'

A woman of mystery. I smile as I follow her back.

I'm not sure what to do with myself as she disappears to the fringes with Jono. It's obviously a conversation I'm not supposed to be part of.

And then I see Annie.

'Do you have a minute?'

We move towards the food stalls where the music isn't quite so loud. I can't remember the last time I spoke to Annie by herself. But this is important. And I might not have another chance.

'Did you call Harriet a pathetic fraud?'

To be fair, she looks horrified. 'Oh no! She told you?! I did – it really just slipped out.'

'Look, I know she can be frustrating.' I try my hardest not to come off as aggressive. It's not like Harriet would thank me for bullying her friends. 'Believe me. I get it. She goes along with things. And at the same time, she's going round in circles in her head. It can feel impossible to break in and know what she actually wants. Until she takes you out with some drastic act of self-preservation.'

'Yes, really! That's so exactly it – that's just what I meant.'

'But that's not what you *said*. A pathetic fraud?! You can't fling crap like that around, Annie. She doesn't shake it off.'

She doesn't respond right away. She watches the band for a minute. I think I've hit a nerve.

'I'll apologise.' She smiles at me, shrugging. Clearly, she feels bad. 'I'll apologise properly.'

I nod. I find myself wanting to confide in her. 'I've been thinking about Harriet. A lot. The way she can get paralysed – maybe worrying about how things might play out. Do you think it's down to that whole thing with the photos?'

She nods slowly. 'That could totally explain at least some of it. Ugh, that was so awful.'

'Yeah.' I hate this subject. 'Anyway, I'm not saying you shouldn't tell her stuff she doesn't want to hear. I just . . . I don't know what's coming next. Where I'll be. I really need to ask you to be kind to her.'

I suddenly feel desperate. I'm clinging to a cliff edge, asking Annie to break my fall.

'Can you please just be extra kind to her?'

She smiles. 'I will, Ben. I promise.'

'Thank you! Hug it out?'

She hugs me side-on. A textbook 'hugging my friend's boyfriend' hug, and I have to smile.

'I don't mean to lecture you, Annie. I know you love her too. It's just . . .' I can't decide whether I really want to keep pouring my heart out.

'You hate the thought of not being there for her.'

'Exactly.'

She nods, but she's distracted. She takes out her phone. 'Ooh, it's time!'

'Time for what?!'

'This way – let's go!'

She bounds off, away from the main stage, through an arch to another section of the ruins. There's someone on security and, when everyone else arrives, Harri scans some tickets on her phone and we're all ushered through.

It's like a VIP area. The music still carries over to us. It travels, muted, on the wind. But the atmosphere is different here. Like a mystical hide-out. An outside lounge in a secret garden. There's a sign: apparently, we have a reservation. A string of lanterns hangs from a canopy. A sofa is tucked in the corner. There's a table with drinks and snacks. But the central feature is a firepit. The flames are irresistibly welcoming. We all gather round it – a basic instinct.

Harri hands out drinks.

Everyone seems to be in on something.

She finds her way back to me. My heart is hammering out of my chest. What's going on? She wraps her arms around me, still smiling. Elated.

'Ben. We both know that people saying nice things at a funeral is just rubbish timing. So, I wanted to get everyone together so we could tell you the good things we think about you to your face.'

I look at them all. They're grinning. And I'm stunned.

It's beyond thoughtful.

The things she's erasing. The gift she's giving me.

This is hands down the most romantic thing anyone has ever done for me. Vintage Harriet – something only she would come up with, and no one else could pull off.

I'm completely blown away.

forty

HARRIET

Ben's facial expression is a slideshow of dazed joy – appreciative and a little bewildered.

I'm just glad to have *finally* made it here.

For me, this whole moment is about as far from spontaneous as it's humanly possible to be – I've planned and thought obsessively about how to curate it all. And that's why I asked Jono to start: he has the highest EQ of anyone I know and he's confident without needing to steal the show – he'll set the right tone. Everyone else is just tipsy enough to avoid being super awkward, and not so wasted they'll mess everything up. So far, so good.

'When Harriet mentioned this idea, it was so perfect. Because it's exactly what I want to thank Ben for.' Jono nods at Ben. 'The way you never miss a chance to say the good things you see in people. And I reckon you probably learnt that the hard way. Which must be tough. But it makes such a big difference to us. Knowing someone who will encourage us all. So. To Ben!'

We all toast and cheer.

'Who's next? Freddie?'

'Yeah, all right.' Freddie puts down his drink and rubs his hands together – the loose cannon. I'm slightly concerned about what will come next. 'Some of you won't know this, because he seems pretty sensible, but Ben can get up to some pretty dumb shit with the right person.'

Ben laughs – and it's a throwback to when he was about twelve: his stupid little kid laugh.

'The trade-off is he keeps me out of trouble. He's definitely pulled me back from the brink when things could've got seriously shady. Even this term, with the new freshers, I find myself thinking – *What would Ben 'the Monk' Wilkins do?* So, despite my best efforts, you're slowly making me into quite a decent person.'

Charlotte interrupts. 'Can I just say, that's actually true – I know it sounds far-fetched.'

'See, witnesses! And I appreciate it. To Ben!'

We cheer and toast again – it's like the world's most affirming drinking game and I'm so grateful they've all bought into this.

'I'm Annie – think I've said hi to everyone by now. Ben and I, we're not especially close – I've kind of come along for moral support. When I met Ben, he wasn't in a great place.' She turns to him, holding his gaze. 'And I guess I was disappointed because I'd heard a *lot* about you. Maybe you've carried on thinking I don't really approve of you? So, I just want to set the record straight. I'm Team Ben, all the way. I've never seen anyone change as much as you have in the time I've known you. And I hope you'll be happy, whatever that means. To Ben!'

I feel Ben's deep breath.

I look at him, tightening my arms round his waist. I've been so fixated with whether everyone else seems comfortable about speaking, I haven't paid much attention to his reactions. He's going under – nearly overwhelmed; I can see it in the clench of his jaw. He pulls me closer, kissing the side of my head.

'Um, OK, my turn?' Paige seems emotional too. 'So, we've already done a whole term without you. And there's a massive gap – you've left a big hole. The thing I've realised I miss the most is the way you pay attention when we're talking. You're not on your phone or, like, looking over my shoulder to see if there's someone more important around.'

There's knowing laughter from the Oxford group – she turns to the rest of us, elaborating. 'Oh, it's totally a thing – "Hey, there's a princess. Hey, there's a sultan" or whatever. So, Ben, whether you're genuine or just really, really great at pretending' – she laughs, dabbing her eyes with the back of her hand – 'it's so nice and so rare to feel like you have someone's full attention. To Ben!'

All eyes turn to Paige's boyfriend, Tim, standing quietly alongside her. I'm not sure I've ever heard him speak.

'Me? I'm sorry – I don't think I can do this.'

'Ah, c'mon, Tim!' Freddie is brutally unsympathetic.

'No, it's not like I don't have anything to say. And Harriet gave us loads of warning. But I'm just . . . it's just –'

'It's all right.' Ben lets go of me. 'I know what you need, Timmy-tim-tim.'

He hands me his drink and approaches Tim. It seems like Ben's offering him a hug and Tim couldn't be more petrified. But at the last minute, Ben flips a switch. He's a magician – I have no idea how it happens, but Tim is in a headlock and Ben's messing up his hair. For some reason, Freddie decides to jump on them both, and they're all laughing and pounding each other like five-year-olds in a soft-play centre.

'Watch the fire!' Paige breaks them up – borderline affectionate.

'Well, that was unique.' Charlotte sips her drink, watching as Ben comes back over to where I'm standing. 'I wasn't sure about coming tonight. It was really nice that I wasn't automatically excluded. But. You know. And then I thought, whatever.'

I sense the collective intake of breath – all of us wondering if she's about to fall off the rails. I'm still so amazed that she has the courage to be here for this.

'What I liked about you, Ben, when we first met, was your confidence. You were confident *and* sober. Which, in freshers' week, was like finding a unicorn or something.'

Ben waves his can of lemonade in the air, taking a mock bow.

'And then, as time went on, I realised that this confidence also translates into you being horrendously stubborn and monstrously pig-headed.'

He laughs and she smiles too.

'But anyway. Even though we had to agree to disagree on some pretty fundamental issues . . . what I appreciate now is you at least let me say everything I needed to say. Several times. So. That's more than a lot of people would do.'

It's hard to tell if she's finished; she's just looking at him.

'To Ben!' Annie moves the moment on.

'Yes, exactly!' Charlotte recovers – or does a heroic impression of it anyway.

'Which just leaves Harriet.' Jono beams at me, and I feel my palms instantly start to sweat.

Why did I think this would be a good idea? To invite a whole bunch of people to witness me say things I've spent months struggling to get out? I want to hop back in my time machine and rethink the strategy.

But then I look at them – light and shadows dancing on their faces as the flames of the firepit flicker. They're smiling. They're half-drunk. No one is here for an Oscar-winning performance. No one is filming this for the internet to judge. It's supportive. A private circle of trust – and love.

I look at Ben.

God, he's beautiful.

It honestly feels like I'm about to recite wedding vows – I've practised this so many times in the mirror. I put our drinks to one side. I hold both his hands in mine – like he did in that moment before I took the ferry home, when he asked me what I want from him and I couldn't articulate a single syllable.

'Do you remember when I used to be afraid of the dark?'

He nods. 'Yeah, of course. It was pretty bad.'

I turn outwards to give them all the context. 'So, I went through a phase when I was quite old – maybe twelve?'

Ben nods; I love that we're telling this together.

'I was terrified of the way all the colours disappear in the dark. And Ben was so great about it when I used to stay over in the holidays – because it properly freaked me out. I'd cry and have these meltdowns, almost panic attacks. And Ben would reassure me, and tell me that it was all still there, and it wouldn't be dark for long, I just needed to wait it out –'

Ben bursts out laughing. 'There's *no way* I was that eloquent. Or philosophical. I was, what? Fifteen?'

'Excuse me!' I have to laugh too – there's a small chance I may have embellished this memory with all the rehearsals I've been doing. 'Who else got heckled?!'

There's more laughter and Paige squeals and drinks. 'To Ben! So romantic!'

'*Fifteen*, Paige, calm down.' He's cracking up.

'Also' – Tim speaks, briefly silencing us, because we can't really believe it – 'that's not quite accurate, is it? Because if our experience of colour is due to matter absorbing and reflecting the different wavelengths of light that humans can perceive –'

Charlotte groans, and starts to giggle hysterically.

'Argh!' Freddie punches Tim again. 'Who invited the biophysicist?!'

'Does no one get that I was fifteen?'

'Then, maybe, technically, colour *isn't* still there in the dark. At least for us.' Tim finishes his thought anyway, smiling quietly at the rising tide of laughter – the inevitable domino-effect of slightly drunk people trying to keep a straight face.

'Everyone, shut up already!' Annie's shouting over the noise, waving her arms in the air. 'Harriet's talking! Some of us have waited years for this!'

'Thank you. *Anyway.* The thing is, Ben, you've always made me brave –'

'Wait, wait!' He interrupts me again, and I can't stop smiling – it's like a comedy of errors, and I love that I feel relaxed enough to enjoy all the ways this is not going as I hoped.

'I don't make you brave.'

'Do you see what I've had to live with my *entire* life?!' I appeal to our audience. 'So argumentative!'

They laugh again, but it dawns on me that he's serious.

'Harri' – he holds my hands again – 'I don't *make* you brave.' He shrugs, looking at me – all of his intensity trained on me like a laser. Everyone gets very quiet very quickly. 'You *are* brave. I just remind you sometimes.'

I nod.

I know what he's telling me. In his incisive, spur-of-the-moment way – he's telling me I don't need him like I think I do. And he might be right.

But that's not the point.

'The point is – the thing I really want to say is . . .' I look him in the eyes; I realise he already knows. 'Ben, I'm *so* in love with you. I have been for the longest time. I should've said something before now, but –'

forty-one

BEN

I kiss her. I have to kiss her.
>I stumble into it, and she's not ready, and she laughs a little.
>It's awkward.
>And then it's epic.

My guess is this:
>Paige and Annie are the ones cheering.
>Jono gives Charlotte a hug.
>Freddie's miming something inappropriate.
>And Tim moves everyone on.

But, really, there's only Harriet.

forty-two

HARRIET

This is actually happening!

It's real and happening.

And it's Ben, so I'm caught up in a paradox – he's this careful force of nature: one hundred per cent present, and unapologetically wholehearted.

And, apparently, there are totally different dimensions to the sensations I'm capable of experiencing – whole worlds I've been carrying around, buried somewhere secret inside myself. I had no clue. No clue that I've been sleepwalking until now – feeling only a fraction of what's physically possible.

No clue I could be this awake.

I love him so much it's a deluge, and I'm drowning, and I say it with my mouth and my arms and my hands – my fingers finding his skin, warm under his clothes. I would say it with my entire body, but this is an open-air gig.

And I picked this spot for a reason. So that we'd have at least some hope of slowing things down. Because there are lines. There are lines I definitely can't cross. Not now.

Not if he's leaving.

forty-three

BEN

It's pure oxygen. More than my body can take.

I'm so hard so fast it's embarrassing. But, also, I completely don't care. This is probably the most honest 'conversation' we've ever had.

There are fireworks.

Actual fireworks – I pull away, laughing. I need to come up for air. Harriet's grinning at me, and a thought crosses my mind.

'Did you time your confession so that, if we kissed, there'd be genuine fireworks?'

She laughs and I don't know what's more amazing – the fact that she'd do that, or the fact that I'd know. 'I wanted it to be memorable.'

I have to laugh. 'Serious points for effort.' I kiss her. I stop. 'But there's no way this wouldn't be memorable.' Does she know how long I've felt like this? Maybe not. 'I've been dreaming about this for weeks.'

'Really?' She beams at me, deeply and obviously intrigued.

'Yeah.' I'm blushing. 'Literally.'

I pull her closer. Close enough to feel me and she bursts out laughing.

'That's . . . upfront.' Her laugh has an edge I've never heard before. And I realise there are sides to her I've never seen. Things I know *nothing* about. And we would have so much fun.

She wraps her arms around me. Retreating into a classic hug.

We watch the fireworks for a while. Following the colours as they spark and fade. Taking everything back to a more manageable tempo.

'Happy New Year, Harri.'

'Happy New Year, Ben.'

We're not in the moment. Not anymore. Our minds are on the future. And we still need to talk.

I don't know what stage we're at in this incredible night she's constructed. Does she want to go back to the flat? If she does, will we have sex? Because I want us to. I absolutely want us to go home and have sex. But I'm done with one-night stands. And, besides, this is Harriet. There's no way – no imaginable scenario – where I could *ever* sleep with her and then leave her.

Am I really ready to stay?

'What happens now?'

The fireworks are finishing. She's reluctant to look away from the sky.

'You can't stay. I'm not asking you to stay.' She turns to me, winding her arms around the back of my neck, bringing my head close to hers. 'You should go and see whether it works out at the monastery. I know it's important to you.'

I hold her. I'm struggling to breathe. It's all happening too quickly. 'You're important to me.'

She smiles, but it's sad. 'This is more important. This is everything.'

I won't argue with that and she knows it.

'Ben, I've fought it and I've been horribly selfish and so scared of losing you. But I love you. I want you to be who you are – whatever that ends up looking like. Whatever that means for me.'

I can tell she's really thought this through. And she means it.

'Harri, you can't wait and see. I'd hate myself for that. Holding you back.'

She nods. Our foreheads bump.

'I know. I'll be OK.'

'More than OK?'

'Ah, now you're really asking.'

I can't laugh. My heart is shattering and she sees it.

'No, I will. I'll try.'

'I'll miss you. So much. Every day.' I can barely talk.

'I'll miss you too.'

And then we're kissing again.

It's raining tears.

It feels like forever.

And it tastes like goodbye.

forty-four

HARRIET

I'm painting all the time.

I'm 'doing a Krasner' and using the grief – the compositions pour out of me in torrents I can't tame. Inspiration to spare. Enough to reignite my A level projects. More than enough for my portfolio.

Everyone is looking after me. Mum is cooking my favourite foods – all involving meat, and carbs, and things that are fried. Justin helps me run it off. I binge on bad TV with Dad, curling up with him like I'm eight, just grateful for his existence. I disappear to Clara's for ginger tea – or something stronger, depending on our mood. Jono checks up on me with messages. Annie's basically moved in.

She makes art with me in the evenings – spreading our things out all over my bedroom floor, always with the right playlist to rage, or weep, or dance and reminisce to. Honestly, she deserves a medal – I had no idea she had it in her to be so patient with me. I can't thank her enough.

The thought of Ben is like a bruise I keep bumping into – fresh jolts of pain in every collision. We're trying to find a way to keep in touch without overwhelming each other; it's arguably impossible and not at all clear what that will look like in the months ahead, but for now we've settled on letters. His handwriting is terrible. I've realised I can't spell without a computer. But taking turns to transcribe our thoughts – it's surprisingly lovely. Intimate enough to matter, slow enough to let the space expand.

I have to think about the future.

It's hard – but decisions need making.

I'll hopefully end up in art school. But I'm not going to London.

Not because I'm running away from the memories – although there are a *lot* of memories. But because I didn't choose London. I chose Ben and assumed he'd be in London. Thinking about it, for myself, the city doesn't excite me. I'll always love it but I've been there and done that.

So, I've applied elsewhere – I'm keeping an open mind, but my joint top three are Manchester, Bournemouth and an English-speaking school in Berlin. The paperwork to study abroad is ridiculous. I've just about got my head around the different fees, eligibility requirements – everything that goes with being an international student. It's not the easy option. But it has real possibilities. It feels exciting.

Part of me wants to know what Ben would think about that.

But I haven't mentioned it to him. Not yet.

I don't want to end up inadvertently asking for his permission. And I know he just wants me to be happy.

Actually.

I'm not sure he would say that. Happy. I don't think he'd use that word. Or he might – but he wouldn't mean it like most people do. More like 'authentic'. Alive. I don't know how he'd describe it.

But I know what he would mean: the standard he would hold me to.

I'm getting there.

And, sometimes, it does feel good.

forty-five

BEN

The beach is the only place where I pray about Harriet.

Otherwise, she'd be the only thing we'd ever talk about. And that would be totally self-absorbed. There's too much going on in the world.

It's difficult today. Some days are easier.

I'm sheltering in the bay. Watching the water. It reminds me of my baptism. I'm not entirely sure why – I wasn't baptised in the sea. I was baptised in an under-floor tank at the church Mum and Maggie grew up in. We had moved on to a different church by then. But it was a big deal and Mum wanted to go home.

I was thirteen.

It was total immersion – total commitment. I felt invincible when they raised me out of the water. Raised to new life. I genuinely felt immortal. And Dad told me to remember the feeling. To 'remember this "yes". They won't all feel this good.'

It massively annoyed me.

I thought he was so negative – putting a downer on this awesome moment when I was taking my place in the most exceptional narrative I'd ever heard. Now, I'm so glad he was straight with me.

Because, today, the 'yes' is a killer.

The struggle to mean it is real.

They sang a song – all the aunties. The little old ladies. Wearing their Sunday best. Clutching their handkerchiefs and weeping, overjoyed. It's echoing in my head. In my heart. In the rhythm of the sea.

I have decided to follow Jesus.
I have decided to follow Jesus.
I have decided to follow Jesus.
No turning back. No turning back.

I have to believe there's something in this for Harri.

Something positive.

The fact that I know anything about art is completely down to her. She messaged me once – ages ago. It was completely random. She'd read something. She wanted to share it. I can't remember who discovered it, or wrote about it – Albert? Joseph Albert? Something like that. But: colours interact.

You can take something that's one colour. A fixed colour.

And if you put it on a different background, it will seem like it's been remixed.

But it hasn't. It's exactly the same. Your eyes just alter their perception, depending on what it's next to.

Mind. Blown.

I think maybe this is like that. Maybe Harriet will get to see other things in herself. All the things she's capable of. Without me literally holding her hand. I hope so, anyway. I need some kind of hope.

It's not all bad.

Sometimes, it's nearly all good.

And the thing that's really changed is the fear.

I've done the thing I was convinced was impossible. I've chosen trust. It's not like I'm fearless. Not exactly. But I've pushed through to other realities. The things on the other side of being shit-scared. And, it turns out, on the other side, there's life. So much life.

I don't think about the future.

> I can't look that far ahead.
>
> I'm just trying to do my best with the days as they come.
>
> And I guess, in time, we'll see.

Acknowledgements

Writing and self-publishing are solitary experiences – but it would be a lie to say I've created this novel alone. It's amazing to reflect on all the people who have come alongside me, at different stages, with their expertise and support.

Thank you to Dr Catherine Humble and the other participants on the Goldsmith University short course I took in winter 2018, for teaching me that writing is rewriting and ambiguous endings are allowed. And to Claire Wingfield, for your perceptive manuscript assessment and unselfish championing of the book's potential.

Thank you to Anne for the extraordinary way you've noticed and nurtured other people's gifts over your entire teaching career – not just in me. It's an honour to still be in touch. To the readers, judges and organisers of the SI Leeds Literary Prize 2022 – thank you for your encouragement and critiques.

Sarah, thank you for the commitment you made to remember me in the obscurity. Love and deep gratitude to Janet and Jeff, for your wisdom and practical support; Chris and Julie, for your enthusiasm and prayers; Ali for being a true believer, facilitating the dream, and for being the voice of reason calling me back from whatever emotional cliff-edge I find myself on.

I'm so grateful to you, Hannah – for your faithful friendship in the whole journey, and for our conversations that continue to give me courage. Thank you to Emma, Emily, Abielle, Hannah, Lucy, Charlotte: I loved talking about Ben and Harriet with you – such a special evening! And to Pauline, for taking on the sensitivity read at short notice – your notes and reassurance have been invaluable.

Julia Koppitz, Kiana Palombo, Becca Allen, Emma Pidsley and the rest of the whitefox publishing family – I could not have done this without you. Thank you so much for changing the system. Jacira and Josh – thank you for investing your time and talents to support me as I venture into the world as a published author.

The work to make this book a reality is ongoing as I write this. So, to everyone else whose contribution is vital but currently unknown: thank you.

And to every single reader bringing your imagination to these words I've given you: we are co-creators. I appreciate it.

Finally, eternal gratitude and imperfect devotion to Jesus.

Questions for readers

1. What were your favourite moments in the book? Which characters were you particularly drawn to, and why? Were there any characters you disliked? Why?

2. Harriet and Clara initially view Ben's decision to become a monk as extreme and inexplicable. As the story moves on, we learn more about his motivations and the process involved in making a commitment to monastic life. What was your response to his decision? Did your reaction change as the novel progressed?

3. How did the use of different timelines and viewpoints affect your reading experience?

4. Although Ben's dad is constantly referred to throughout the novel, we never meet him. How does his influence and his absence shape the story? What does this show us about Ben's grief?

5. Ben and Harriet have a long, shared history and are familiar with each other from spending so much time together growing up.

   - How do they support each other? Does their interdependence seem healthy? Why or why not?

   - Did you believe in their potential as a romantic couple? Why or why not?

   - Ben talks about his faith in relational terms, and the story could be seen as a twist on a classic love triangle. Do you think this description is accurate? Why or why not?

6. Ben and Harriet are both multifaceted people. What are some of the seemingly contradictory aspects of their individual characters? Did you find their complexity believable?

7. Conflict is a central theme of the novel. Ben's choices cause hurt and trauma. Harriet also hurts Justin, and is hurt by Annie. Were you able to empathise with the characters in their worst moments? How did you react to the examples of forgiveness and reconciliation in the story?

8. The characters' experiences cause them to reflect on aspects of everyday life, like social media use and our relationship with the rest of nature. The book also explores numerous non-fiction themes as part of the narrative – including Christian theology, legal philosophy and art history. How did these wider themes impact your reading of the story? Did you notice all of them? Did they engage or distract you?

9. Many of the characters in the novel could be described as 'underrepresented' or 'diverse'. At the same time, they are just people living their lives. In your opinion, did the novel strike a balance between highlighting societal dynamics and telling personal stories? Give some examples to support your view.

10. By the end of the novel, both Ben and Harriet have been honest about their feelings and made significant decisions about their next steps. Do their choices seem authentic? Why or why not?

11. What is the significance of the title?

12. Did you find the ending satisfying? What do you imagine happens in the future?

13. Are there any lingering questions from the book that you are still thinking about?

References

'I Have Decided to Follow Jesus' Traditional Hymn attributed to Simon K. Marak (1877 – 1975)

Lee Krasner: Living Colour monograph edited by Eleanor Nairne

References:

'[I]n 1957, Krasner decided that she would take over Pollock's barn.' – page 119 *Night Journeys*

'fraught with foreboding' – page 111 *Prophecy* NB: This is part of a longer Lee Krasner quotation cited in the text. Full quote: 'Prophecy was fraught with foreboding. When I saw it, I was aware it was a frightening image, but I had to let it come through.' Original source is cited in the monograph as Lee Krasner, quoted in Eleanor Munro, *Originals: American Women Artists* (New York: Simon & Schuster, 1979), p.116.

First published in the United Kingdom in 2019 by Thames & Hudson Ltd in association with Barbican Art Gallery on the occasion of the exhibition *Lee Krasner: Living Colour*, curated by Eleanor Nairne 30 May –1 September 2019

About the Author

Writing has always been an integral part of how Liz Amos relates to the world. Her previous work mainly consists of personal reflections, written to make sense of her everyday relationships and non-linear professional life. *All the Truths Between Us* is her first novel and is self-published. It's the book she needed to find.

A curious introvert and sensitive thinker, Liz loves gatherings that feel hospitable, and deep chats with kind people. You're welcome to join the conversation.

#allthetruthsbetweenus

@liz.amos_writes

liz-amos.com

Printed in Great Britain
by Amazon

28073974R00164